LESS THUNDER, MORE LIGHTNING

THE BENEDICTION OF PAUL

BOOK TWO

PATRICIA MCCLURE

WAYZGOOSE PRESS

To my other parents,
Beverly Jean Brown Coolidge
& Reverend Alfred Hulscher

CONTENTS

Foreword   vii

1. The Monastery of Saint Alberic   1
2. Harvest Time   12
3. Epiphany   19
4. Ungodly Acts   28
5. Cycles of Sins   36
6. Saint George   45
7. Confession   55
8. Saint Clare   64
9. Azuline   74
10. His Abbotship   83
11. Meaningful Work   90
12. Father Jacob Returns   97
13. Incense   103
14. Jacob's God   110
15. Halloween   117
16. Treaties   127
17. Not-So-Junior Monk   135
18. Confessions   139
19. Silent Screams   146
20. Powwow   156
21. Broken Chalices   162
22. Jesus Mug   167
23. Staying   177
24. Spoken Evil   184
25. The Beating   194
26. What Now?   203
27. Front Door   210
28. Greenhopper   215
29. Home Sweet Home   224
30. Bad Boy   232

31. Waiting   239

32. Acceptance   247

33. Despair   254

34. Sins of the Mother   262

35. Election   270

Acknowledgments   283

The Series: The Benediction of Paul   285

FOREWORD

There is a lot of trauma in this story: trauma experienced by Father Jacob as a child and as an adult, trauma endured by the other Native Americans in his life, and trauma by Paul, the young ward of St. Alberic's Abbey.

None of us escape trauma, though some experience a deeply permeating, multi-generational trauma, while others of us experience individual, situational traumas. In writing this story, I felt compelled to showcase the physical abuse that is often ignored or downplayed in our society.

I have heard it said that caring adults are needed to help a child overcome adversity. I believe there is truth in that. Being blessed with a neighbor who became my mother figure and a man who became my father figure helped me fill the gaps in my life. Without them, I could not have told this story.

I hope that I have conveyed in these pages that the adverse childhood experiences, the substance abuse issues, the deep poverty faced by this land's first peoples, and the multi-generational trauma that afflicts so many Native Americans results from the horrors inflicted upon their nations by the now-dominant society and its government over hundreds of years.

CHAPTER I

THE MONASTERY OF SAINT ALBERIC

Psalm 31:8
I will instruct you and teach you
In the way you should go.
I will give you counsel
With my eye upon you.

Father Jacob Mackenzie rode his motorbike through the darkness on Montana Highway 87 to Saint Alberic Monastery. His braid thumped like a whip on his back. He could see the faint shadow on the hilltop against the predawn sky. He pulled off the road and wound his way past the college and through the apple orchard. The dorms were quiet. In a few weeks, the young and eager would arrive. Jacob enjoyed the students. Their arrival always brought a buzz contrasting with his tranquil rhythms of monastic life.

Father Jacob slowed as he came to the cemetery. He leaned his motorcycle against the enormous stone wall and pushed through the protesting iron gates. The graves looked cold in the predawn light. Jacob made his way to the hedges, setting the toppled urn of fresh yellow roses upright on Father Lucian's grave. Hidden to the right was a smaller graveyard, hardly visible from the road. This was the secular burial ground for the monks' widowed mothers and spinster sisters. Jacob's wife, Faith, and his children lay there. Another lifetime, yet the emptiness lingered. Time had not erased his pain. Perhaps healing wasn't possible. The birds chattered. Jacob stood and breathed in the cool morning air.

"I love you and miss you all," he said, pivoting away.

Father Jacob avoided Brother Mellitus's grave, for he felt that the old trickster would trip him in the dim light. Try as the monks might, they could not keep that headstone level.

As he revved his bike, his thoughts turned to Paul Warner, who had loved the elderly monk. Two deaths for one so young. The community had buried Paul's mother, Sarah, in the secular graveyard when they became his guardians four years ago.

Father Jacob still couldn't decide if the boy's mother, Sarah, had been wise or foolish. The deal was "Raise my son, and you will have 1.5 million dollars." The kicker was that the monks accepted, believing the child was the answer to their prayers for financial help from God.

As far as Father Jacob could tell, nothing substantial came from the financial agreement. He didn't drive a fancy car. The parish where he worked at Saint Clare still had heating issues. There wasn't a hot tub in the monastery's backyard or shiny new tractor in the barn. Not that it mattered. But, for all they had to endure raising Paul, where was the monetary reward? He sometimes pictured the Abbot locked in his office, counting the coins like Scrooge. The only change was that getting approval for expenditure took much more paperwork.

At the brewery, he parked his bike. The smell of hops swirled on the breeze. The one benefit of Saint Alberic was that beer was abundant. They would never get rich from the three brews of Absolution Ale, nicknamed "Redemption in the bottle—an ale for every sin," but it supplied a modest income. The wool from the sheep and the weave shop kept them one step away from living the true meaning of poverty—ale and weaving. There was not much to offer young Montanans, yet the institution had the best theologian in the state, Father Joannicus Brookes. That drew many scholars to the college. The man who lacked social skills had students flocking to him.

Jacob sniffed the air, smelling the aroma of breakfast. Temptation spoke as a hot cup of coffee before morning prayers. Instead, he entered the monastery. Two angels on the iron gates, Michael and Gabriel, flanked the entrance. He greeted them with a slight bow. They allowed secular people past these two shadowy angels but not past the wooden doors that led to the monastery proper. Jacob slipped through into the dim light of the hallway. The first floor had a few cells reserved for visiting monks. They devoted the rest of the space to the Abbot's office, the community room, and the Chapter Room.

He took the stairs to the third floor and entered his cell. He tossed his small satchel on the bed before switching on the light. His room was ascetic compared to those of the other monks. A dream catcher hung in the window. On the nightstand stood burned candles sticking up from the multicolored puddle of wax on a tarnished silver tray. Half of a brightly colored geometric-patterned blanket covered the bed. It had been his wedding blanket, but when Faith died, he buried part of it with her.

A coupstick stood silently in the corner, and three books on the otherwise empty shelf leaned against a vase with a flower long since expired. A shiny sculpture of a raven perched on the highest ledge, looming in its claws, was a beaded rosary. Tiny Stones in the River gave him two small rocks marking pivotal moments in his life. The traditional crucifix, along with the brilliant blue Apsáalooke nation flag, hung on the wall by his bed. This flag was old. The modern design of a pipe, a hat, a medicine bag, war bonnets, a tipi, and three mountains had replaced the Big Dipper that adorned his worn banner.

Father Jacob ran his fingers through his long hair and re-braided it. Echoes from yesterday's conversation rattled in his mind. The young couple's plea, "We didn't even get our three years. You're the blue-eyed one. Heal us. Bless us so this doesn't happen again." They had just lost a child to SIDS. Jacob knew loss five times over. His family had died over the course of a weekend because of a drunk, Mitchell Davis, and twilight. His life irrevocably changed.

They wanted answers, and they wanted hope. Sometimes the tasks of priesthood sucked.

What could he tell them? *Your child is in heaven with God*, or *she is with the Great Spirit*. Which did he believe? He was neither a good Apsáalooke nor the blue-eyed anomaly they sought. There are no miracles for them, no magic tonic. He could tell them to set her spirit free, to move on. What a hypocrite. To be Apsáalooke means to say goodbye. He hadn't done that.

He rubbed the finger where his wedding ring had been and sighed. He wanted to tell the couple he had no gift, but they invoked matriarchy, saying, "Your grandmother, Taima Knows the Song, sent us."

He would talk to her; she needed to stop telling people he had the power. The comparison to Jesus was not a happy ending story. He was not a healer.

He knew his history. He was a throwback. His white ancestor, a French trader, Cold Feet, gave him his blue eyes. He stayed with Sings in the Night and fathered several children, and many generations later, one had blue eyes.

Jacob could hear his wife Faith scolding him as if she were in the room with him. "You can't run away from what you are. We are Indian, and no amount of washing will change our brown skin."

The burden of the past clung to him as he changed into cutoffs and a tee shirt before putting on his black habit. The material rubbed against his bare legs as he zipped the cassock closed. He pulled the long cloth scapular over his head and straightened it between his shoulder blades.

"Now I am official," he chuckled. Who would have believed that, at age 35, he would end up being a monk? He was an odd mix of Apsáalooke and Catholic, never fully embracing either. He was happily married twelve years ago, expecting his fourth child while finishing seminary classes. God had a wicked sense of humor if he had one at all.

Father Jacob walked down the hall from the monastery to the church, stopping to pick up his prayer books from the wall slots. With a Psalter in his hand, he paused, letting his eyes adjust to the dim candlelight as he made his way to his choir seat. Each monk had an assigned place according to when they entered. At other monasteries, they separated the monks and the congregation. He liked that the church had an open concept about it, not your traditional rows of pews facing to highlight an altar. He noticed that the first row was fuller than usual. Then he remembered. Discernment week. *Oh joy, young hopefuls.*

Just as the bells rang, the lights illuminated the church one by one. Father Jacob noticed a few more monks were sitting early. Usually, Father Joannicus sat alone in the first hours before prayers. Jacob took his place in the choir. He reflected on the irony of life.

He knew he had nothing to offer these men. There is no vocation story here. He was here because he never left, more realistically, because God dumped him. God ripped his loving family out of his arms, and these monks scooped up the empty shell of a man and waited. We are all waiting for that burning bush.

Jacob smiled ruefully. This wasn't the tale a young hopeful wanted to hear.

Abbot Gordon had been wise enough to make Father Vincent the Vocation Director and Father Joannicus the Guest Master. They were the monks to emulate, not an Apsáalooke with freakish blue eyes.

Brother Moses bobbed in like a cartoon character, complete with a grin. Never a negative word came from his mouth. His world had only cheerful faces and rainbows. Eager and ready, he did every job, and Jacob remembered sharing his three years of junior formation with him. Obedience and grateful service took on a new meaning. Brother Moses nodded in contentment as he passed the discerning ones, some of whom shifted in their chairs.

The opening proclamation began. "Oh Lord, open my lips."

"And my mouth will proclaim your praise," responded the community.

A few seconds later, Paul appeared, somewhat disheveled, taking his seat behind the row of senior monks. Apparently, Paul needed more time than five minutes between the summons of the bells and the start of prayers.

Praise ended. The monks bowed in pairs at the altar, silently heading to the building housing the refectory, kitchen, and guesthouse.

They stood in the hallway waiting for the Abbot to lead them into breakfast, a practice that was more ritualistic than practical. Paul raced past the line of black robes to be in front.

"What are you doing here?" Paul asked, stopping next to Jacob.

"Discernment week. I am discerning."

"You're a monk already," laughed the eight-year-old boy.

"Really? Damn, when did that happen?" Jacob said, turning and seeing the Abbot.

"The Lord be with you, Father Jacob," Abbot Gordon said.

Abbot Gordon was a tall, thin man balding in a neat circle. If not for the black robe, he reminded Jacob of a Franciscan.

"And with you, Father Abbot."

"I'm glad to see you with us. Let's try to encourage our discerning guests this year."

Jacob smiled. He hadn't discouraged last year's eager men. He had let them see the soft underside of community living, a horde of men with lax manners and personal baggage. That reality often sent idealistic hopefuls running away.

"I will remind Brother Ambrose not to lick the honey off the outside of his mug," Jacob said with a wry smile.

The Abbot shook his head as he entered the refectory.

Mid-afternoon brought heat and humidity.

"Where are the wannabes?" Father Jacob asked Brother Ambrose.

"If they are smart, they are napping. I introduced them to farming."

The hairy hulk of a monk grinned, and Jacob understood he worked them hard. They sat in the shade on the patio.

"So, how many are reconsidering their vocation?" Jacob asked.

Droplets of water glistened on Brother Ambrose's massive beard, yet Jacob still detected the faint odor of farm and tobacco.

"The Rule says *Ora et Labora*. They need to realize that. I think two of them are hearing a second calling."

"Ah, the call of God versus the hand of man," Jacob said, handing Brother Ambrose a glass of iced tea.

"What the heck?" Ambrose grumbled as he smacked his lips at the sweetness in his glass. It lacked any tinge of alcohol.

"You do not want them to get the wrong idea. They are not joining a boys' club."

Brother Ambrose frowned, dug into his side pocket, pulled out a small flask, and poured the contents into his glass. "Yes, they are, but we have a higher purpose than any ordinary boy's club."

"Are you complete dummies?" Paul's not-so-quiet voice traveled to the backyard through the screened window. It had a small kitchenette stocked with coffee and snacks, a large fireplace, sofas, and tables. It opened out onto the patio and yard.

"How rude. What's a kid doing here, anyway?" a nasal voice asked.

"I'm Paul Warner. I live here. For your information, monks don't just wear habits. This is their home, where they wear other clothes. And do lots of things. You don't know much about monks, do you?"

"Look, kid, I've been Catholic all my life. I know all about religious orders." Condescension punctuated each word.

I am not voting him in, thought Jacob, drinking his tea, recalling the look of disdain he had received from this man; a look that said God only called white males to monastic life.

Paul needed more lessons in manners, but then again, most kids did. Paul had the misfortune of living with intellectuals who were mostly socially stunted men. Their focus was not on the social graces; sometimes, that association was reflected in the child's attitude.

"No, you don't. Brother Ambrose says you know nothing about cow poop until you step into it. You're just standing at the barn door looking in," Paul said.

Father Jacob's eyes widened as Brother Ambrose gave a thumbs-up. His fist pumped the air.

A distinct voice surfaced. Jacob peeked through the kitchenette window and placed the voice with the pock-faced young man. "I expected a little more praying, silence, and fasting."

"We pray four times a day. Father Jonah says you can pray everywhere cuz God isn't just sitting in the church waiting for you. Don't you know about the deathly silence at night? You can pray a lot then," Paul said with the monastic authority of an abbot.

"Who's Father Jonah?"

"He's called Father Joannicus, the Guest Master. Only I call him Father Jonah," Paul said, exasperation filling his voice.

Joannicus appeared, dressed in his light cotton habit. Jacob saw trousers peeking out from under the long, flowing, wrinkled cassock.

"It's ninety-eight degrees out. Why are you wearing that?" Ambrose asked, fanning himself with a meaty hand.

"We have guests. It's important to portray ourselves properly," Joannicus explained, pushing his frameless glasses up his nose.

"They will figure that out soon enough. Hiding in a habit does not change that," Jacob said, wishing he had spiked his own tea.

Father Joannicus headed toward the community room, but Brother Ambrose pulled him back.

"There is a lot of togetherness time. I'm looking for more strictness, solitude."

Good, thought Jacob, *the nasal man won't stay.*

"Have you read the Rule?" Paul asked.

Father Joannicus frowned and shot his eyes heavenward. Jacob could tell that he wanted to stop this conversation.

"Yes. Have you?"

Paul laughed. "Yes, every day. It says a lot about balance and *modernation*."

"Don't you mean moderation?" came the deep voice of the oldest discerner.

"Yeah, that's the word. This is a community. We do things together, or you can become a Trappist," Paul said.

"Or a Jesuit."

Jacob decided he wanted that man to join.

"No, they want power," Paul said, obviously quoting something he had overheard.

Ambrose smacked Father Jacob's arm.

"I did not say that. I would have said cardinals are power-hungry, one step away from Popeship. It was probably Brother Mellitus. He did not like the hierarchy. He believed Benedictines were the only true monastics in the world."

Paul continued, "If you want to be someone special, community isn't for you." The three men looked at each other. Had the child really said that? What an astute observation from someone so young. If Paul were in formation, he would be a junior monk. Ironically, some juniors were still unclear about what community life meant.

"Maybe we should let Paul be the Vocation Director," Ambrose whispered.

"What do you think monks do? Walk on water, drink wine, and pray?"

"I didn't think they shoveled manure," Nasal Man retorted.

The screen door squeaked, and Paul said, "Well, they do, and they laugh, and they cry, and they fart, and they burp, and they pray... a lot."

"What's wrong with that Moses guy?" the pock-faced man asked.

Paul turned, half in the room and half outside.

"Nothing is wrong with Brother Moses. Father Jonah said he's the heart of the community."

"He's a little retarded."

Joannicus moved to break up the conversation, stepping around the corner and revealing his presence to the group.

"Paul, Brother Ambrose is looking for you," Joannicus said, pulling Paul outside and pointing him toward the large man.

Paul approached Ambrose, pleased with his ability to teach. "They can't tell the difference between a father and brother."

"And you do?" Jacob asked, goading the boy.

"Yes, a father is a priest. A brother is not. The Abbot is in charge, and everyone is a monk."

"Such a smart boy," Ambrose said, ruffling Paul's head of brown curls as the child beamed.

"What's retarded mean?"

"Slow and kind," Ambrose said with authority.

"What's wrong with that?" Paul asked as he tried to climb Ambrose.

"Nothing at all. He's jealous that Brother Moses is here, and he isn't. God calls all kinds of men."

"I don't understand what that means, calls. Is it like when Father Jonah tells me it's bedtime, or is it like when the bells call us to prayer? Can you tell me what it is?"

"Good luck," Jacob said as he turned to exit the treacherous discussion.

"Where do you think you're going? This question involves you.

You have a story," Ambrose said, setting the monkey child on the table in front of him.

"You go first," Jacob said. "I would love to hear how you got here. Besides, my story has little to do with a call from God."

CHAPTER 2
HARVEST TIME

Psalm 66: 7
The earth has yielded its fruit,
for God, our God, has blessed us.

F ather Pius Carrington sat in the abbey's refectory, finishing his coffee and listening to the movement in the hall. This was harvest time. Every year, the community gathered, and those out on parish assignments arrived home. As the pastor of Saint George, the biggest Catholic parish in southeastern Montana, Pius felt blessed with the support of his confrères. If he had opted to be a diocesan priest, he would be alone in his vocation to serve. Father Pius looked forward to this time with a holy purpose. Father Joannicus appeared in the doorway.

"Paul, let's go."

"I'm not going."

"You're not staying here. Brother Barnabas will not allow it," Father Joannicus said.

Father Pius smirked. After last year's fiasco, when they had harvested peaches and Paul was packing, he left his mark on each peach by taking a bite. Nobody could believe the number of half-peaches the child consumed. Christmas peach preserves were a gift that anyone associated with the monastery received that year. It amazed Pius that Brother Barnabas could devise so many ways to disguise peaches.

Father Joannicus Brookes was younger than Pius. Joannicus had arrived at the monastery at age eighteen with two suitcases lengthening his skinny arms, and he never left. Pius was a novice then, and he thought the newest arrival was too young. New to Catholicism and raised by a Baptist minister, Joannicus had become an expert in Church theology. He was a teacher, yet he opted to do physical labor.

All parish-assigned monks were required to visit the monastery once a week. Sometimes, the task was a feat of juggling, but Father Pius understood the need to stay in contact with his fellow monks. The Abbot was wise to insist they come for a visit. Jacob had a parish, too, but his parish was Apsáalooke. Pius often worried that Jacob allowed too many Indian beliefs to trump the Church's protocols.

Jacob let sermons become discussions, which did not sit well with Father Pius. Saint Clare was small. The people claimed they were Catholic. Yet the few times Pius had visited, he was appalled. The statue of the Virgin Mary was adorned with feathers and hides, as if she were a doll dressed according to Apsáalooke beliefs. Father Jacob conducted Mass dressed as if he were going to a powwow. The sound of drums and the gibberish "hey yea" singing. Blackfoot, Cheyenne, or Crow—it all sounded the same. They all looked the same. Shiny black hair, tanned skin, and a funny aroma--if only they would embrace modern living instead of dwelling in tipis.

Father Pius found the odd mix of Crow and Catholic disturbing. He also found Jacob's appearance startling: dark complexion and high cheekbones contrasted with his blue eyes. Pius understood the recessive gene sequence that would have taken place, and he knew the whites and the natives intermingled.

"I want to harvest. I don't want to sort. That's for old monks," Paul said as he trailed after Ambrose.

"And little boys," Brother Ambrose said, his voice businesslike.

"Aw, please, I want to help."

"Paul, you're not strong enough to move the sacks," Ambrose said, ruffling Paul's curls.

Paul batted his hand away. "I can do it. It's not fair you never let me do anything important."

Brother Ambrose looked at Paul and then shrugged his shoulders. "Okay, you can try."

Father Pius shook his head. How could Brother Ambrose allow Paul to manipulate him?

"You know, setting limits and sticking to them works better than giving in," Pius told Joannicus. "He will never learn if you capitulate to his every whim."

Father Joannicus sighed. "Paul is strong-willed. Sometimes, it's better to save the fight for more important things. Like silence at prayers."

Father Pius knew kids. Although he was not fond of them, he felt he had a handle on orderliness and discipline. He helped run the parish school at Saint George.

Trucks took the monks down the hill to the farm and orchard. Father Pius watched as Paul ran to the trees with an empty sack.

Paul's efforts to move the apples to the truck proved fruitless. Still, Paul tried. He pulled and pushed the sack, but it did not move, and yet, he continued amazing the monks with his persistence.

Stubbornness that borders on willfulness, thought Pius as he carried his full sacks to the packing station.

Pius watched Brother Moses attempt to help Paul.

"Let me help you with that," Moses said, lifting the sack.

Paul glowered at him, pushing his hands away and renewing his effort.

"Please, Paul, let me help."

"Brother," Joannicus said, approaching the two. "He's not ready for help."

Moses stepped aside.

"Child, really," Pius said. "You'd have more success running one apple at a time than a sack full. Give it up. You'll not succeed."

Paul growled and kicked clods of dirt toward him. Dust rose and settled.

"Paul Warner," Ambrose bellowed, his hairy arms bulging as he hauled two sacks. "Cut that out. I warned you, this work was not for you."

An apple flew past Brother Ambrose. How the child missed such a large target baffled Pius. Ambrose laid down his sacks. A struggle between the two ended with a sharp swat to the posterior and a threat.

"If you ever throw fruit again, you'll be on the hilltop, peeling fruit till you're forty-five," boomed Ambrose before continuing his trek to the truck.

Paul wailed. Brother Moses skirted around Father Joannicus and attempted to pick up the scattered apples.

"No," Ambrose said. "He wanted to do this job. It's for him to finish."

"But Ambrose," Moses pleaded. "He can't do it. You're being mean-spirited."

Brother Ambrose stood, crossing his arms, blocking Moses. "One must learn one's limits."

"Ambrose is right. He chose the work," Pius said. "Failure isn't all bad."

"But he's a boy," Moses said.

"We are doing ourselves a disservice when we let him act like he's in charge. It's time for him to learn his place. He should be hilltop or packing, not underfoot distracting us from our work," Pius said.

Paul wiped his tears, streaking mud, like war paint, across his cheeks. Joannicus dropped a second bag next to Paul.

"Try fewer apples in the sack," Joannicus said, moving his load with ease.

Father Pius shook his head. He disagreed with this lesson. He headed to the orchard, reflecting on the last three years since Paul's arrival. He, like Joannicus, had found the child unsettling. He watched as Paul interrupted every routine in Father Joe's day. Lately, Joannicus was more at peace with the burden. Paul lived a Benedictine life of balance, prayers, work, and silence. Father Pius couldn't help but think monks had no business raising a young boy. The potential for disastrous results loomed clear. He knew the Church itself had many issues with children and women.

Paul removed some fruit from the bag but still struggled as the load carved a gully in the soft dirt behind him.

Paul sat down and moaned. "I need help."

Brother Moses moved to help.

"No, Brother, this is the boy's task," Ambrose said.

"But he's asking for help," Moses said, stomping his foot in a rare flare of temper.

"That's good, but he needs to finish the task on his own."

The large man stood with his arms crossed. Brother Moses grew red in the face before he stomped off. "You, Brother, are a mean, mean man."

Poor simple Moses—everyone knew when Brother Ambrose said "no," the discussion was over.

The heat rose as they worked. Town folk came helping and hauling. The community gave a lot of canned and fresh produce to anyone in need. Pius took a break and drank ice water from the cooler. Ambrose mopped his head with a sponge of cool water. He reeked of tobacco and sweat.

"What a stubborn mule," Pius said as he watched Paul roll the apple sack down the trail.

"Brother Moses or Paul?" Ambrose asked, shaking his wet hair.

"That boy is always tenacious. I would say there was hope for him, but Scholastica was easier to train." Upon hearing her name, the shepherd dog resting in the shade raised her head, looked about, and then returned to her nap. "And I'm torn between natural consequences and saving him from himself. More times than not, I must prevent Moses from rescuing him. That man's an enabler."

Pius nodded. "Natural consequences are well and good. But I wouldn't wait until he fell in the river before cautioning him to stay away from the edge."

"That's our job to save him from himself. He's a kid with little experience," Joannicus said, entering the shade and removing his glasses to wipe the sweat from his face. "Seriously, Moses was just trying to help."

"They will both survive," Ambrose said.

"I'm with Ambrose. Perhaps Paul won't be so demanding next time," Pius said, cracking the knuckles on his right hand. He watched Joe's face turn sour as if he were responsible for every annoying behavior the child exhibited. "I don't blame you. Children are challenging work. But Paul has been here three years. I would think him capable of learning discipline."

"Many of us believe if you spare the rod, you spoil the child," Ambrose said, rubbing his sore, muscled arm. "Do you want me to end his struggle?"

Father Pius noticed Joe's hesitance. He hoped Father Joannicus would back off and not undermine Brother Ambrose.

"Seriously," Joannicus said, looking at Ambrose. "Paul is learning our ways. We give adults five years to become Benedictine."

"I'm not stubborn," Ambrose said, turning and lumbering off to the orchard, the dust following his massive body.

Could Pius put himself in that category? As Benedictines, they were obedient to an abbot, one elected by them to be their leader. Willful. Yes, he could admit that his will struggled sometimes. Still, Paul's attitude was hard to tolerate.

Paul let out a long, mournful sound and cried. Joannicus turned away from Pius and walked to where Paul sat, casting a shadow over him.

Paul wailed, "I can't do it."

"Seriously, are you sure?" Joannicus said. "Seems to me you're almost there."

Tearfully, Paul pulled his bag of bruised apples up to the crate and dumped them in. Then he sat down, holding his knees.

"Well done," Joannicus said, bringing Paul water.

Paul collapsed onto the soil. "I only did one bag, and everyone else did hundreds."

"It was your first try," Joannicus said. "You'll improve."

CHAPTER 3
EPIPHANY

Psalm 84:5-6
Revive us now, God, our helper!
Put an end to your grievance against us.
Will you be angry with us forever?
Will your anger never cease?

Father Pius Carrington walked into the community room. The lights twinkled on the Christmas tree. The smell of pine and baked treats filled his nose. His parish duties were over, and now he could partake in the joyous atmosphere with his confrères. He looked for a new decoration on the large pine tree. It was a tradition that the newest members, who made solemn vows, contributed an angel to the tree. Pius spied the cherub among the green branches.

The celebration brought everyone together in a relaxed mood. Pius heard Father Jacob laughing and turned to see him and Brother

Ambrose toasting, their bottles of ale clinking. In Pius's opinion, Father Jacob Mackenzie was a moody fellow. Even as a young man, before his official entry into monastic living, he flamed and embered.

Paul ran around the room, handing out gifts. At the start of Advent, the monks selected names and shopped. Pius poured himself a glass of port as he remembered the year that Brother Mellitus, Merlin as Paul called him, drew Father Jacob's name. The gift Father Jacob received was a box of coal and a note about getting used to the eternal fire early. Jacob's reaction impressed Pius for the first time in their monastic years. Father Jacob thought the present was acceptable. Pius felt it was uncharitable. But then Brother Mellitus picked on everyone. If you dislike someone, you need a reason. Life within a community meant you learned to be charitable to others, even those you didn't like.

Jacob held a plate full of sugary treats and sat beside Pius. They watched Paul opening his many gifts.

Paul's godparents, Gracie and Patrick, fretted about Paul. The stack of wrapped packages told Pius they had worried needlessly. Monks found themselves showered with presents, ending up with more than what they wanted. Saint Benedict believed each man should receive what he needed. So, in that spirit, there was a community donation table.

Paul opened and tossed another present aside as "Away in a Manger" played softly in the background.

Pius cracked his knuckle as he watched the ungrateful child.

"Ah, the joy of the season, wantonness, and good cheer," Ambrose said, raising a bottle of Absolution Ale. "I wanted a new piece of machinery for the farm. I guess Santy Claus put me on the naughty list this year."

It wouldn't take much to place Brother Ambrose on that list, Pius thought. Today, he stood in front of the fireplace, out of habit, clad in a plaid wool shirt, making him look like a man from the Ozarks. All that was missing was a hunting knife and rifle. The fire crackled and sparked.

Father Joannicus glared at Brother Ambrose over the top of his round, frameless glasses. Pius knew the glorification of a man dressed in red handing out gifts irritated Joannicus. He glanced at all the pagan symbols displayed in the room, from the Christmas tree to the five-pointed star. He hoped Joannicus would let it rest. Catholics were good pagans. Father Joannicus couldn't dispute that.

"I asked Santa for something, and it's not here," Paul said as Father Pius flinched.

"When did you communicate with Santa Claus?" Joannicus asked, tugging on his scapular, attempting to even it as it hung over his shoulders.

"Gracie took me to see him. And I wrote him a letter in secret," Paul said.

Joe's face reddened, and the vein in his neck pulsed as he removed his glasses. Brother Ambrose hurried to where Paul's wrapped gifts were and handed the boy a large box while snatching a red-bowed package from the pile. Pius observed the gift slip behind his back as Jacob intercepted the package, tucking it under his scapular, the apron-like part of the habit. With the present concealed, Jacob headed toward the outside door.

Pius realized Jacob and Ambrose were playing Santa Claus.

Paul opened a large parcel from Martha Van Horn, the Abbot's mother, and groaned out displeasure.

"I didn't want this. I wanted a skateboard, not dumb rollerblades. These are for babies. Didn't anyone listen? Why didn't I get what I asked for?"

"Excuse me, but you had better not be complaining about your gifts. Do I need to remind you what we are celebrating today?" Joannicus said.

Paul crumpled up the paper. "I wanted a skateboard."

With his jaw set, Joannicus stood, straightening his scapular with a sharp tug, and gathered up Paul's gifts, wrapped and unwrapped.

"Hey, what are you doing?" Paul asked in amazement. "Those are mine. You have no right."

"Ungrateful children do not deserve gifts," Joannicus said, his voice quaking.

Pius sat astonished at both Paul and Father Joannicus.

Paul screamed and kicked the sofa. "You're so unfair. Those are mine."

Arms full of presents, Joannicus stopped and looked at Paul as if seeing an apparition.

"I want my presents."

Father Joannicus waited. Paul stomped out of the room. Joannicus placed the gifts in a cabinet with a lock and pocketed the key. Paul returned calm and composed as if someone had pushed the "off" button. He stood in front of Joannicus, looking angelic.

"Can I please have my presents?"

"May I, and the answer is still no." Joannicus breathed, arms crossed under his front scapular. "When you can show me what it means to be thankful, we will talk."

"You're wicked," Paul yelled, pushing Joannicus away.

"Oh, that is out of line," Ambrose said, rising from his seat. Paul exited the community room.

Smart kid. Pius listened as Paul's cell door opened and slammed several times. It reverberated in the silent halls. Christmas had ended early.

Brother Ambrose frowned. "Sorry, Joannicus, but I didn't take him to see the jolly old elf. I only intercepted the request. Ah, he's just disappointed. Kids get that way. Come on, Joannicus, don't be like that. Be mad at me. I won't give him the Santy present. I think you're missing an opportunity. God's gift to humanity, that's what it's about. Kids need an example to understand that kind of generosity. Good ol' Saint Nick shows that."

Father Joannicus stood silently, trembling and gripping the back of the chair.

"Seriously, he's not being very Benedictine, wanting so much,"

Joannicus said through clenched teeth as Mitch Miller and his gang sang "Must be Santa" in the background.

"He's a kid, and who ever heard of expecting too much from God?" Ambrose said as he headed out to the patio.

Disappointed was one thing, but the attitude was what Pius found annoying.

Was it the lack of consistency in expectations and control? These were men whose lifestyle was based on discipline and moderation.

Teaching one child these values should be easy.

Paul re-entered the community room with paper, a pen, and a poorly wrapped gift. He pulled up a chair and wrote.

The sliding glass door opened. Father Jacob entered with Ambrose. Snowflakes whooshed in as if trying to escape the frigid temperatures. Brother Ambrose appeared more buffalo than a monk as he shook himself off.

"Good comeback, Little One," he said to Paul, snowflakes falling on the stack of envelopes.

Paul finished writing his thank-you note. He took them to Father Joannicus.

"I'm done," Paul said, wiping his nose on his sleeve. "Are you going to open your present now?"

"Thank you, but no thank you," Joannicus said, glancing up momentarily from the newspaper he was reading. He slid the package toward the giver.

Father Pius twisted the ring on his little finger. Jacob cringed. Although it looked harsh, Pius believed in Joannicus. The man seldom acted without reason, even when cornered. He must have a bigger plan than just making the child and us miserable.

"What do you mean, no thank you? I made it for you," Paul said; his voice squeaked with pain.

"Yes, I know you did. Thank you, but I don't need it."

Paul's mouth hung open. No words came out. Joannicus left the present and the room. Paul fell to the floor, and a wail escaped his lips.

Was the sadness real, or was Paul trying to manipulate him?

"Holy Mother of God," Ambrose said as he bent over and scooped the child up.

Father Jacob gulped his sherry and shivered. "This is slow torture. At least with a beating, you know when it is over."

"True," Pius said, recalling a young man with bruises. He knew with certainty that Jacob's bruises were partly deserved punches. Like Paul, Jacob often spoke without forethought.

"He hates me," Paul sobbed from Ambrose's massive shoulder.

"No, Little One, he doesn't hate you. He's just trying to teach you something. What the hell it is, I don't know," Ambrose said, thumping Paul's back.

"I think the message is about being grateful," Father Pius said. "Joannicus has a point, and I admire his fortitude."

"There is no lesson learned when the spirit is crushed," Ambrose grumbled. "Bring that man back here. Paul is not in the novitiate. This instruction is over."

Father Pius walked down the hall to Joe's cell.

That's the problem here. They expect Paul to act like a monastic candidate, someone eager to learn the ways of Benedictine living. That explains Paul's meltdown.

Ambrose was right. Paul was not a novice. He was a child who needed direction. The door to Joe's cell was open, so Pius stuck his head in.

"Rose wants you, and it wasn't a request."

The bells rang, calling them to prayers.

Father Joannicus rose and straightened his habit. "It's time for prayers. I'll deal with that later."

In silence, he and Joannicus headed toward the church. Father Pius was a little stunned that his confrères were critical of Joannicus.

Dealing with the boy's cheeky responses was a challenge. Paul often said things that bordered on insolence.

Before they entered the church, Paul ran up to Joannicus and grabbed hold of his scapular, the part that hung down his back.

"Why do you hate me?" Paul said, eyes puffy with sadness.

Father Joannicus untangled himself from the boy. "I don't hate you."

"But you didn't want my present," Paul choked.

"I did as you did."

"But they..." Paul gasped for air. "They didn't hear me."

"I did, and so did God," Joannicus said, handing Paul a handkerchief.

Father Pius smiled. *Nicely done.*

Father Jacob stepped around them, mumbling, "That is if he was listening."

Pius felt himself bristle. Doubter and revolutionary. Couldn't he, for once, have faith and obey?

Several days passed, and Pius enjoyed the peacefulness of the monastic life. Paul appeared angelic, not rebellious, having accepted a giftless Christmas. More baked goods filled the community room tables. Pius feared he would have to loosen his belt a notch before year's end. Packages trickled in. The "white elephant" table was cluttered with items. Paul had even contributed a few toys.

After Sunday Mass, the monks lingered in the atrium, greeting those who had attended the service. Pius and Jacob inched their way from the crowds. They paused as a stately woman approached.

"Merry Christmas, Father Hilary," Mrs. Kane said as she handed him a wrapped package. "Where is that little man? I have some Christmas cheer for him, too." She handed Paul a box.

"Thank you, Mrs. Kane," Paul said.

"Well, open it, boys," Mrs. Kane said.

Pius smiled to himself. Why is it that older women see monks as boys?

Father Hilary was the same age as the widow Kane. He was the prior second in command under the Abbot—a quiet and elegant man. Nuns had raised Father Hilary, so being a monk suited him. Yet Mrs. Kane referred to him as a boy.

Father Hilary opened the package. Inside was a beautiful, hand-knitted sweater; triangles of sable, gray, and chocolate brown formed an attractive pattern.

"Jean, this is lovely."

"I hope it fits."

Father Hilary tried it on. The woman knew her sizing.

Paul unwrapped his box and quickly closed the lid, a look of panic on his face.

"What did you get?" Joannicus asked, walking toward Paul.

"A sweater," Paul said, backing away.

"Let's see it."

Dismay touched Paul's face as he removed the sweater, which vibrated with a hideous combination of pink and red. Jacob shielded his eyes as if the colors hurt. Father Pius witnessed Father Joannicus working hard to hide his expression of horror.

"You should try it on and see if it fits," Joannicus said, choking on his words.

Paul's eyes grew wide with disbelief. Father Pius held his breath, trying not to say the obvious.

"Let us hope it does not fit. That is one ugly sweater," Jacob whispered to Pius.

Paul stood paralyzed. Jacob stepped forward.

"Oh, pretty, let me put that away for you," Jacob said.

Joannicus took the box from Jacob and handed Paul the sweater. Paul hung his head as he put the sweater on. The pink contrasted with his complexion, making him look as sick as Father Pius felt.

"Seriously," Father Joannicus said, stumbling over his words. "It fits, and it's... it's... dazzling."

"What color is that?" Pius whispered, admiring Father Joe's kind words.

"I do not have a clue. Off-pink?" Jacob suggested. "Crimson-bismol, maybe?"

26

Ambrose snorted as he leaned between the two, startling them. "Cerise."

Pius and Jacob exchanged stunned looks.

"It is not an actual color if you say it in French," Jacob said.

Father Hilary invited Mrs. Kane to dine with the community in the refectory. Fathers Jacob and Pius vied for a seat that didn't face Paul.

After lunch, Pius and Jacob walked in the crisp afternoon air and couldn't help but notice the cerise-draped child making a snow angel.

Father Pius shook his head. "It's obscene. What was that woman thinking? Someone needs to give her yarn from our sheep. Yarn that is dyed in pleasant colors."

"Black is not a color for a child," Jacob quoted, doing a fair imitation of the grand woman. "Paul, Mrs. Kane has gone home. You do not have to wear that god-awful thing anymore."

"I know, Father, but it's warm," Paul said, running and sliding on the iced walkway.

Father Pius smiled. Although he would have dealt with Paul more swiftly, Joe had learned his lesson.

CHAPTER 4
UNGODLY ACTS

Psalm 40: 8
My enemies whisper together against me.
They all weigh up the evil which is on me.

Father Jacob sat at the long table in the conference room, listening to the voices drone. Jacob leaned back in his chair to look at the display case, which held an ancient bible, a chalice, a paten, and an old Ithaca rifle.

Newly appointed, Father Jacob was now on the Senior Council, a group of monks that helped the Abbot in community matters.

Abbot Gordon wanted him home. Unlike Father Pius, Jacob liked to spend his non-parish days at the Rez. Today, he had to bring concerns and listen to details about things he'd rather not know. He wasn't a good choice for fatherly community advice, but his confrères had selected him. The Abbot's only comment on his appointment was, "We all need an advocate."

Abbot Gordon was a reasonable middle-of-the-road man. He often took the stance of 'let's see what will happen' rather than risk losing a candidate or a struggling monk. He had veered left when he decided that allowing Paul into the community was a gift from God. The time Gordon insisted that the monks kneel during the Eucharistic prayer—despite the Church's move to lax and lazy ways —that was to the right.

It's too bad we could not debate that decision at this meeting. Does modern man still need to kneel before his Creator?

Warm sunlight absorbed itself into his black habit as Father Jacob suppressed a yawn. This meeting was odd. This wasn't a Senior Council meeting. Vincent and Moses were not here. Jacob didn't care what color the bed sheets should be to replace the old worn ones. He didn't care what kind of cereal, bran or sweet, should replace the discontinued one. This discussion didn't concern him. Maybe this was a hint. Was he going to be reassigned?

Don't be ridiculous, Jacob, nobody wants Saint Clare's parish, whispered the voice of Faith in his mind. He leaned back in the chair, and his eyes grew heavy as the voices buzzed from one minor concern to another.

"Now," Abbot Gordon said. "There is a matter concerning Paul. The matter will remain in this office."

Father Jacob opened one eye and glanced at Father Joannicus for a clue, but Joannicus held his glasses in his folded hands. Jacob heard Paul was unwell, but this now didn't seem like the whole truth. The tone of the Abbot's voice caused Jacob to sit up straight.

"Paul is fine. This will not occur again."

"What are you talking about?" Jacob asked, anxiety racing through him.

"There has been a minor incident," continued Abbot Gordon.

"Incident? What kind of incident?" Jacob asked as Brother Ambrose elbowed him.

"Shush, let the Abbot talk," Ambrose said.

"A monk became overzealous in his discipline and left marks."

Father Jacob felt the floor tremble as if a stampede of buffalo thundered by.

"I recognize this is a serious matter, but we do not need unwanted attention. We need Paul, and Paul needs us. I'll not risk losing him by calling in others. We can handle this on our own."

Jacob's tongue stuck to the roof of his mouth, making it difficult to speak. His stomach churned. He feared the contents of lunch would spew out if his mouth became unglued.

Abbot Gordon continued, "I'll take care of the monk, and we as a group will attend to Paul's needs, assuring him that this will not occur again."

"Are you telling me that Paul has been beaten?" Jacob said; his normal tenor voice sounded pinched even to his ears.

"That is a rather harsh term for this incident," Abbot Gordon said as if ordering breakfast.

The men at the table had heard of his non-existent relationship with his mother, Judith, and his volatile and violent relationship with his stepfather, Terence Mackenzie. Some even knew of his biological father Endow's drunk violence toward Judith. Yet here they sat as if they were discussing Cheerios flavors.

"Who?" Jacob stood.

"That is not your concern," Abbot Gordon said.

"It is. You are telling me that someone beat Paul?"

Father Joannicus stood up, his frame sagging, his scapular hanging crooked. "Jacob, calm down. Paul is fine. He has no broken bones, a few marks, and the bruises will heal."

"If he has a bruise, call that Carr woman."

Brother Ambrose smacked the table. "No, that would be an over-reaction. Accidents happen. We all get a little angry, you, me, and others."

Jacob stood, leaning over, placing both hands on the table. "I do not beat Paul."

"You have spanked him," Ambrose said, his eyes narrowed.

"So have you," Jacob said, leveling his gaze at Ambrose.

Why was Ambrose, who protected him from Terence, justifying this event? Paul needs protection.

The Mackenzie clan was not happy when Jacob first arrived at the monastery. The Mackenzie family's dynamics involved shouting and physical contact, not hugs. Ambrose planted himself like a bulkhead to keep the peace. Any attempts to hit Jacob had to go through Ambrose. Over the years, monastic celebrations where the Mackenzies were present moved from dangerous to palatable tension and now to uncomfortable moments.

Brother Ambrose stood rubbing the top of his head with his calloused hands. Like a volcano erupting, Jacob couldn't control himself.

"What is this meeting about? Are you accusing me of something?"

"Nobody is accusing you," Joannicus said far too quickly for Jacob's liking.

"Fine," Ambrose said, leaning on the table. "Are you guilty of something?"

"I would never hurt Paul. How dare you?" Jacob said, feeling as if Ambrose had sucker punched him.

"Stop. We are keeping this information between the five of us. I'll not be the Abbot of a house divided. Gentlemen, sit down."

"I agree with the Abbot," Father Hilary said, making his presence known. "We don't need Ms. Carr thinking Paul is in danger and removing him. That would be a disaster. He's so much a part of us."

Father Jacob collapsed into the chair. Brother Ambrose mirrored his movements, his chair protesting the man's weight.

Jacob fingered his braid as if it were a talisman. The rhetoric of the past flooded him. It was always the same. Fools believe children are protected. People looked the other way and justified the act of broken bones, citing that parents had rights and a child belonged at home no matter what.

Jacob swallowed the acid in his throat. All the excuses didn't change that Jacob wore bruises like a badge of honor.

"Then why bother her? It would only upset Paul and the community," Joannicus said, his eyes appearing larger behind his glasses.

"Because the evil monk must be punished," Jacob said.

Everyone stared at him as if he had summoned Lucifer.

"Punished," Ambrose said. "Are you ready to punish Terence, turn him in for beating you as a child? You didn't then, and you wouldn't now."

A slap would have hurt less than the mention of his stepfather. Jacob held the table, watching his vision become cloudy. Beads of sweat formed at his hairline. He tried to tell, and it got a second beating. And even with a broken bone, he could not stop it. The childhood emotions collided with adult reasoning, running circles in his mind. Endure or give up the best home you ever had.

"My stepfather is not who we are discussing. Child abuse is a crime. You act as if we are discussing the color of new sheets. I want to know who?"

"Paul isn't telling," Joannicus said.

"He will talk to me," Jacob said. "I am done. I will not be your victim, nor will I let this happen to Paul. I will sort this out."

"I forbid you to further traumatize Paul," Abbot Gordon said.

Jacob clenched his fists. He could not believe his ears.

The door to the Abbot's office opened, and Paul walked in, sporting a shiner.

Jacob rose and ushered Paul out of the room.

"Father Jacob," Abbot Gordon said, "stop."

Once inside the privacy of Paul's cell, Jacob released him. Paul darted to his bed and glowered. He and Paul always had a hot-and-cold relationship, a fact that didn't bother Jacob. Kids were fickle. Father Jacob recognized Paul was jealous of anyone loving Father Joannicus, and it was obvious to Paul that Jacob and Joannicus were close.

"What happened? Tell me who beat you," Jacob said, trying to sound gentle but knowing his voice sounded angry.

Paul glared.

"Let me see."

"No, leave me alone. Get out."

Jacob expected to see the Abbot when the door opened.

"You told," Paul said, anger mixed with confusion. "You promised."

"I had to," Joannicus said, his voice lacking conviction.

"Fine, I hate you. Look, it's just bruises," Paul said, showing the marks on his thigh and buttocks. Greenish blue and crusted over welts. "Happy now?"

"No, I am not happy. Tell me who did this so I can stop it."

"I don't want to talk to you," Paul said, and to make his point, he dove into bed and buried himself under his blankets.

Joannicus sat down on Paul's bed, placing a hand on the lump of blankets. A cloud of silence filled the room. Father Jacob wondered if Joannicus was praying or evoking a healing cure. The urgent meeting of the Senior Council, minus Brother Moses and Father Vincent, the community heralds, told Jacob this wasn't the first gathering to discuss the issue. Father Jacob looked around the room. Toys and stuffed animals littered the floor, along with mismatched socks. The walls held a menagerie of fantasy creatures and Catholic icons. Twinkle lights brightened the corner.

Jacob stooped to pick up the blue blanket and folded it before placing it on the chair. This can't be happening. He estimated from the discoloration that the abuse had occurred earlier in the week. Did Paul act strange on Monday? He couldn't recall.

Father Jacob looked at the door.

"They aren't coming," Joannicus said, rising. "We are leaving you alone, Paul. If you need me, I'll be in my cell."

The muffled response came under the blankets.

Jacob followed Joannicus to his cell across the alcove.

"Are you accusing me?" Jacob asked, searching for the nearest chair that wasn't piled with books or clothing. "Just because I was abused doesn't mean I'm an abusive person."

Father Joannicus closed his cell door.

"Nobody is accusing you. Certainly not me, but..." Joannicus stood gazing at the pile of clothing. "You're the one with the history, and you have used corporal punishment. Even with my limited parenting skills, I realize it's not good practice to get obedience with fear."

"Works for God," Jacob said, regretting the words as they left his lips. "I never suggested others use spanking. It is my form of correction, not a community policy. This is not my fault. What about Ambrose? He yells and thumps Paul on the head."

Anger, like a festered wound, radiated through Father Jacob. How dare they think he could hurt Paul?

Joannicus sat behind his simple wooden desk. "Why are you so angry?"

"Someone beat Paul. I do not understand why you are not angry," Jacob said, surveying the usual cluttered mess of stacks of papers, books, and laundry.

"Anger isn't the response to fix this issue. Pointing fingers just makes everyone a victim. I think we need to help him. What you learn about a person changes how you view them. This event could fracture the community. You know that."

Jacob stood up and paced the room.

"I am aware of the Church's policy of shipping evil men to distant parishes. We do not have that choice. We need to protect Paul." A variety of meaner monks sprung to mind.

Father Joannicus looked away. "This is not that kind of abuse, and I wish you wouldn't refer to him as evil. He made a mistake, one mistake."

"This is only the beginning. It will not stop. We have to intervene."

Joannicus moved a textbook to the side of his desk.

"You don't know that."

"Yes, I do. I lived with this beast. It will happen again. There could be broken bones next time," Jacob said, sorting through a pile of Paul's artwork. Didn't Joannicus toss anything away?

"You can't be everywhere. Paul can't live under a microscope. We will find help for this monk. Everyone is a child of God, worthy of redemption. It sounds like you want revenge rather than justice," Joannicus said.

The half-opened metal blinds at the windows clanked as a breeze blew into the room. Guilt splashed over Jacob. People make mistakes. Joe was right; he couldn't be everywhere.

"We need to focus on Paul," Joannicus said, clicking his red pen as his hand hovered over a stack of student papers.

"I am. Come down from the hilltop. The world is full of repeat sinners. People do not stop sinning because you forgive them."

"I need not leave to recognize the world is sinful. I pray every day for them," Joannicus said.

Jacob clenched his jaw. "Yes, let us pray for world peace. How long have we been doing that? So, you will pray?"

"And forgive him."

"Some acts are unforgivable," Jacob said, his throat constricting.

Joannicus looked up from the papers. "Nonsense. God forgives all. This man is a monk. He's one of our own. We must forgive him. We can't destroy his life with this. Even Christ forgave his killers."

Father Jacob didn't like the comparison.

"How many chances does he get, Joannicus?" Jacob asked. Scripture verses of seventy times seven whispered in his brain as he gripped the desk, fearing if he let go, he would find his hands wrapped around Joe's neck.

"I don't know, but I must obey and trust that God's hand is in this."

"Some things require more than obedience," Jacob said, baffled by the Christian rhetoric of forgiveness in the face of evil. Does the devil deserve redemption?

CHAPTER 5
CYCLES OF SINS

Psalm 58: 4-5
See, they lie in wait for my life.
Powerful men band together against me.
For no offense, no sin of mine, Lord,
For no guilt of mine, they rush to take their stand.

F ather Jacob sat freezing and sweating on the little porch off the south side of the third floor. The clouds chased the sun in an endless game of hide-and-seek, and the snow glistened around him. The February days were still bitterly cold, even with the sunshine. Since the big meeting, Jacob had avoided the monastery and, when home, avoided them.

"There you are," Ambrose said, stepping onto the deck.

"Here I am. Did I slip from your watchful eye?"

The porch was small. The big man stood, blocking the sun. Jacob sensed the cold creeping toward him.

"You're not that interesting to watch. I'm not monitoring you. We are starting Schola practice for Easter Sunday. Are you planning to sing with us?"

"Always."

"Why are you avoiding us?"

"I don't want to be accused."

Ambrose grunted and rubbed the top of his head. "Stop brooding. This isn't about you. Besides, Paul is doing well."

Bounced back? Jacob wasn't sure that was the term he would call Paul's behavior, which Joannicus had informed him consisted of nightmares and clinginess. The adults held the event on hold. Yet, he sensed a current of tension. Was it all in his mind? Were they waiting for him to confirm that the abused became abusers?

"I am not an abuser," Jacob hissed.

Brother Ambrose marched the length of the porch, making a wide path. Snow-like dandruff dusted the hem of his habit. He turned to face Jacob.

"I would have to see for myself that you beat Paul to believe you are the one. We need to find the real culprit. I find myself suspicious of everyone, and that includes you and Joannicus. I'm embarrassed to say I'm just another doubtful Thomas."

Doubting Thomas, thought Jacob. "I feel the same way. Everyone appears guilty."

"Not good for the community or Paul. I want the boy to talk." Brother Ambrose rubbed his arms for warmth, and the rip around the shoulder of his habit exposed his red long johns.

"Paul will talk when Paul is ready," Jacob said, unbraiding and braiding his hair.

Brother Ambrose stepped away from Father Jacob. "You should cover up, snow glare and all."

"I do not burn. That is the afterlife."

Puffs of fog rose around Ambrose's large, wooly face as he spoke, making him appear ghostlike. "No doubt about that. Christian up. What's wrong with you? Nobody said you are guilty."

"No, they just thought it. Two against me, two for me, and I am the tiebreaker, but nobody believes me."

"So, you are a mind reader now?" Brother Ambrose said, clipping his hands to his waist belt, causing his habit to rise above his ankles, exposing his mismatched socks.

Jacob shivered in the cold as the sun hid behind a snow cloud.

"What do you want from me?"

"I want you to protect the boy, just as I am doing," Ambrose said.

"You were here, and it happened," Jacob said.

"Come on, Jacob, we've been down this road. Stop acting like a little boy."

Could he stop being the little boy abused, the emotions like a wild bird trapped in a house of glass that kept beating its wings, hoping for release? Jacob thought he had grown away from the fear and turmoil of abuse. This event seemed to have chipped the windows that encased emotions, causing a spiderweb-like crack.

This big oaf is pushing. But Jacob knew something wasn't right. Coyote came and visited his dreams. Coyote heralded a change between duality and connection. The world was abruptly complicated.

Jacob's inner walls crumbled. Like a magnet picking up iron shavings, Brother Ambrose had a gift for releasing Jacob's emotions with the right amount of push and pull.

"It is my fault. If only I had practiced restraint," Jacob said, his voice wobbling with emotion. "This man might have done the same."

Brother Ambrose roared with laughter. Jacob gasped.

"My, I wasn't aware you were so powerful. Get a hold of yourself. Are you telling me that Terence was a puppet in your hands? I call holy cow pie. Shame on you. Now you sound like that old monk, Father Lucian, a man riddled with regret. He was before your time with us. The poor man muttered all the time, 'I'm sorry.' None of us could figure out what he had done to be that miserable. Don't do that to yourself."

He had tortured that man.

The mention of Lucian's name caused Jacob to taste bitterness in the back of his throat. Father Lucian was the Benedictine monk who ran Saint George's parish when Jacob was a boy. The children of Saint George's went to confession every week, and Jacob would confess to Father Lucian every beating, accepting the blame for his stepfather's actions.

"Bless me, Father, for I have sinned... my father beat me again. I'm sorry I made him so mad. I should be a better boy. Then, my father would not beat me. Will you pray for me, ask God to make me obedient?"

"Child, don't speak so brazenly," Father Lucian would say.

Father Jacob remembered the sound of the monk shifting and clearing his throat, but as a child, he didn't recognize the man's discomfort. Jacob was aware of the power it gave him. The nuns, Father Lucian, and his own family were aware of the abuse. They were all members of the circle of silence. Everyone repeated the excuses, dismissed, and forgave. If they couldn't or wouldn't help him, they could suffer with him once a week, starting with Father Lucian.

When Jacob grew up, he recognized the cruelty of what was a child's attempt at control. It was too late to take back his actions. Father Lucian was deaf and blind by the time Jacob made amends. He was unsure if the man knew that Jacob had forgiven him.

It was his burden of guilt.

"You need to tell Paul it's not his fault, even if he is obnoxious. Let me state that again. It's not your fault your father beat you. Say it with me," Ambrose said, sounding like a state-paid social worker.

The sun caused the snow to sparkle. Beads of sweat formed on Jacob's temple. Sometimes, he made Terence beat him. He had control.

"It is not my fault. My father beat me."

"Good. We need to figure out who."

That was a good idea, but how? They couldn't just go around accusing or get Paul to talk.

Jacob smoothed his hair back, sensing the coldness of his hands on his head.

Ambrose stomped his feet as if marching. The little porch vibrated. "Then help Joannicus. He's floundering. Explain to him why Paul is being stubborn."

Jacob realized that Paul's refusal to talk was more fear-based than stubborn. What had the monk threatened? Or did Paul want the man's love?

Despite Ambrose's confidence in him, he didn't know how to fix this.

"Yes, you do," came the voice of his wife, Faith.

"Go away. You are bothering me," Jacob said.

Brother Ambrose growled, and a blast of warm air filled the porch as the large man made his way back inside.

The past leaned against Jacob. The fear that he was guilty left a shadow on his heart that refused to leave. He wanted to move into the monastery and protect Paul. Yet, he sat miles away, making excuses, believing the impossible, riding the waves of guilt that he was responsible for this event. Ambrose was right. This wasn't his story, but the events transported him back in time.

Terence spoke of love, but his action betrayed that. Hadn't Jacob done the same? He loved the child and justified his spankings by saying that the child needed discipline. He baited Terence. He forced him to strike. Did he ever feel as conflicted? The child was still ashamed despite knowing who to blame. He was one step away from being his father, stepfather, or that monk.

There was little doubt in Jacob's mind that Terence loved him. He recognized his mother did not love him, never did, and never would. Jacob's free spirit and fierce loyalty to his heritage reminded his mother, Judith, of what she didn't want to be: Apsáalooke. Jacob resembled his father, Endow. This man beat her when he drank and died, leaving her with four children. Without a father, Jacob turned to Terence. The man showed Jacob love. *Was the man beating Paul a friend or a foe? Did Paul like him? Did it matter?* The Elder within him played with the whys, but the Warrior wanted to act, and Faith was silent.

Hours passed. The temperature dipped. The sun on the patio burned warm. Like one with a fever, Jacob melted and simmered, contemplating the situation as the heat of indignation burned inside him as hot as the sun. The debate raged on. What should he do? When should he do it?

This was not his problem, for they had ordered him to stay away from Paul. He knew the event would happen again, and so he would disobey.

The door to the patio opened.

"You have no shirt on. Do you know it is winter?" Paul said in a motherly tone.

"I am getting a suntan."

A cool finger touched his shoulder.

"Sunburn, you mean. And you're crazy. Abbot Gordon is looking for you."

"Where is your zookeeper?" Jacob asked, noticing Paul was alone.

"I don't need a keeper. I don't need a guard. You can tell Abbot Gordon that. He won't leave me alone. He's always making me check in before I can go anywhere. I can't go to the farm. It's not fair," Paul said as he crunched the outer crust of snow to the soft underside with his foot.

"He wants to keep you safe," Jacob said, thinking Paul didn't sound recovered, not with the Abbot hovering.

"I'm safe."

Time had passed. Nothing had happened. Maybe Abbot Gordon was right. Perhaps the evil monk had learned, but experience told him it was a lie.

"I'm eight now. I can take care of myself."

Father Jacob nodded, wiping the sweat from his face. Not against angry adults. "I am sure you can, but can you escape from watchful monks?"

"I can, that's easy."

"Apparently," Jacob said, wondering what lie Paul had told them.

"I told them I was taking a nap. When they left, I got up. I don't have to be watched constantly. I'm not a baby." Paul leaned on Jacob's chair. "You don't believe me, do you?"

"Sneaky boys need watching. I believe you, but you should do what the Abbot asks, you know, obedience and all."

"I didn't disobey."

"No, but you make it hard for those watching you to protect you. It would be so much easier for everyone if you just talked," Jacob said, brushing Paul's face with the end of his braid.

Guilt danced momentarily across Paul's face. "No, you don't understand. He's powerful."

"He is a man, not God. I figured you would have learned the difference by now," Jacob said.

Paul's eyes darted around. Sadness settled on his face and pierced Jacob's heart.

"You all need to forget," Paul said, waving his arm in a sweeping gesture.

The slight breeze caused Jacob to shiver. "You need a wand for that."

"You buried the wand with Merlin."

The intricate wooden staff that had belonged to Brother Mellitus Hahn, known to Paul as Merlin, had intrigued the child from the first time he saw it.

"That was not a wand. That was a cane, and we did not bury it with Brother Mellitus." Jacob rose and put on his shirt.

Paul's eyes grew wide. Jacob had captured the boy's curiosity.

"I need that wand."

"Interesting. What will it do for you?" Jacob stood, his body stiff from the cold.

"Make you all forget."

"And the bad monk? Will it make him forget too?"

Paul shrugged his shoulders. A look of consternation creased the boy's brow. Jacob could almost hear Joannicus tsking. Don't cater to magical thinking. Was it magical thinking to hold an amulet or a medal of a saint? If Paul had faith in the cane, so be it. Besides, Paul could use it to whack the shins of the evil monk.

"Do you have it?"

Jacob stepped into the little TV room, which held a large sofa and several chairs. The heat of the room wrapped around Jacob, embracing him. "Tell me who, and I will tell you where I hid it."

Paul followed him in as he picked up his habit. "Not fair. I can't tell you."

"Why? Did the bad monk say he would keep you from eating oatmeal if you told?" Jacob said, knowing he was poking a badger.

Paul stared at him. "We haven't had oatmeal lately."

"Nonsense. What did he threaten? I will make sure you have oatmeal."

"I can't. Leave me alone," Paul said. "You're going to jinx me."

"Paul, this is not magic. I cannot protect you if I do not know who to punch."

"You can't hit him, your fathers, and the Abbot wouldn't allow it."

"He hit you."

"Stop it, just stop it." Paul covered his ears with his hands.

Father Jacob unzipped his cassock and stepped triumphantly into it. He learned the man was a priest. "We can talk later. Did the Abbot send you?"

"No, I heard him ask about you, and I knew you were hiding."

Father Jacob slipped his scapular over his head and tugged the long black cloth so it hung straight over his shoulders. Knowing where the evil monk was was clever, but it was only a temporary solution to safety.

"It would be more effective if you stayed in a large group rather than isolate yourself with one monk," Jacob said.

"I'm with one monk now," Paul muttered.

"I am not the one you need to stay clear of."

Paul shrugged his shoulders.

The Warrior, the Elder, and Faith all hung their heads. If only the advice were true.

CHAPTER 6
SAINT GEORGE

Psalm 50: 5-6
My offences truly I know them.
My sin is always before me.
Against you, you alone have I sinned.
What is evil in your sight, I have done.

onight was the First Confession for two classes of second graders at Saint George's parish. Some children attended parochial school. Father Pius Carrington had invited Fathers Joannicus Brookes and Vincent Mackenzie to help him listen and absolve forty eight-year-olds of their sins. Sitting in a small room, sliding a screen back and forth, and smelling children's rancid or bubble gum breath for an hour drained him. Saint George wasn't doing face-to-face confession. That is good because he wasn't sure he could sit straight-faced in front of children when they confessed to telling a lie.

The side door to the church opened. Father Joannicus and Paul entered the church.

"I'm sorry, but nobody was available to watch him. He has things to keep himself busy."

Father Pius frowned, cracking his knuckles. There was a house full of monks and nobody to watch Paul, and more likely, nobody wanted to watch him.

Paul frowned and slipped into the last pew of the large, ornate church. The red carpet led to an altar on a marble platform.

"You could go to confession here," Father Vincent said.

"No, I'm going to confession at Saint Clare's with Father Jacob," Paul said. "Abbot Gordon said I could."

The change in where Paul would make his first communion surprised Pius. Paul's godparents, Patrick and Gracie, were members of his parish here at Saint George. Pius himself had recommended the childless couple for the honor of godparents. Yet Abbot Gordon had announced that Paul would attend Saint Clare's for his religious education. He wondered if the decision had to do with Joannicus placing Paul in a predominantly Native school and Jacob's parish was Native.

Father Joannicus put on his stole. The children filed into the church. Excited voices filled the vestibule but were soon hushed.

Father Pius stood next to Paul and leaned down. "This is Saint George's, not the monastery. This is where I'm in charge. You will behave."

Paul scooted down the bench away from Father Pius.

Pius rubbed his eyes as a little boy entered and took his seat. He would scream if he heard one more rendition of the Ten Commandments. His head rang with petty sins. "I murdered an ant, I kissed my Ken doll, I did adultery because Mommy said to clean my room and I didn't." Stealing, lying, wanting their sibling's toys, and an occasional curse, he could tolerate, but these children didn't understand sin.

He wondered if Jacob, at Saint Clare's, had this problem with children confessing to sins they couldn't have committed. As the child droned on, Pius wondered what Paul would confess. Disobedience? Paul had few opportunities to break the big ten. With his daily prayer schedule and Sunday attendance, the first four commandments were a given. Pius fiddled with the ring on his right hand, a gift from his bishop uncle. He hoped that number five translated into honor thy fathers and brothers. Paul told lies that began with a sheep and ended with a miracle.

"Father, are we done?" the little boy asked. Father Pius stifled a yawn. He hadn't heard the child's sins but knew they were forgivable.

"Yes, say two Hail Marys and an Our Father," Pius said, standing. The child quickly left the confessional. Father Pius straightened his habit, opened the confessional door, and stepped into the church. The scent of lingering incense filled his nose. Father Pius listened. The heater vents hummed. Paul was nowhere in sight.

Fathers Vincent and Joannicus emerged from their confessional, stretching and looking as exhausted as Pius felt.

"How many acts of adultery did you have?" Vincent asked.

"Nine," Joannicus said. "What are they being taught?"

Paul's head popped up midway through in a pew. "Look what I found. Money for the poor."

Father Pius noticed all the books in the pews lined up. Father Joannicus glanced at Pius for approval. Pius nodded. Joannicus smoothed the front of his scapular, which barely showed a wrinkle, and stepped into the church's vestibule as Paul ran to make his deposit.

"How come the kids weren't smiling after confession? Especially those that went to him," Paul asked, apparently unaware that voices carried in the vestibule.

"He has a name: Father Pius," Joannicus said, his voice weary and a little hoarse. "Perhaps he hopes that this will be their last confession."

"Does he want them to die?" Paul said.

"No, I meant that Father Pius hopes that if they feel bad enough, they won't need to come back," Joannicus said as he entered the church proper.

"He's just plain mean," Paul said, running to catch up to Joannicus.

Father Pius frowned at Paul's rudeness.

"You'll have a lot to confess if you keep talking like that. You need to stop saying everything that comes into your head. Seriously, get your coat, it's late," Joannicus said.

Since Father Pius was due for a visit to the monastery, he took the free ride home. He walked over to the rectory with Father Vincent.

The rectory was an ample three-bedroom house with a recreation room where Pius held teen socials. Father Pius felt at ease with the teens and awkward with children, thankful that others in the parish found the younger group entertaining. The furniture in the rectory was dated but comfortable. He reserved the largest bedroom as his suite since it had a private bath and a nook he used as an office. He used the other bedrooms for guests and visiting monks. He liked offering them a place to stay away from the monastery.

"This place has changed little since Father Lucian was the pastor. Only he used this space for his office," Father Vincent said. "I remember the long walk to his desk, twice as long when you were in trouble."

Father Pius laughed. Lucian must have used dread as a persuasion tactic. The nuns liked to use guilt, but Pius preferred a quick and direct solution when dealing with errant children. Father Pius grabbed his overnight bag, and they headed to the car together.

"Oh no," Paul wailed.

"Now what?" Father Vincent said.

"I want Father Jonah in back with me."

"Jiminy Christmas, honestly," Vincent said, leaning against the car. "I hope I wasn't this persnickety when I was a boy."

"Knowing your brother Jacob, he would've put you out of your misery if you had been," Pius said as he walked toward the backseat. Although Vincent and Jacob were half brothers, they differed in temperament and humor as far apart as Custer was from the Sioux.

"Are you really Father Jacob's brother?" Paul asked.

"We are half brothers," Father Vincent said. We have different fathers. Father Jacob's father was Endow Knows the Song. He's the father of Jimmy, Rebecca, and Marie. Terence is my father and the father of Terence Junior, David, Thomas, and Victoria."

"Who's Jimmy?"

"Jacob's older brother."

"Marie is Sister Marie, right? You have too many fathers and sisters. I think I will stick to my family—only fathers and brothers. Father Jonah, please sit in the back with me."

"Joannicus, you give in to his demands far too often," Pius said as he got into the front seat.

"I prefer to think of it as picking my battles," Joannicus said, sounding irate.

Paul climbed into the back and kicked the seat with a mighty force. Pius lurched forward.

"Paul," Joannicus said, astonished. "Seriously, what is wrong with you?"

"Sorry, sorry," the boy said. "My foot slipped."

"Fine, but you need to apologize," Joannicus said.

"I did." Paul shrugged. "I'm sorry, really sorry."

Father Pius knew a lie when he heard it but was impressed with Joe's ability to influence Paul.

But he was too forgiving, thought Father Pius as he folded his hands in a tight grip on his lap.

The ride to Saint Alberic's was uneventful. Joannicus carried a sleeping Paul into the monastery. *They coddle him too much*, thought Pius, now understanding the grumbles of backaches among his confrères.

Father Pius walked down the dim hallway to his cell on the third floor. The hour was ten o'clock, most of the monks were asleep, and the halls echoed with muffled snores. A sharp shout caused Pius to jump. Turning toward the sound, he saw a flash of light from under Father Jacob's door. That's odd, Pius thought. Jacob visits on Tuesdays. The light switched off.

Pius softly closed his cell door. This was a sanctuary to him, where he was surrounded by objects that brought him joy. His books on spirituality, three icons, one of Saint Pius, one of Saint Benedict, and one of Mary, were all given to him as gifts. The glow from the Tiffany night-light cast the shadow of a large crucifix in front of him. He hung his habit up and slipped out of his slacks. From his dresser drawer, he took out a pressed set of pajamas. Father Pius lingered momentarily to smell the freshness before donning the cotton navy-blue nightwear. He climbed into bed, set his alarm, and prayed the rosary until he drifted off to sleep.

The alarm clock buzzed, waking Pius from sleep. He rose and prayed as he brushed his teeth and shaved, carefully conserving the water. The morning bells rang, and he slipped into his habit. Pius walked from the monastery to the church as Paul raced by him.

"Stop," Pius said.

Paul skidded to a halt.

"Go back to the end of the hall and walk," Pius said.

"I'll be late," Paul said, turning to leave. "And you're breaking the grand silence."

Father Pius grabbed Paul's arm, turned him toward the monastery entrance, and shoved the boy. "You're late already," he said.

Paul stumbled forward and then stopped. Pius felt his brow becoming hot. "Don't make me walk you back."

Paul stood, not moving. Pius marched the child to the end of the hallway. Paul protested. Father Pius clamped a hand over Paul's mouth and continued into the monastery. The ornate doors that separated the hall from the cloister thumped shut, taking the muffled protests that grew louder as they approached Paul's cell away from the community.

Father Pius entered the church, pushing Brother Fabian's wheelchair. The old monk had been wandering in the hallway, muttering about where they had moved the church. Paul arrived quietly and humbly in the middle of the first psalm.

A visit to the monastery meant a chat with the Abbot, so by early afternoon, Pius knocked on the door of Abbot Gordon's office.

"Father Pius, the Lord be with you," Abbot Gordon said as he looked up from the papers on his desk.

"And with you, Father Abbot."

"How did confessions go?"

It impressed Pius that Abbot Gordon, with all the other pressing matters an abbot dealt with, remembered this insignificant event.

"Thanks to the help of Fathers Vincent and Joannicus, things went well, and we saved souls. I noticed Paul wasn't at breakfast this morning."

"Yes, he came and told me he wasn't well."

"He was up late, way past a decent bedtime for a child. I don't know why Father Joannicus brought him last night."

"Father Joannicus has sole responsibility for Paul," Abbot Gordon said. "I'm considering changing his teaching responsibilities so he can focus more on Paul. I'm sure you're aware he has a positive influence on the boy."

Confusion filled Pius. Hadn't Joannicus always been the monk in charge of Paul?

Monastic training kicked in. Pius pursed his lips. Paul didn't need constant supervision. The boy negotiated his way through the monastic day with ease and finesse. As for Joannicus, anyone hanging around the man couldn't help but convert. Yet Pius knew Father Joannicus would not like this news. He loved teaching.

"Consistency is good when dealing with children," Pius said, having seen the boy get from one monk too often what the other denied him.

"Exactly," Abbot Gordon said. "With one monk in charge, like our Novice Master is in charge of the novices, there will be less confusion for the boy and all of us."

"I'm not questioning your decision, but is Joannicus the wisest choice? Brother Ambrose or Father Jacob seemed to bring Paul to mind quicker than some."

Abbot Gordon rubbed his chin and nodded. "Paul loves Father Joannicus. Love begets obedience, too."

Pius nodded. Joannicus does not love Paul. He sees the boy as a duty.

Father Pius excused himself from the office. He was now free to spend his day as a monastic rather than a pastor. A sadness filled Pius, for he knew Joannicus would obey the Abbot even if the task was doomed to failure.

Pius wandered into the community room and smelled the heavy odor of deodorant and shampoo. He saw Brother Ambrose leaning over Father Joannicus like a vulture over a carcass.

"Just because I work with animals doesn't mean I can't read people. When the sheep are nervous, the predator is out there, and my sheep are nervous," Ambrose said.

"Seriously, I don't know what is wrong with your sheep. I've got a degree in theology, not animal husbandry," Joannicus said, looking like a scolded child.

Pius pushed his lips together, suppressing a laugh.

"So, I ask you again, where's Paul? He always helps at the farm after school," Brother Ambrose said.

Father Joannicus moved his chair back into Ambrose, trying to escape the large man's intimidation. "I assumed he was with you?"

"You're supposed to know where he is at all times."

Joannicus stood and looked up at Ambrose. "As I said, he's with you; if he isn't, it's your job to find him."

"But he didn't get off the bus," Ambrose said.

Joannicus glanced at his watch. "Are you aware of the time? What did you think he was doing taking a taxi home?"

"I wasn't done with the sheep," Ambrose said, crossing his arms.

"Hey guys, I think he had a case of school-itis."

"Seriously, he was here all day?" Joannicus said, throwing his arms up.

Ambrose glared at the surprised Joannicus.

"Look, if nobody tells me these things, like he's sick, then how am I supposed to keep track of him? I've classes to teach," Joannicus said.

"Fine caretaker, you're turning out to be," Ambrose said, moving toward the coffee pot.

"I said it once before. This isn't a one-person job. I'm going to talk to Abbot Gordon. This is not working," Joannicus said as he shoved his student's red-marked papers into his satchel.

"Aren't you going to check on Paul?" Ambrose said.

Joannicus headed out of the community room.

"You were pretty harsh. Paul's care should be a group activity. It takes two parents in the secular world," Pius said, thinking the raising of Paul was a community project.

Ambrose scratched his beard. "Guess I was. Between Paul and Jacob, I'm feeling stretched."

"What's wrong with Jacob?"

Ambrose's minty tobacco breath filled the space between them.

"I don't know, but he has been sleeping here and returning to Saint Clare's in the morning. Rebecca says nightmares. So, help me, Saint Rita. I need to understand what's bugging Jacob, for it seems to affect Joannicus."

Saint Rita was the patron of hopeless cases. Pius watched the man lumber out. Good luck with that. Pius didn't think Jacob's problems were affecting Joannicus. The issue was Paul. Father Jacob wasn't a hopeless case—more of a lost cause. He would have gone with Saint Jude.

CHAPTER 7
CONFESSION

Psalm 102: 3
It is he who forgives all your guilt,
who heals every one of your ills.

F ather Jacob stood in the doorway of the second-grade class, a small class of ten children. Paul and several boys ran, bumping into each other—playing musical chairs without music. As the children noticed his tall, lean frame, dressed in a black habit, in the doorway, they quickly found seats. Quietness filled the space as they transformed into angels, halos held up by little horns. Paul was the last one seated.

The teacher, Mrs. Spotted Horse, motioned to the children. They all stood and chanted, in sing-song unison, "Good evening, Father Jacob." Paul, who was not familiar with this parochial school custom of respect, instead switched seats. The children sat with their heads tilted upward as Jacob stood in the front of the class. He smiled, enjoying the moment, excited for these children he had known since baptism as they took the next step in their spiritual development.

"Who can tell me what sin is?" Standard catechism answers erupted, but Jacob hoped there would be more.

A little girl with big brown eyes raised her hand. "Sin is when you do something, and someone gets hurt."

"I like that answer, Annie," Jacob said. "So, does anyone have questions about the sacrament of reconciliation?"

Paul raised his hand, his sleeve slipped, and Jacob noticed a bruise. Had Abbot Gordon noticed it?

"How come sin only counts now?"

Father Jacob scanned the boy's face as he walked the length of the room. "What do you mean, only counts now?"

"I've said mean things in the past, but now it's a sin. It wasn't a sin before. What changed?" Paul asked, sounding like the academic scholars he lived with.

Jacob smiled, suspecting the monks had something to do with this theological question.

"You did. You can only commit a sin if you understand right from wrong. You have reached what the Church calls the age of reason."

"What if the Church is wrong? What if I don't understand?" Paul challenged.

Mrs. Spotted Horse stood up. Her chair banged on the back wall. "Give others a chance to ask questions, Paul."

Jacob stepped toward Paul and said, "The Church is never wrong. Ask Father Joannicus."

Jacob exited the room and entered the auditorium, where parents and Father Joannicus waited. Joannicus looked up from reading something by Saint Augustine. Guilt ran through Jacob. He had avoided the monastery, hoping to avoid questions about his nocturnal visits. What could he say? Confess he was having nightmares of Terence beating him. That sounded stupid. He was supposed to protect Paul, yet he feared he would be helpless in defending him.

Rebecca, his sister, had told him to seek a healer. She was a healer but told him, "Our tears are too mingled." She meant that she was too close to help him. Was he too close to Paul?

"You don't need to hang around. Paul will be okay," Jacob said, sitting at the table.

Joannicus glanced around the room.

"Seriously, I know."

"I am surprised you did not insist on coming into the classroom with me. Did Gordon insist you stay?" Jacob didn't wait for the answer. "Did you see the bruise on Paul's arm?"

Father Joannicus shifted in his chair. "Yes, he told me he got it at the farm. Something about that gate."

"And you believed him?"

"I will not perform an inquisition whenever he has a bruise."

Joannicus sounded sad, as Jacob thought Abbot Gordon would question everyone again.

"Why is he here? Saint George's parish is closer and where his godparents are."

"Abbot Gordon sees demons in all of us. I am to keep Paul in sight. Do you have any clue what that's doing to my spiritual life? To answer your question, Paul asked to come here. Abbot Gordon thought he could get a name out of Paul if he gave into Paul's request."

A baby cried, and its mother paced in big circles, attempting to soothe it.

"Foolish man."

Joannicus winced. "Perhaps, but Abbot Gordon doesn't give up."

"Too much time has passed. Paul will not talk," Jacob said, erasing a pencil mark from the table with his thumb.

"Seriously, keeping Paul with me is not working for either."

Jacob nodded, seeing the dilemma.

Father Joannicus rubbed the letters of the book in his hand.

"It is still going on?" Jacob asked.

"Maybe, okay, probably. This has to stop," Joannicus said, avoiding Jacob's face.

"What happened to the forgiveness clause?"

"Seriously, forgiveness requires repentance. How does a man achieve conversion if he's removed from temptation? A temptation isn't always overcome by running away or avoiding."

Father Jacob smiled. "Seems to have worked for centuries so far."

"You're playing the devil's advocate. Stop. One should avoid sin. But if you keep committing the same sin, something isn't working," Joannicus said, frustration tingeing his voice.

The doors opened, and the room flooded with children's voices. Paul ran around the auditorium as Jacob stacked chairs, and when the only sound left was Paul, Joannicus packed his book. Paul skidded to a stop.

"Father Jonah," Paul said, leaning against the monk. "I'm not ready, so do we have to come back next week?"

"Yes," Joannicus said, crossing his arms. "What makes you not ready?"

"I'd rather not go to hell. If I don't go to confession, then I can't go to hell. Cuz I can say I didn't know I was sinning."

Father Joannicus raised his eyes heavenward and then peered over the top of his glasses.

Father Jacob chuckled at the cleverness of the child. "First, the whole thing is about forgiveness, not hell and eternal damnation. Second, you are old enough to pay for your actions."

Paul's face contorted, full of seriousness and innocence. "But what if I'm not forgiven?"

"If you confess your sins, you are forgiven," Jacob said, trying to imagine a sin that an eight-year-old could commit that condemned him to hell. Most of the sins he heard involved bubble gum, horror movies, and siblings.

"No matter how horrible?" Paul challenged.

"No matter how horrible. Your worst sin is speaking before you think," Father Jacob said.

"What does that mean?"

"What does Brother Ambrose tell you?" Jacob asked.

"Don't say mean things, or I'll thump you," Paul offered, his voice sincere.

"I will tell you a secret. We all sin," Jacob said. "So, we all need to ask forgiveness and try again."

Paul glanced at Joannicus. Father Jacob knew Paul didn't believe Joannicus was capable of sin.

"I don't believe that. You shouldn't talk like that," Paul said as he picked up his coat.

Father Joannicus hung his head as if in defeat. "Don't repeat the sin."

Paul rolled his eyes. "Yeah, right, like Brother Moses and chocolate. He comes to confession every week and says the same sin. To me, the whole thing sounds dumb."

Father Joe's jaw dropped. Jacob cleared his throat. Thankful he had figured out that Paul spied on people years ago. He now checked where the boy was before discussing sensitive matters.

"What is confessed is sealed. I cannot discuss it elsewhere," Joannicus said, with a slight trace of a growl.

Paul stood on the chair to be the height of Joannicus. "Really? So, if I tell the priest something in confession, he can't tell anyone?"

Jacob wondered where Paul was going. Did he think naming the evil monk during confession would keep that monk from finding out? Clearly, the man had convinced Paul not to speak his name.

Cautiously, Joannicus answered. "Correct."

"What if I stole a penny that rolled away from the collection box? You can't tell, so I can't get punished, right?" Paul asked, leaping off the chair.

A soft noise of impatient disbelief escaped Joannicus. "Seriously, even if you confess, it doesn't make the sin disappear. Eventually, people find out."

Jacob and Paul's eyes met, and he recognized the look of total disbelief. Jacob didn't envy Joannicus's job of saving this soul.

. . .

Father Jacob sat in the confessional, a walk-in-closet-sized space with two chairs, a small table, and a kneeler. A crucifix adorned the wall with one low-watt bulb glowed in the sconce, giving the space a soft, cozy feeling. Jacob remembered the small box with a kneeler and a screen wall. The glow of the light silhouetted the priest, giving him an angelic appearance. Jacob recognized the shadowy figure and addressed the priest by name—so much for anonymity in the confessional.

This was post-Vatican II. They replaced the stale darkness and screened shadows with something lasting: another person's face. The change, although complex for many Catholics, seemed right to Jacob. In his Native American culture, if you wronged someone, you faced that person. You didn't whisper "sorry" in the dark outside of the tipi. Catholics were cowards. None would have survived the old monastic practice called *chapter of faults*. In this practice, a monk or nun would confess to the entire community every minor infraction they committed while attempting to abide by the Rule. He thought of his wife, Faith, and smiled. He could see her shaking her head at both of these cleansing rituals, and uttering it accomplished nothing.

The troublemaker, Larry Hawk, entered the room. Three times, Jacob leaned forward with a soft and dangerous voice. "Is that all?"

Larry crumbled; his defiant attitude was now replaced with remorse. Jacob suppressed a smile.

Jacob removed his stole, a thin, long cloth draped around his shoulders, stepped out of the small space, and stretched. The smell of beeswax candles lingered in the air, and the confessional seemed bright compared to the church's dim light. Even though he liked this part of his job, ten first-time confessions in one night exhausted him.

"Father Jacob, I'm sorry to do this to you, but we forgot one," Mrs. Spotted Horse said.

Jacob turned to see Paul shaking his head no.

"He says he'll do it at home, but I think not," Mrs. Spotted Horse said with a smile. Paul hung his head.

"Come along, Paul." Jacob opened the door and switched on the light. The mustiness lingered. He wished he could leave the door open. Jacob sat down, straightening his robe, placing his stole over his shoulders, and folding his scapular in his lap.

"Get in here," he said, slightly annoyed that Paul was not sitting in the chair reserved for the penitent.

The little boy stood pressed to the dark wood panels.

What happened to the bold little boy who stood in front of everyone last Sunday night and shouted, "I hate you"? Gone was the child who hotly argued his rights when he had none.

"Paul, come over here and sit, please," Jacob said, crossing his long legs and rubbing his tired eyes. Paul swallowed audibly.

"I don't have any sins that I can tell about."

Blue eyes met brown.

"Make them up," Jacob said, knowing Joannicus had coached the child in sins one could commit.

"I don't think Father Jonah would approve."

"Thank you, Brother Ambrose." Jacob reached for Paul's arm to guide him to the chair. Paul leaped backward, tripping, landing on the floor, narrowly missing the low shelf edge, and scrambling to the corner, hugging his knees.

Jacob glanced at the door, hearing shuffling beyond, holding his breath, expecting Father Joannicus to open it any second. Paul's labored breathing broke the heavy silence. A shiver ran down Jacob's spine.

Jacob patted the worn, velvety cushion and waited in silence, left hand supporting his chin. Paul moved toward the chair but stopped short of it as if sitting in it would loosen his tongue.

"I don't want to be punished for confessing the wrong thing," Paul said.

Good God, what have my confrères been telling the boy? Did they counsel hell and damnation over love and forgiveness?

A frown appeared on Jacob's face. "Paul, I do not know what you think will happen. In confession, there is forgiveness, not punishment."

Paul's head drooped as he whispered, "Bless me, Father, for I have sinned."

Father Jacob dipped his thumb in holy water, making a wet sign of the cross on Paul's forehead and nose.

"What are you doing?"

"You asked me to bless you. I am blessing you."

Paul smiled faintly and then frowned. "This is serious."

Jacob folded his hands and waited.

"I make people mad, and they do terrible things. How can I stop? I don't mean to be so bad."

Jacob's jaw tightened. "Paul, nobody has the right to harm you. Anger is their sin, not yours."

"I didn't listen."

This confession had the stench of secrets, the words of a man guilty of sin trying to blame a child for his actions. Father Jacob shook his head.

"I turned on the light. He said no, but I did it. The mean monk said bad things would happen if I talked. I don't want that."

Father Jacob squeezed the armrest. "You are confessing their sin."

"But I made them do it," Paul said. "I disobeyed."

"No, you did not make him hurt you. The only disobedience I see is that you have not given us a name."

Tears formed in Paul's eyes. "Abbot Gordon wants me to tell him, but I can't. I can only talk in confession."

Jacob held his breath. The child was clever, using confessional methods to protect himself.

"So, this monk is threatening you?"

Paul looked at Jacob for as long as a hummingbird's visit. Jacob's mouth went dry. Paul stared at the crucifix on the wall as if Jesus would step down.

"I'm sorry."

"For what, Paul?" Jacob asked, his chest constricting.

"For lying to Father Joannicus," Paul whispered.

Jacob's patience was waning. "About?"

"I told him it was you."

CHAPTER 8
SAINT CLARE

Psalm 36: 8
Calm your anger and forget your rage.
Do not fret, it only leads to evil.

" I told him it was you."

The words still haunted Father Jacob as he sat in his office several days later. Who had Father Joannicus told? Brother Ambrose? No, Rose would be here. Joannicus told someone. Abbot Gordon? Had Abbot Gordon sent Paul to Saint Clare's before or after Paul had lied to Father Joannicus? Where were his accusers?

Jacob looked out the window. The sun had shone brightly this morning, but now the snow was falling. A late storm with predictions of record snowfall and wind gusts was all speculation and guesswork. Even as the snow fell, they were still making estimates, just like his confrères.

He hadn't done anything. If he said, "It was not me," who would believe him? The hard part was that he couldn't say anything. A priest was saddled, burdened with everyone's sins.

"No, it does not make me kin to Christ," Jacob said to the large crucifix on his office wall, feeling a piercing pain at the thought of Paul and the mean monk.

"You gave him good confessional advice," the Warrior within preached. "Run and find protection," argued the voice of the Elder. Like that will keep him from harm, countered the voice of his dead wife, Faith. *It is all a lie. God won't protect Paul any more than he protected me.* Jacob could almost hear Joannicus sighing. When had he become such a skeptic? Jacob let out a laugh.

He had always been a skeptic.

The secret confession clashed with Jacob's Native American beliefs. He faced the people he had wronged, never hiding in a box, whispering mistakes to a stranger using pronouns instead of names.

His conversion to Catholicism differed from Joannicus's. As a teenage convert, Joannicus left his Baptist upbringing to embrace the Catholic faith completely. During his years of monastic formation, Joannicus accepted the Church and all of her teachings as if handed down by God himself.

Joannicus had once been a Baptist. He grew up Apsáalooke. At eight, they baptized him Catholic, and for him, the whole thing seemed fake. The nuns and priests didn't have answers to his questions, nor did the warriors or elders of his tribe. They also tried to get him to abandon his Apsáalooke beliefs. As a child, Jacob could see the inconsistencies of religion. Paul's conversion began with a baptism at age five. Was he young enough to accept the Church's teachings without question?

No, Paul questioned when the ideal and reality didn't match. This skeptical view reminded him of himself.

"Father Jacob," roared a voice that bounced and echoed down the halls of the parish house. The hairs on the back of Jacob's neck stood at attention. "Reverend Jacob Mackenzie."

Jacob realized who was calling him, and he exhaled with relief. The voice belonged to Brother Ambrose.

"Rose?" Jacob called, surprised. Ambrose was called Rose not because he smelled good but because he had thorns.

Brother Ambrose approached, his eyes wide. He was dressed in his work coveralls and smelt more pungent than normal. Snowflakes dotted his head and beard. As Ambrose turned, Jacob saw he was not alone. Next to him, in a tight grasp, toes barely touching the ground, was a pale and wide-eyed Paul.

"I need you, Father Jacob," Ambrose said. His tone sounded menacing.

"Of course you do," Jacob said.

Seeing the anger etched on Ambrose's face, Jacob thought this could not be good. *Damn, Joannicus told him what Paul said.*

"What can I do for you, Rose?"

"You can punish him. I'll kill him if I do it. I'm very, very angry."

"What do you want me to do?" Jacob asked. Sure, he had misunderstood.

"Paddle his behind."

Had Brother Ambrose lost his mind, talking about physical punishment, knowing less than a year ago, Paul had been so abused? Abbot Gordon had said no more spankings. Jacob knew Ambrose hadn't followed the order.

"Come," Jacob said, leading Brother Ambrose down the hall and outside. Jacob pushed Ambrose's arm down so Paul could walk.

Damn, what has Paul done to tick Ambrose off? He had seen the two square off before with loud shouts and crossed arms. Ambrose was winning the battle, and Paul, like a geyser, spouted and fizzled out.

The snow plopped on them as they entered the backyard, making their way to the rectory. Jacob noticed that the statue of St. Clare was quickly being encased in white.

He liked the statue. Clare was a Franciscan, not a Benedictine—a mismatched saint to a parish. The primarily Native parishioners could not swallow the whole Catholic theology without some fry bread.

When they entered the kitchen, Ambrose let go of Paul's arm. Jacob was sure the child's arm would be bruised.

Should that be reported? It was another unclear situation.

Jacob bit his lower lip. The small kitchen smelled like a campfire. "What happened?"

Brother Ambrose paced the small kitchen, rubbing his sooty head.

"I don't know. One second, I'm feeding the sheep, and the next, the barn is filled with smoke, the fire bell is ringing, the sheep are kicking, and the dogs are barking. Cats and rats are running like bats out of hell."

Paul pasted himself against the wall, trying to dissolve into the woodwork.

Jacob glanced at Paul, who looked paler than normal. His cheeks and arms were covered in black smudges, like war paint.

"That boy. I know it in my bones. He's as guilty as they come. He needs a good throttling." Ambrose stopped and took a step toward Paul.

"Rose, calm down." Jacob stepped between them. "You are not making sense."

"Oh, I am. You need to take care of this." Ambrose's voice reached a thunderous peak.

"Sit," Jacob said, hoping he sounded as threatening as the man he faced. Paul whimpered, sliding down the wall to the floor. "You drove an hour in this weather for me to spank the child? That is crazy talk."

Ambrose's brow knitted together as he clunked a chair, wood scraping wood. He coughed a dry, raspy cough.

Jacob moved to get him water. There was a fire. They both reeked of smoke.

Paul sat silently, his red-rimmed eyes staring at Ambrose.

Ambrose's hand shook as he drank, and then he closed his eyes.

"This child will be the death of me. I teach him and train him, and then this. He's always been obsessed with fire. He'll burn us out of house and home one of these days."

"Stop. Take a breath, start at the beginning."

A coughing fit racked Ambrose, and in a rough voice, he said, "Fire in the barn."

"Is everyone okay?" Jacob asked.

"Okay? Brother Moses left in an ambulance. He was on fire." Ambrose sat, running both hands over the top of his head. Burned hair like pine needles fell to the floor. Skin glistened and blistered on a bare arm.

Jacob rushed to the sink and soaked a towel in water. Then he grabbed Ambrose's waving arm and wrapped it in the damp cloth.

Jacob looked closer at Paul, and he noticed he was missing a shoe and that his wet, soggy sock was making a puddle where he sat.

Ambrose covered his face with his good hand.

"Scholastica's dead. I told you she was smarter than that TV Lassie. She ran into the smoke and flames and led me right to Moses. I got him out." Ambrose's voice cracked. "She didn't come out. I called her, but she..." A sob crinkled up his face, and the top of his mustache glistened. The table shook. Jacob listened to Paul sniffling in the corner. This was bad, terrible.

"Why did she play hero?"

"Paul, take a shower," Jacob said as he turned to Ambrose. "Rose, I am so sorry."

Ambrose wiped his face with his hand. "She was just a dog."

Rivers of moisture watered his beard. Jacob stood and bent over, embracing part of the man whose pain was tangible.

Minutes passed, and then Ambrose pushed Jacob away. A fur-wrapped figure appeared at the window of the back door. The door opened before Jacob could register who it was. Snow clung to the parka. He peered at the person, recognizing his sister Rebecca. She unzipped her coat, draping it on a hook next to the door and handing Jacob a set of child-size clothing. He looked at her questioningly.

"I was listening to the news and saw Rosie's truck. What's wrong?"

"Fire. He and Paul are here."

Ambrose choked and coughed violently. His breath seemed labored. Rebecca pushed Jacob aside, her nursing skills taking over as Ambrose tried to catch his breath.

"Rosie, Great Thunder Beings," Rebecca said. "I'm taking you to the hospital."

Although the large man protested, he rose and followed Rebecca out of the house. Jacob watched as Ambrose filled the front seat.

Snow coated Jacob as he stood outside. Rebecca paused. "The boy?"

"He looks fine. There was no coughing or burns that I noticed," Jacob said. "I will take him home."

She nodded and slipped into the driver's seat. Jacob glanced at the sky. The clouds had grown dark and heavy.

Jacob entered the kitchen and shook off the layer of snow. Paul stood in the living room wrapped in a towel, giving Jacob an unobstructed view of the boy's body, which he scanned for bruises and burns.

Jacob gathered Paul's clothes, put them in the washer, and handed the boy the clothing Rebecca had brought.

"Where's Brother Ambrose?" Paul asked.

"He had to see if Moses was doing okay," Jacob lied.

Paul's lower lip trembled. "If Brother Moses dies, will I go to hell?"

Jacob clenched his jaw. *Catholics and their hell.* "Hell is for terrible adults, not children. Grab that blanket. We need to get you home."

Paul took the folded clothing and wandered into the one bedroom. Jacob shook his head. Paul whimpered in the other room.

"Do dogs go to heaven?" Paul asked, swimming in the oversized shirt.

The correct answer was no. But how could a child believe in a benevolent God who didn't take beloved pets to heaven?

"Where else would she go?"

Paul looked sadder than on the day that Brother Mellitus had died. Paul moved from the doorway to the sofa.

"My stomach hurts."

"You are fine. It is just guilt."

"No, my head hurts."

Just the effects of smoke, Jacob assured himself. "We need to get you home."

"I don't want to go home. I really can't go home. I ruined everything."

Tears ran down Paul's cheeks.

Jacob wanted to shake Paul and shout, "Stop with the over-exaggeration; these guys forgive almost everything. Ambrose just blew his top, but you know he loves you and has probably forgiven you. The barn is just a building!" Instead, he sighed and went to the bedroom to pack his overnight bag. He knew if he made it to Saint Alberic's, he would not return to Saint Clare's tonight.

Jacob stepped back into the living room with Paul's discarded wet towel and saw Paul standing at the window.

"Father Jacob, I don't think we are going anywhere."

Jacob looked out the window and saw the snow-like meringue drifts obscuring fences and bushes.

"Crap."

Paul scowled and then moved back to the sofa. "Bless me, Father, for I have sinned."

"Oh no, we are not having this discussion in confessional form. Tell me what happened," Jacob said, opening the kitchen cupboard.

"I set the fire," Paul said in a whisper. "I read that you could fry an egg by the sun and start a fire with ice."

"Who gives you these ideas?"

"Brother Ambrose. Merlin told me you can start a fire with a magnifying glass, and he said you could start one with a rock."

Jacob remembered seeing a flint with dried buffalo dung in the case in the meeting room and wondered if it was now missing. He placed a pot on the stove. Venison stew sounded right for a chilly winter night.

"I didn't have a magnifying glass, so I took Brother Robert's glasses. It worked," Paul said, his chin falling to his chest. "But the wind blew the straw around, and it landed next to the bales." Paul's face wrinkled in pain. "They just blew up."

"Okay," Jacob said, trying hard not to correct the story or laugh at the vision of Brother Robert groping around for his glasses.

"I tried to put the fire out with water, but the wall was smoking. I ran to the yard and rang the fire bell. Everyone came running, and the dogs were barking, so much noise."

"That was smart," Jacob said, taking the stew from the fridge.

"People shoveled snow into the barn. The fire department came too. I saw Moses burning." Paul winced. "I hid in the truck. They were looking for me. I was scared."

Paul sobbed. Jacob watched and placed bread into the toaster.

The temptation to console proved hard to resist, but he knew the boy needed to feel the pain he had caused. Tears were a part of the process.

"What am I going to do? I'm an orphan now."

Jacob smiled. "You were an orphan long before this. You are on the right track. What can you do to fix this?"

"Fix it?" Paul squeaked. The look on Paul's face showed he was just grasping the meaning of sin.

"I see you have found your penance. Realizing your actions harmed many people you loved."

Jacob buttered the toast and filled two bowls. Paul sniffled and ate very little. *The burden of guilt is often heavy*, thought Jacob.

The back door banged open, and Rebecca stepped in, stomping her boots on the mat. Snowflakes tumbled down, melting on the tiled floor. She removed her furry parka and transformed from a bear to a seal, her shiny black hair shimmering down her back.

"I left Rosie at the hospital. I nearly didn't make it back. I'm glad you didn't leave," Rebecca said.

"Damn, Rose," Jacob said. "I do not need this."

"It cannot be that bad."

A moan escaped Paul. Rebecca and Jacob looked over as Paul doubled over, holding his stomach.

"I don't feel good," Paul said as lunch made a second appearance. Jacob pinched his nose. Rebecca snickered.

"Fine *basaake* you must have been," Rebecca said.

"Very funny. I do not deal with the sick kids," Jacob said, fearing that the walls would collapse around him. He knew that Paul would not die from the flu, yet the images of children, his children limp and pale, shook his foundation.

"You'll be fine. Sick kids sleep. This is just a virus. Twenty-four hours at the most."

"Nobody told me."

"The same stuff has been on the Rez. It's probably hit the monastery, too. I know you are having a challenging time. Will you be all right here tonight? I can stay," Rebecca said.

"No." Jacob wished he could say yes. The nightmares were more frequent. She had come over several nights to comfort him, but the storm outside would prevent that. She needed to be with her family.

He could manage this.

"I would start a fire now. Looks like it will be a camping storm," Rebecca said as she walked a stumbling Paul to the bedroom and tucked him into Jacob's bed. She turned around and looked at Jacob. She tilted her head. Her large brown eyes surveyed him.

"Are you going to be all right?"

"Yeah," Jacob lied.

Rebecca put on her parka. Her dark face, framed in white fur, looked up at him.

"Do you want me to stay?"

Jacob kissed her cheek, wishing he could say yes. "Nah."

Rebecca hugged him, her fragrance of summer roses, a light sweetness.

"Smoke signal me if you need me," Rebecca said with a laugh as she headed out the door.

CHAPTER 9
AZULINE

Psalm 108: 26-27
Help me, Lord my God.
Save me because of your love.
Let them know that this is your work.
That this is your doing, O Lord.

Father Jacob gritted his teeth as Paul whimpered, tossing covers to the floor. After what seemed like hours, the child calmed and slept. Jacob made the sign of the cross on Paul's forehead before leaving. Images of his children crowded his mind as he glared at the crucifix over his dining room table.

"Not fair. You know I cannot deal with the sick."

The three days of dying family members had left Jacob damaged. He found it nearly impossible to minister to the sick in a hospital. The smell, the uniforms, the moans of dying people sent him to the edge of panic. He avoided that part of his ministry, even though it was a priest's duty. Sometimes, he couldn't evade the Anointing of the Sick or the giving of Last Rites, as many lay people called it. He would steel himself to administer this sacrament when he had to and then pay the price of reliving the event that changed his life and canceled out his fatherhood. Sadness, dreams, fragments of last words spoken, and a cloak of depression always followed, even when the person receiving the sacrament didn't die.

The demons of the past stood in front of him, challenging him to fight. Jacob chanted the names of his children, "Katie, Elias, Rosie, Almost Joan. Elias, Rosie, Almost Joan, Faith, Katie." Birth order and then death order. A starry night, a drunk driver, and the station wagon rolling, rolling, rolling down the ravine, screams, and bodies tossed from the car.

The phone rang, startling him.

"Are you bringing Paul home?" came the worried voice of Father Joannicus.

"Have you looked outside?" Jacob asked, shaking himself free of that terrible day. "I will be there when it's over. How are you and the others?"

"We're fine. Brother Moses is in the hospital. You know Paul can't be with you. Can I talk to him?" Joannicus asked.

Irritation crept up Jacob's spine like a tickle in the middle of his back. Joannicus should have known Paul was lying. The child was prone to tall tales and exaggerations.

"Why? I am not the one trying to hurt him, and besides, he is asleep."

The silence on the other end lingered.

"Seriously, asleep?" the tone in Joe's voice called *liar*. Anger washed through Jacob. He imagined Abbot Gordon standing next to Joannicus.

"He was not feeling well. Rebecca said it looks like a virus, twenty-four hours at the most. How many others are sick?" Jacob asked, knowing how 'bugs' seemed to run through the monastery, a hazard of living together.

"Seriously, I'm not sick," Joannicus said.

"That's not what I asked." Jacob untangled the phone cord, which was twisted like a slinky. "Paul is asleep. But he will have a bruise on his arm from Ambrose dragging him around."

"A bruise from Brother Ambrose?" Joannicus said, doubt leaking out of each letter.

"Yeah, Ambrose, the one who brought Paul here. Both were pretty upset."

"What happened to Ambrose? Why isn't Paul with him? This is not good."

Jacob gave up on the tangled mess and tightened his grip on the phone.

"Look, you are worried. I get that. Paul will be fine. Rebecca took Ambrose. He is spending the night in the hospital.

"Seriously, Paul can't stay there with you," Joannicus said firmly. The tone made Jacob wish he could reach through the phone and wrap his fingers around his friend's neck.

"Why not?"

"You know Abbot Gordon has limited Paul's interactions with others," Joannicus said.

That meant him.

"If you are that worried about him, come on out and fetch him yourself."

Warrior rage filled Jacob as he slammed down the phone and yanked the cord from the wall.

He was not the evil monk.

After checking on Paul, who continued a fitful sleep, Jacob busied himself with preparations, making a quick dash to the church and office to make sure everyone had left. As he entered the kitchen, he noticed that Rebecca had left her medicine pouch on the counter. Had she brought it for Ambrose? The pouch was an Indian first aid kit, but she wouldn't just leave it. Maybe she will return and take care of Paul. He fished out a container of willow bark powder and stirred it into a glass of water.

The snow made the world full of unidentifiable white humps. The wind howled, and the windows shivered. Jacob built a large fire. Soon, the room felt feverish as the stove gave off an eerie red glow.

"Are you trying to burn the house down?" Faith asked with a smirk.

Shame filled Jacob. Was Joannicus on his way here? He hoped not.

Jacob sat at the table and tried to repair the plastic insert on the end of the phone cord. There was no dial tone when he pushed it into the wall jack.

"Crap. Serves me right," Jacob said, looking at the crucifix on the wall. "Your hand or mine, either way, is a good punishment for being mean. Now, I can add guilt to my sins if anything should happen to Joannicus."

The afternoon crept at a slow pace. Jacob lit sweet grass, smudged, and prayed aloud for protection from his sorrow. He fingered his rosary beads, forgetting to pause and reflect on the mystery in hand.

"It is your own fault that your children's faces haunt you. Let them go," Jacob said to the twisting flames in the wood-burning stove. "You are a bad Crow and monk."

Paul cried out, and Jacob ran to the room. The child sat on the edge of the bed, shaking.

"I couldn't catch the fish. I'm wet," Paul muttered, his eyes heavy with fever as his head bobbled from side to side.

"Here, drink this," Jacob said, cupping his hands around Paul's hot fingers. Jacob had laced the water with willow bark for just this moment. An aspirin would have worked, but he preferred natural herbs. Paul drank without complaint as his fiery breath seared Jacob's hand as he pulled the covers up.

"Owls dance funny. I like monkeys," Paul mumbled. Then he sighed and fell back asleep.

Poor kid—at least in sleep, you do not know how miserable you are, thought Jacob. His mind focused on his own children and the few times he had to fever-sit. His oldest, Katie, was the hardest when ill. She wanted to deny and defy the illness with willpower. Paul reminded him of her, bold in her approach to life and yet still needing her *basaake*. He wondered if he would have been a grandpa if she had lived.

Jacob paused at the door, his emotions colliding like rabbits when an eagle circled overhead. Why did he perceive such overwhelming dread? This is crazy. Paul would recover. He needed to pull himself together and stop overreacting. Paul was sick, not dying. But the owl always heralded death. And a monkey, like a coyote, means trickster. It was just fever dreams.

Jacob growled, raising his eyes heavenward.

"You play dirty. I thought we understood each other. I am not the protector of children. Four lives died during my watch, and now you send Paul. What did you expect?"

Jacob knew the answer as he moved to the kitchen.

To unlock his heart and make him love again. The Elder inside him nodded.

"It hurts too much. I dislike seeing kids suffer. You made me watch them die. You took them away, and now you hand me this kid. It makes me think I am the only one who can protect him. I cannot."

After washing and drying his hands, he tossed the towel on the counter. Dizziness gripped him. One after the other, placed in his arms, broken, bleeding, struggling to breathe, eyes dark and hopeful, then glazed and gone. Jacob shook himself, his long hair whipping from side to side.

"Enough. Fine, you win. I admit I love the boy, I care, and I want to help. Now, give me something to work with. I do not think I can protect him alone. I could not protect my own kids. Gordon and Joannicus think I am the bad one. How do I convince them otherwise? This is lame, a storm, and illness. I will do it, but you better hold up your end of the bargain. So, Lord, do we have a deal?"

There was a sudden pop and then silence. Darkness shrouded the room—the power had gone out. Jacob fumbled for the flashlight as he listened to the howling wind.

"So, was that a yes or no?"

The silence amplified the fevered child's movements and sighs. Father Jacob placed a cool washcloth on Paul's forehead. Paul shivered and cried out but did not wake up. Jacob was curled up on the sofa. The springs in the cushions poked him. Sleep avoided him. He sat up.

What time is it? Jacob grabbed the flashlight and made his way to the bedroom. He dug in the drawer beside his bed for his great-grandfather's pocket watch. The tarnished silver lid easily opened as he surveyed the time—*eight o'clock*. With the beam of light, he glanced at the sleeping child.

Jacob lay on the bed, making the sign of the cross and continuing his rosary. Sometime later, a hot arm smacked his face, startling Jacob awake.

It is not safe to sleep with the sick.

He rolled out of bed, stumbled to the living room, and whipped the flames to glowing. He got a pot, filled it with water, waited for it to boil, and then placed the eggs in it. Once cooked, he set the pot aside to cool. Day was dawning through the drapes as he opened them to watch the snowfall. He ate a box of crackers, checked on Paul, gathered candles, and played with the hot wax, making little crooked dream catchers. He made tea, danced, forced Paul to drink water, and checked the light switches by turning them off and on. By the afternoon, Jacob had written his sermon for Sunday. The silence grew ominous, so he sang hymns and played solitaire as he waited. Paul still lay quiet and dripping from sweat.

Evening came early as Jacob blew out the lanterns. He glanced at the crucifix over his bed and then at Paul.

"Both of you are not holding up your share of the conversation." Jacob lay on the bed next to the restless boy. He hummed and then prayed aloud until his eyes shut.

Jacob dreamed troubled dreams of children and happier days until soft crying woke him up.

"Hush," Jacob said. "Hush, go back to sleep. *Basaake* will be home soon."

Father Jacob sat up, wide awake. Blinking at Paul standing next to him, his mind still painted with his children's faces. Paul rattled with a cough. Jacob swung his legs to the floor.

"I'm cold. Do you always sleep on top of the covers?"

Paul followed Jacob to the living room. The low glow and lack of heat from the stove indicated time had passed. He stuffed a log into the embers. Outside, the snow blew in crazy circles, creating an eerie fog of gray light as Jacob tried to assess if it was day or night.

"How are you?"

"Thirsty, and my head hurts," Paul said as tears tumbled. "I want Father Jonah."

"Me too," Father Jacob said, as he placed a hand on the still-feverish brow before wrapping Paul up in a soft wool blanket. The room heated quickly.

"Hold me," Paul demanded. "Sing to me."

Jacob sang a Lakota lullaby, "*Cante waste hoksila ake istimba, hanhepi kin waste.* Good-hearted boy, go back to sleep. The night is good."

His mind drifted to other times he'd sung this song to Elias—remembering his lifeless body. He hummed and chided himself, *Knows the Song, indeed.*

That was his actual surname—Knows the Song, not Mackenzie. He didn't use that name often. Father Jacob worked better than the formal Reverend Mackenzie Knows the Song—so many names in one lifetime.

Jacob switched to hymns as they sat on the sofa close to the fire, and Paul drifted back to sleep. The wind had subsided, and the silence grew stronger, only broken by a pop or crackle from the burning wood. Paul's head rested on Jacob's chest, drool escaping down the boy's chin. How many times had he sat with a sleeping child on his lap? The weight and the warmth felt good. Jacob listened to the rhythm of Paul's breaths, peaceful like the few breaths that Almost Joanie had taken. Her first breaths had been her last breaths. Jacob's heart ached.

Jacob pushed the sweat-coated hair from the child's brow. How could anyone hurt a child? He had asked that question in various forms since the first bruise. Paul could be annoying and rude but also endearing and sensitive. *A child*, the Elder inside him said. Children meant everything to the tribe. They were the future. The birth of his nephew rejuvenated his will to live after losing his family. Jacob knew from his own childhood that children could manipulate situations that would cause a beating. However, Paul lived to please, not to fight. Even Joannicus, who lacked child-rearing knowledge, figured that out.

The light in the bathroom glared, and the refrigerator hummed. The power had returned, and Jacob felt no urgency to move.

He needed to be at the monastery to protect Paul. The Warrior within cheered. His innocent confrères lived under the umbrella of false hope that this bad monk would change. The heart of an abuser didn't soften on its own. He could see Faith nodding in agreement.

The phone rang, piercing the quiet.

Paul's fever must have broken, for his tee shirt felt damp as Jacob moved to answer the call.

"Oh, thank God," Joannicus said.

"Hello to you, too."

"Is everything all right? We've been without power. I guess you were out, too. Paul doesn't like that much silence. We tried to come and get him, but the storm prevented us from leaving."

Jacob smiled, remembering the story of Saint Scholastica. She was the sister of Saint Benedict. When her brother refused to spend more time with her, she prayed to God, who sent a storm, forcing Benedict to extend his visit.

"Yes, we are both fine. Thanks for asking. I am surprised you did not hitch up the sheep and arrive by sheep sleigh."

"Seriously, Jacob, don't be petulant. Abbot Gordon and I were concerned."

The truth at last. *More like panicking beyond reason*, thought Jacob with a shiver.

"Is that Father Jonah?" Paul asked, sitting up and rubbing his eyes. "I want to talk to him."

Jacob looked at Paul as he handed Paul the phone. The correct color had returned to Paul's cheeks.

"I was sick. Seriously, I'm better. Father Jacob took good care of me. We'll be home tomorrow. I'm fine, really fine. Is Brother Ambrose still mad? Okay. Well, I'm going to fix it. I got a plan," Paul said, looking at Jacob.

Brother Ambrose would look at things differently. He could not hold a grudge. He might be angry, like a bear woken up early from his winter nap, but the big man had a bigger heart. His daughter Katie had named the man the Bear, and she had been right. He was *daxpitchee*.

Paul hung up and said, "He can't talk to you. He's in his grumpy mood."

"Shower time," Jacob announced, realizing that this protection thing would require him to be one step ahead of Paul if he wanted to assure Paul's safety. But could he do that? Perhaps nobody escaped childhood unscarred.

CHAPTER 10
HIS ABBOTSHIP

Psalm 52: 7
O that Israel's salvation might come from Zion!
When God delivers his people from bondage,
then Jacob will be glad, and Israel rejoices.

J acob waited for the phone to ring again. It did not.

He sent the boy to shower and sliced some cheese while hunting for chicken noodle soup.

The cure for everything.

Rebecca entered with an avalanche of snow. She unlaced her snowshoes and shook herself off.

"It is spectacular out there. We should make snow angels."

"Are you kidding me?" Jacob said, happy to see her.

"Brought chicken noodle soup for Paul," Rebecca said, looking around. "You didn't forget him, did you?"

"You should have come sooner," Jacob said, getting a frying pan out.

"Was it that bad? I left you my medicine. Sick kids sleep."

"Sick kids spread bad dreams."

Rebecca stopped teasing and hugged Jacob.

Paul came out dressed, smelling faintly of aftershave. Jacob placed bread and cheese into the pan, covering it with a lid.

Paul submitted to Rebecca's motherly once-over. "I declare you cured, Father Jacob's first miracle."

"I'm still hungry and tired."

"You have time to rest before my *bachuuke* takes you home. The snow has stopped, the sky is clearing, but the roads are not yet drivable, especially in Rosie's truck."

Paul's head fell to his chest as Jacob poured the chicken soup into a pot, setting it on the stove to boil.

"What's my punishment?" Paul said, climbing up to the counter.

"No punishment. You need to make amends for your poor choices," Jacob said, placing a warm sandwich in front of Paul.

"A punishment is better." Paul poked the warm bread, causing the melted cheese to ooze from the sides.

Rebecca laughed. Jacob stirred the soup as the aroma of chicken filled the air.

"You realize Father Jacob can't be a saint, right?" Paul said as concern creased his face.

Rebecca shook her head. "All he needs is a few miracles and testimony. How old are you?"

"I'm nine and a half, give or take a few days," Paul said.

Jacob tossed another dollop of butter into the pan, watching it sizzle.

Rebecca scowled and said, in Apsáalooke, "Jacob, you cannot let this go on. It's not normal. Children don't talk like that. It's unnatural."

"What do you expect when he is surrounded by intellectuals? He does not pontificate at school."

"He's a kid. He needs to be a kid, not a mini-Joe." They watched Paul bless himself and pray over his cheese sandwich.

"They have entirely too much influence on him," Rebecca said.

They had influence, and they were his family. Monastic living was not a terrible thing. Sarah Warner, Paul's mother, had picked them. They were not a bad tribe to live with.

"He picks up part of the teaching. That is not what worries me."

A wicked grin filled Rebecca's face. "Children reflect their families."

"You are such a pop psychologist. Paul is too mouthy for his own good," Jacob said.

"Sometimes I wonder what planet you came from. That doesn't give anyone the right to harm."

Jacob knew he shouldn't have confided in her about the beating, but how else would he have explained to her the nightmares he was having? He flipped the hot sandwich onto a plate. "He needs a few lessons in discretion."

"He's only nine," Rebecca said, poking a smiley face into the cheesy sandwich.

"Give or take a few days. Just because you're talking Crow doesn't mean I don't know that you're talking about me," Paul said, through a bite of sandwich. "What are you saying?"

"That this soup will cure all," Jacob said in English as he ladled some soup into a large cup.

"Get some rest, both of you." Rebecca put on her coat and gloves, waved goodbye, and entered the white world.

"What do you want to do today?" Jacob asked, savoring the first bite of homemade soup.

"You could read to me. We are finishing Mark, Chapters 15 and 16. This year, Father Jonah and I started with the New Testament."

"You need a bigger reading list. How about we read a story about a bear, a boy, and the hundred-acre woods?"

"Is this an Indian story?" Paul asked as he climbed onto the sofa. "Okay, just don't tell Father Jonah."

"I will not tell him."

"Even if he asks, tell him it was about Barabbas and purple clothing."

Jacob sat on the sofa and opened the book by A.A. Milne.

"Okay, my throat hurts," Jacob said after an hour and a half of reading.

"You are getting sick?" Paul placed his hand on Jacob's brow.

"I am not getting sick, but it is nice to hear you care. I was convinced you hated me."

"Sorry, you're not that mean. There are meaner monks."

"So, I have heard, but I find it hard to believe."

"I'm going to find something to read," Paul said.

"I have a book about a boy who lied, and his nose grew. It has a fairy in it." Jacob rose to clean the kitchen.

"You're just being mean now," Paul said from the bedroom.

Was he being mean? The whole situation was a mess. Did Joannicus believe Paul? He could force Paul to confess. But to what? Who the real mean monk was, or that Paul lied? Bumps and bruises, active boy or mean monk? How does one assign a degree to a beating? It wasn't murder.

Paul appeared, carrying a stack of board games. "Let's play Monotony."

He unfolded the gray board with colored rectangles. "I'm the shoe. I always get to be the shoe. So, I can kick butt."

Several hours passed as they played and filled up on crackers, cheese, fruit, and hot tea.

"How come you don't pray?" Paul asked, straightening his red hotels on the red and yellow side of the board.

"I pray just as much as anyone," Jacob said, feeling defensive. It was true he had not prayed before this meal or the one earlier. He prayed, just not for things. His prayers were full of gratitude. Prayer was about communicating. God knew his needs, so all that remained was casual conversation.

"You're not like other monks, and I don't mean cuz you're brownish and have tattoos," Paul said. "You don't say the same things as Father Jonah."

"Not everyone's faith is as strong as Father Jonah's," Jacob said, rolling the dice and counting his ill-fated steps into the hotel alley.

"I know," Paul said. "But are you Catholic?"

"Yes," Jacob said, smiling, "I am a Crow Catholic dipped in Benedictinism."

Paul's eyes narrowed. "Is that a real word? You owe me $1050, and it's still your roll. You got doubles."

"I said it. You understood it. It is a word. I am a mixture of all I have experienced. Apsáalooke spirituality was where I started. I did not throw out the old for the new. I like my Apsáalooke beliefs. Sometimes, they explain things better than the Church."

Jacob paid and rolled, landing on Marvin Gardens.

Paul grinned. The game was over. "Sometimes, there is no explaining. That's what Father Jonah says. You must believe in the mystery of it all."

Jacob nodded.

Paul collected the game pieces as Jacob cleaned the kitchen. Paul peered at the clock and asked, "Is that the correct time? We should be praying."

Jacob rolled his eyes and wiped his hands. "There is a Psalter on the table."

"Aren't we going to the church?"

"Paul, it is freezing over there. You just got over being sick."

"I have a coat. We'll appreciate the heat more afterward," Paul said, sounding like an adult. "You shouldn't lie," he added, putting on his shoes.

"I am thankful now," Jacob said, raising his hands heavenward like a televangelist. "Oh Lord, maker of all that is good, thank you for my nice warm house." He stopped and stared at Paul. "Seriously?"

"Seriously," Paul said as he shook his head. Father Jacob swore he looked like a miniature Father Joannicus. Jacob opened the door and looked out. Even though the church was near, the frozen air made it seem far. The snow came up to his knees as he made a narrow path between the rectory and the church. Jacob wished he had worn gloves as they entered the darkness, which was lit only by the shimmering votive lights. Their frosty breaths lingered where they stopped as Jacob turned on one spotlight over the altar.

"You are choir two." Jacob took a seat in front of the altar, started the Office with a song, and then paused. "You are not singing."

"I like listening to you."

Father Jacob flipped open the Psalter. "Psalm 8," he announced, slipping one frozen hand under his armpit.

Paul cleared his throat. "No, it should be 136. This is week two. Psalm 8 is a morning psalm. The Rule says so."

"You do not know that. You were sick for days," Jacob said, finding it hard to accept that Paul had memorized the sequence of four weeks.

"It is," Paul said in an exasperated tone.

Jacob shivered. What choice did he have? Freeze or capitulate. "Fine, you pick a psalm."

Paul smiled. He began with Psalm 136.

"I suppose you do not need a book," Jacob said, snapping his Psalter shut and hugging himself for warmth.

"I need a book, silly. Father Jonah doesn't. He has them all memorized, just like the olden days when Saint Benedict was a monk."

"Father Joannicus does not have all the Psalms memorized," Jacob said as he rubbed his hands together to keep them from aching. He was thankful the evening prayers were shorter than morning prayers.

"Yes, he does."

"No, he does not."

His brain was frozen. Why was he arguing?

"Yes, he does. He doesn't have a book when we go out and pray the Office."

The tip of Jacob's nose felt numb, so Jacob obeyed the little abbot and finished prayers, running for the exit as soon as they said the last *amen*. He stood next to the stove.

He had experienced hell freezing over.

Paul came in and hung up his coat. Jacob banked the fire for the night. He stacked a pillow and blanket on the sofa. Jacob entered his bedroom and noticed that Paul was in his bed.

"You cannot sleep in my bed with me."

"Why not? Father Jonah lets me sleep in his bed sometimes."

But he's not in it. The words of protest froze in Jacob's mouth. Who would know? Jacob shook his head, grabbed a blanket, and rolled it up, placing it between them in the bed. "Your side. My side."

"You're weird," Paul said.

"You are a little odd yourself," Jacob said, turning off the light. Shadows from the fire wiggled through the open door.

"I can't sleep," Paul said. "I'm sad. I killed Scholastica. I really messed up."

"Yep," Jacob said, smiling in the dark. "How are you going to change that?"

"I don't know."

"You could start by putting the flint and stone back into the cabinet in the Chapter Room."

"Who told you?"

"Never mind that," Jacob said. "You could read to Brother Robert to give his eyes a rest. Moses always loves to play checkers."

"Those are promising ideas," Paul said, yawning. "I could also get Brother Ambrose a puppy."

"Perhaps you should start with the idea of a puppy," Jacob said.

"A nice, soft, cuddly puppy. I will call her Gertrude, like the saint of Bingham, or Gertrude of the barn."

CHAPTER II
MEANINGFUL WORK

Psalm 36: 4
If you find your delight in the Lord,
he will grant your heart's desire.

T he late spring storm transformed the hilltop into a frosted cake. Early buds stood shrouded in snow blankets. During the storm, Father Pius enjoyed the company of his fellow monks instead of hurrying back to his parish. The air was warm, and the snow stood triumphantly all around. He made his way down the hill to the college.

The college seemed frozen in time and the dorms glowed like a Thomas Kinkade winter painting.

Excitement tingled his frame as he opened the door to the large brick building of higher learning. An odor of beeswax varnish filled his nose. How many hungry minds had wandered through these halls on their journey to adulthood?

Now is my time; I'll be teaching. He had aspired to teach not English or philosophy but theology. Once he had earned his degree, the Abbot assigned him to the parish of Saint George. The Benedictines had always lent a hand to the diocesan, supplying monks when needed. He was an obedient monk who hid his disappointment at not being allowed to teach in the theology department.

The old floor underneath his feet creaked and groaned as he headed to the stairwell. Wide oaken steps beckoned him to climb. Abbot Gordon's words rang in his ears, "You will teach three classes, all of them in theology. This will ease the workload for Father Joannicus." Worry filled him as he walked down the long hallway on the fourth floor. Would Joannicus resent this change?

Pius sighed. This change could be a challenge.

Giggling coeds broke the silence of his reflection. He turned to see one dash out of a classroom. As he passed the opened door, he saw Father Joannicus attempting to gather a melting snowball.

It was half past, and only one student was in the classroom.

"Do you need help?" Pius asked.

"Silly girls. Shouldn't they be in class?" Joannicus said, wiping his wet hands on his scapular. A dusting of snow-like chalk trailed down the black wool habit where the snowball had hit before landing on the floor.

"They canceled classes. It's snowmageddon out there."

"Seriously, why aren't the students who live here in class? I'm here. We have power, and they are just across the courtyard."

Father Pius smiled. Snow day was not on Joe's radar. The student's face pleaded with Pius—please explain *canceled*.

"Perhaps they are ill," Pius said. The lone student coughed. Joannicus frowned and pushed his glasses up his nose.

"Fine, then. You can go. Thank you for coming to class," Joannicus said as the student made a mad dash out the door.

"Seriously, they are not ill. The class is a few yards away. They are lazy." Joannicus gathered his folder and placed it into his black satchel. A crease appeared on his forehead as he looked out the window. "What is taking Jacob so long?"

Father Joannicus seemed anxious about Paul's return. Did he really miss him? Hadn't he complained about how Paul intruded into his hermit-like desires?

"The snow is deep," Pius said, reflecting that Jacob and Paul seemed to get along fine—how, he was not sure. Paul ran hot and cold, liking and disliking monks according to his own selfish needs.

"I'm sure you're right. It's just that Paul was sick," Joannicus said.

"Jacob's been a father. He has dealt with sick children before."

Father Pius remembered Jacob with his own children. The phrase "acting like a pack of wild Indians" came to mind. The "let them be" attitude of raising children did not impress Pius. Children needed structure.

They headed down the hall, the floor squeaking in time with their steps. Pius searched for a way to ask Joannicus for help.

"I hear you're coming home, and Father Vincent will take over the parish," Joannicus said as he fished his keys from his habit pocket. Pius studied his shoes.

"Yes, that's true. I hope you and I can discuss theological matters, perhaps with the juniors and novices."

Joannicus opened the door.

"I'm no longer a part of the formation team. Abbot Gordon has relieved me of my teaching and my monastic responsibilities."

Father Pius grappled with the question, asking the obvious and not wanting to add to the melancholy that had settled like dust around Father Joannicus.

The musty smell of oldness that comes with opening a forgotten trunk wafted out. Pius thought of it as the aroma of wisdom. He fingered the ring on his right hand. The gold ring belonged to his mother's uncle, who had risen to the honor of the bishop in Denmark only to be murdered during the occupation. He was a bishop and a Benedictine monk. Pius had received it when he entered the priesthood, and Gordon had allowed him to wear it.

"What will you do?" Pius asked as he cracked his knuckles.

Joannicus sat in the wooden chair behind the bulky desk. It grunted in protest.

"Are you planning to write?" Pius asked, not giving Joannicus time to answer the first question.

"No, but that's a promising idea. My only responsibility is to watch Paul; seriously, the boy doesn't require much supervision."

Pius wondered why the Abbot made these changes.

Pius cracked his knuckles on his other hand and focused on the wall, which had a calendar three months behind it.

"Did something happen down here?"

Joannicus looked up from rummaging around in his desk. "No complaints from the college administration have come to my attention."

"I meant coed problems." Pius stole a glance over his shoulder.

Joe's jaw dropped, and shock spread across his face, but his cheeks reddened. "Those are children."

"Sorry. I didn't mean to insult you. But young women wanting to procreate and prove their sexual attractiveness." Pius paused, not having the heart to finish.

Joannicus stacked his papers. "I get it—rumors and whispers. No, this change is not about teaching. I'm struggling with my faith, my dark night of the soul. Everyone has it. I haven't lost God. I've just lost the path. Perhaps Gordon sees that, and this is my time to grow more rooted."

Pius felt a stir in his stomach. He didn't like the words, even if they were true. Not Joannicus. He was the cornerstone, as solid as the Abbot, a religious man of steel.

"How may I help?" Pius asked as the door to the office burst open.

"We're back," Paul announced, tossing his coat on the floor.

Father Pius frowned as Paul entered the long, narrow office.

There was a reason for this crisis. They were monks, not babysitters. One benefit of being monastic is that one didn't have parental duties.

Paul's radiant face turned sour as he moved closer to Joannicus, who gave Paul a detailed once-over.

"Roads are open," Paul said, pulling down his shirt and pushing Joe's hands away.

That's odd, thought Pius. *What is he looking for?* He had heard the boy had the stomach flu, not chicken pox.

Father Jacob appeared at the door, out of breath. "He's fine. It was just a twenty-four-hour thing. Rebecca pronounced him well."

"One lucky boy," Pius said, having heard about the damage Paul had done with his little science experiment. "The charred barn is still standing, and Moses is still breathing. Have you been to the hilltop?"

"Brother Ambrose will forgive me," Paul said, thrusting his chin out. "I'm going to help him on the farm and get him a puppy. May I visit Brother Moses this afternoon?" Paul ran his fingers over the book spines on the shelves next to Joannicus.

"Yes, but don't tire him out. He needs his rest."

"We're gonna play checkers, and I'll let him win," Paul said as he hopped across the room toward the door.

"We all were ill," Pius said, wondering where Paul got his energy.

"Seriously, it was just an upset stomach," Joannicus mumbled.

Paul stopped in mid-motion between Pius and Jacob.

"You were ill," Jacob and Paul said in unison.

"No, not really. There are probably ill effects from the fire and cold. You know I don't like extreme cold. With the power outage, it gets freezing in those stone buildings."

The tension in the room grew thick. Jacob snorted, and Paul glared before coughing in Pius' direction and not covering his mouth.

Anger flared in Pius. *He did that on purpose. What an obnoxious child.* Brother Ambrose should have made compost out of him.

Father Jacob grabbed Paul's arm and bent down, looming over the child. "Quit."

Paul's shoulders slumped.

Jacob had control over this child. Three days together had taught Paul who was in charge.

Paul slunk to the door and exited. Pius heard the thunderous footsteps grow softer as the child raced down the empty hall.

"It's time to face the bear. By that, I mean Rose. I hope he is in a forgiving mood," Jacob said.

"Paul is correct. I believe Ambrose has already moved on," Joannicus said, standing up and retrieving Paul's fallen coat as he headed out the door. "I think we should hold off on the puppy."

Paul's thudding footsteps grew louder as he raced by.

"Coat and no puppy," Joannicus said, holding the down-filled jacket.

"It's not what you want. It's what Brother Ambrose needs," Pius said, giving Paul a stern look.

"He needs one," Paul said.

"He is right," Jacob said. "Do not mention it, and we can discuss it later. Mention it, and definitely no puppy."

Paul growled and raced off, coat in hand, as Joannicus shook his head.

Father Pius felt the energy draining out of him as he watched Joannicus. *This child is crushing Joe's spirit.* Good thing he was home. He could help and spend more time with Joannicus.

"Congrats on the teaching assignments and Guest Master; there are many social duties," Jacob said.

Pius wrapped his winter scarf around his head. In his delight at teaching, he had forgotten that he would soon be the new Guest Master for the Monastery.

Joannicus paused, putting on his gloves.

"You will do well in both positions," Joannicus said, stumbling over his words.

They made a slow ascent on the slippery path to the monastery.

"Joannicus, I will need help with this new assignment. I hope you will be available?" Pius asked.

"Of course. I'm at your disposal," Joannicus said, but it sounded like resignation rather than an offer to help.

"I would not mind a change," Jacob said. "You and I should trade places."

Joannicus stopped at the crazy suggestion, looked at Jacob, and then shook his head. "Seriously, Gordon wouldn't go for it. I know nothing about running a parish. I cannot be a single parent. I need the community to help raise Paul."

A misaimed snowball crashed into the tree. Jacob smiled as he scooped snow and formed it into a ball.

"They run by themselves. You do not need to know anything. Rebecca is there. She knows everything." Jacob threw the white ball at Paul, hitting the boy in the back.

What was Jacob thinking? The notion of Joannicus in a parish didn't fit.

Heavy snow plopped down, making cavernous holes as it slid off branches.

A tickle of shame itched Pius as he followed Jacob and Joannicus into the monastery. The suggestion was troubling. Jacob's presence would be another distraction for Father Joannicus. But sending Joannicus to a Native parish would strip him of the theological discussions he hoped to have with Joe. That thought was more than troubling.

Dear God, please keep Father Joannicus with us. We need him here.

CHAPTER 12
FATHER JACOB RETURNS

Psalm 50: 3
Have mercy on me, God, in your kindness.
In your compassion, blot out my offense.

Father Jacob entered the Abbot's office with a cursory knock. Abbot Gordon looked up from his desk. "Father Jacob, the Lord be with you."

"And with you, Father Abbot. I got the message you wanted to see me."

The Abbot leaned back in his leather chair. The sun glistened off the snow behind him, almost blinding Jacob and encasing the Abbot in a halo-like glow.

"Thank you for taking care of Brother Ambrose and returning Paul." Abbot Gordon spoke slowly. "Please thank your sister, Rebecca, for getting Brother Ambrose to the hospital. He can be a challenge."

Jacob nodded. That wasn't the real reason for the summons.

"Be careful," the Warrior within said.

"I'm told that Paul has a bruise on his arm," Abbot Gordon said, his face a sheen of innocence.

Father Jacob willed his face to remain passive, inhaling slowly. He let the sweetness of the lilies next to the desk fill his nostrils. He would not let Gordon bait him.

"Ambrose lays claim to the injury," Abbot Gordon said.

The small clock on the desk swirled, calling out a gentle tune.

"I realize that I have burdened you these last few months. I'm aware you disagree with my judgment. Every week, I expect to see you. I can't overlook continual absences."

This game will stop if you tell everything about Paul. A slight grin played at the corner of his lips. "It won't be a problem."

A confused expression appeared on Abbot Gordon's face, and Jacob's confidence soared.

Father Jacob relished the words. "I am asking that you consider my returning to the monastery. I have been absent for too long."

He had been pastor of Saint Clare's for the past ten years. Abbot Gordon's eyes narrowed.

"Who could take your parish?"

"Father Joannicus is free."

The Abbot's chair clunked forward. "Excuse me?"

Father Jacob held his smile in check as he looked at the balding man, whose cheeks tinged with red as if someone had slapped him.

"No. This kind of thing takes time, calls to the Bishop."

"There is always Rebecca. She supervised the running of the parish when I was on vacation." Jacob watched Abbot Gordon's face. The Warrior within said, "Sweeten the deal. "

"I fear, since the event, that I need more support. I have been having nightmares." Jacob chose his words carefully, attempting to sound needy and penitent. "The only place I sleep is here." Guilt peeked around the corner of his conscience and quickly ducked back.

Abbot Gordon nodded. Everyone knew the monastery was Jacob's sanctuary.

"I would like to come home. It's time to come home," Jacob said.

The deception was not very monk-like, but he couldn't say he was coming home no matter what. Rudeness never gets you much, a lesson Paul needed to learn. Jacob perceived Gordon would not let him languish spiritually if he asked for help.

Abbot Gordon leaned forward, folded, then unfolded his hands. He rubbed his chin and balding head. "What will you do here?"

"If I have a choice, I thought perhaps, sacristan. I could also help at the farm."

"Paul helps at the farm."

"Paul is there after school. In the afternoons, I will be busy with my duties as the sacristan." Jacob wondered if Gordon would believe this. The duties of a sacristan involved setting up the chalices and hosts for Mass and making sure the colors and garments were ready for the priest to wear. The tasks of cleaning, arranging the flowers, trimming candles, and keeping the schedule updated didn't take all day, but he'd drag it out.

The clock on the wall ticked loudly. Jacob willed himself to remain standing still, keeping his breath slow and even. With a penetrating stare, Abbot Gordon scowled and then said, "Junior Master. We need a Junior Master."

Jacob reeled, resting a hand on the corner of the desk.

Oh no. He didn't want to be responsible for the fledging monks' needs and imagined fears. Gordon's face was now calm. Had Joannicus set him up? Did Gordon want Jacob home to keep a better eye on him?

"There are six Juniors. I'll call them in and inform them they need to report to you. Is tomorrow morning a suitable time to meet with them?"

It looks like he is spending the night.

"Certainly. The sooner, the better," Jacob mumbled acidly. He could do this. His goal was to protect Paul.

"Excellent," Abbot Gordon said, smiling and turning his chair away to face the window behind him.

Father Jacob exited, walked down the hall, and entered the community room, slightly confused and nervous over what had just happened. Several monks looked up and nodded, acknowledging his presence. Jacob made his way to the table where Ambrose and Paul were sitting.

"Are you ill?" Brother Ambrose asked, looking up from peeking at his solitaire hand.

Jacob sat, shaking his head. What had he done?

"What's wrong? Are you getting the flu?" Ambrose pressed. "Did Abbot Gordon blame you for Paul's arm?"

"No, I am fine. Gordon accepted your explanation," Jacob said. "Apparently, I am to be the new Junior Master."

Several heads turned in his direction at the announcement.

"That's crazy talk, man," Paul mumbled as he colored in his saints coloring book.

"Paul, where do you come up with those colorful phrases?" Brother Ambrose scolded as he turned to Jacob. "Who will take your parish? Father Vincent can't run two parishes."

Why did people assume that the parish needed a Native priest? A compassionate man could do the job.

Jacob smiled at the vision of his sister Rebecca dressed in priestly robes. "Maybe Rebecca would like the job."

Brother Ambrose laughed. Abbot Gordon and Father Joannicus entered the community room together. Gordon posted a message to the bulletin board. The two were talking in hushed tones. Father Pius entered the room, checking the board for messages. Jacob watched the man's head snap in Joannicus's direction and then twist, glaring at Jacob.

"Congratulations, Father Joannicus," Pius said, his words seeming strained. I'm sure you'll be a fine pastor at Saint Clare."

"What?" Paul said, springing up from the table and causing cards to fly. "Father Jonah is leaving? No, that can't be."

"Oh, Jacob, what have you done?" Brother Ambrose said.

"I didn't do it," Jacob said, trying to sound innocent. He had done nothing; he had merely suggested it. Father Pius smiled smugly as Paul's protests filled the room.

"I'm going with him," Paul said, running to the Abbot. "He's not leaving me here alone." Paul grabbed Joe's sleeve.

"Paul, you're never alone," Gordon said. "Change is good. Father Joannicus will return."

"Unless women turn him," Ambrose muttered.

"Women will not be his challenge," Jacob hissed. Social obligations and coming back to the community would be more difficult. He wondered if he had just sent his friend into a hazardous situation. Parish life allowed for solitude.

"The world has gone crazy. They have sent the kitten to the wolves," Brother Ambrose said, shaking his head. "At least Rebecca will be there to protect him."

Unless she devours him first. He should warn Rebecca. She didn't like change either. A prickle of nervousness ran through him.

"No," Paul said, stomping his foot. "This can't be happening. We don't need Father Jacob here. Send him back."

Father Joannicus frowned, and Jacob studied his face. Was he angry, happy, scared?

"Paul, that is enough. You need to go to your cell," Abbot Gordon ordered, pointing to the door.

"No."

The elderly monks gasped. Gordon's usually placid face turned hard. Brother Ambrose's chair scraped on the floor. Paul looked at the large man with the bandaged arm. Jacob stood.

Paul crossed his arms. "I'm not going to my room. And even if you get me in there, I'm not staying."

"Oh yes, you are. I'll lock you in if I have to," Ambrose said, sitting back down. "You need to listen to the Abbot and go to your cell."

Paul's jaw jutted stubbornly. Joannicus stood silently. Jacob regretted his rash decision. Protecting Paul was one thing, but correcting Paul was not the task he wanted.

"Paul, I'm in charge. I'll decide who goes and comes," Abbot Gordon stated, his face red and sweating. The man looked ill.

"You're not in charge." Paul pointed to a monk who sat silently pretending to read the newspaper. "You don't know that he kisses girls." Paul turned and pointed to another monk whose eyes grew large with fear. "Or that he drinks the wine while cleaning up after Mass." Paul straightened his arm and spun around, looking for another victim. "And he takes a leak outside all the time." Monks left before secrets became general knowledge. "He has a TV in his cell."

"Enough," Joannicus said as he turned, placing a hand on the boy's shoulder. "You need to obey."

"But, Father Jonah," Paul protested, "you can't go."

"Seriously, I do as I am told," Father Joannicus said, looking at Paul over his glasses with expectation.

Jacob noticed Father Pius standing in the doorway of the nearly empty community room. He hadn't shied away from Paul's little display of power. Jacob couldn't read the look on his face. Was it with a sneer or shock that Joannicus accepted the post of Saint Clare's without protest?

Tangible shame and confusion floated in Paul's wake as he stomped out of the room. The wine wasn't a surprise. Brother Thaddeus was fond of drinking. He felt embarrassed for Father James having his sin announced before the community. He now understood how Paul got himself beaten. The Juniors would be easy compared to teaching a child self-restraint.

CHAPTER 13
INCENSE

Psalm 64:4
Too heavy for us, our offenses,
but you wipe them away.

Father Jacob walked up the hill from the cemetery. The rain dripped from the trees. The odor was dank and intoxicating. He had spent the morning trying to decide the best way to keep Paul safe. He didn't believe this was the life that Sarah Warner had envisioned when she entrusted Paul to them. Even though a year had passed since the bad monk hurt Paul, they were no closer to knowing whom. Jacob figured it was a matter of time, although it felt like he was the only one waiting.

He heard the 1940s truck long before it honked. Brother Ambrose pulled up beside him and stopped, beckoning him in. The door creaked as Jacob climbed into the warm cab.

"Have you moved in already?" Brother Ambrose asked.

"I had little to move," Jacob said, fiddling with his long black braid.

The truck rumbled as it made its way to the monastery.

"You are sending me the Juniors? I could use the help on the farm."

"No, I hadn't thought about that. I was hoping I could help."

Brother Ambrose laughed. "Silly monk, you won't have time to play here. Why did Abbot Gordon send Father Joannicus away?" ·

"Why ask me? Why not ask Joannicus?"

Ambrose applied the brakes. Father Jacob caught himself before his head hit the windshield.

The large man turned and placed a heavy hand on Jacob's arm. "Who is the mean monk? We could have used Joannicus on our team. Unless you're telling me that he's the one."

"Oh, God no, Joannicus might not love Paul, but he would never hurt a child. Why would you say that?" Jacob was surprised that anyone could suspect Father Joannicus.

"It's sometimes hard to tell the good guys from the bad." Brother Ambrose hit the gas, and they continued up the hill. "We all love the boy. Some of us don't know it."

Jacob wanted to argue that letting a child rule or caring out of duty was not love. Instead, he said, "I thought I was the prime suspect."

"We were all suspects if you talk to Abbot Gordon."

"It is not you, is it?" Father Jacob asked, fearful that Ambrose might say he was.

"Is the boy still alive?"

Jacob drew a smiley face on the foggy window. "He gets a lot of bumps and bruises."

"You're sounding like the Abbot. He's an active boy. Not every bruise is cause for alarm. Don't go stirring the tar when we don't have the feathers. You came home to monitor Paul, right?"

"No. I love community life so much," Jacob said, wiping the condensation off the window with his sleeve.

"You're so full of shit, but you make me laugh. You love us, but like Joannicus, you're afraid to admit it."

The truck stopped at the hilltop. Both men looked up, noticing billows of white smoke wafting from the church. They jumped out of the truck and took off running.

The smoke was thick as Father Jacob ran through the hallway toward the sacristy, scapular flying and the skirts of his cassock held up. He placed a hand on the door. It was cool to the touch. A vapor trail of white smoke oozed from under the door. It was sweet, not the musky aroma of wood. This was not a fire. *Damned Juniors can't even extinguish an incense cake properly.*

The sacristy was small, with wall-to-wall cabinets and storage for chalices and candles. Near the stairwell hung incense burners for various celebrations and several processional crosses.

Jacob turned the doorknob, then reached into his jeans pocket for the key. Ambrose's labored breathing came up behind him.

"No fire, thank God."

Jacob pushed the door open. The two stepped back as a wall of white choked them. Ambrose grabbed the end of Jacob's scapular and tried to fan the cloud from the threshold. Billows of incense rolled out like foam as Jacob yanked his scapular out of the man's hands.

"The fog is thick. Help me, Joseph," Paul announced in a loud voice. "Where is Benedict? When there is work to be done, that saint runs off."

Jacob wondered how the child could breathe in the room, let alone move. Relief filled Jacob, followed by irritation. Paul should not be playing in here.

"Joseph, you can't go to the stables now. No, I don't want to sing silly songs to your son. Yes, I know what the angel said. Just give me the magic robe your father made for you. Yes. Jacob's magic robe. Joseph, Joseph," Paul's voice scolded.

Jacob recognized Abbot Gordon's tone of disapproval in the child's voice.

"We don't have a Joseph," Ambrose whispered, wiping his watering eyes.

Paul, oblivious to his audience, continued in a tone of exasperation, "Mary said I could use the robe. I don't have time to argue with you. The monks could come at any moment."

The smoke cleared, and Paul's eyes watered as he jumped around with a long-tapered candle and banged it against the standing candlesticks.

"Take that and that," Paul shouted as he fought his imaginary enemies. "Victory! Alleluia! I claim this cloth in the name of the Father, Son, and Holy Monks of the order of American Cantonese."

At that moment, Jacob saw Paul for what he was: a child with a large vocabulary and mismatched myths. They were members of the American-Cassinese Congregation of the Benedictine Confederation, but that was a mouthful.

"Chinese food, anyone?" Ambrose grinned as the figure of a little boy draped in a striped altar cloth became clearer.

"Time is running out. I must find the treasure." Paul hopped from one rosary bead circle to the next. "Through him, with him, in him, all for one and one for all."

The cupboards banged open as Paul looked for a hidden treasure. He climbed onto the counter and pulled out a chalice with a red, tear-shaped ruby embedded in the base. Paul jumped down from the counter with a loud thump, holding the chalice high.

"Through rain, sleet, snow, and dark of night, I'll find my way back. I'll bring the cup of salvation home and save the monks from the fires of hell."

Paul stood before the crucifix, then knelt, raising the chalice upward.

"Oh no, you won't trick me like you did, Jacob. I will not serve you for another seven years. You better watch out. You better not cry." Paul's voice was low and sinister as he poured the contents of a cruet into the incense urn. The water smothered the burning cake. "I'm melting," Paul squeaked. "You wicked, wicked child."

Ambrose sank to the floor, shaking with laughter. He held a hand over his mouth as tears ran down his cheeks.

"Come home, monks, I've liquefied the terrible king. The bells are ringing. Let's start working."

"We have arrived," Jacob announced.

Paul froze, dropped the colorful altar cloth, and bolted past them.

Brother Ambrose bellowed with laughter, his large girth jiggling with mirth.

Jacob tried to survey the damage as he picked up the discarded altar cloth and chalice. Nothing appeared misplaced as he opened the window by the stairwell that led to the wine cellar. Maybe Joannicus wasn't exaggerating when he complained about a child in the monastery.

"Oh Lord, have mercy," Ambrose said, mopping his face. "One of us needs to speak to the boy."

Together, they walked back to the monastery, a trail of the sweet scent following them.

They found Paul, feet dangling over the sofa arm in the community room.

Father Pius entered the room behind them, wrinkling his nose. "What's that smell?"

"Holiness," Jacob said with wicked amusement, wondering how long he would reek like a feast day service.

Ambrose laughed, heading to the kitchenette to pour himself coffee.

Father Joannicus stood in the doorway and sniffed. "Someone used too much aftershave. Father Pius, do you have time to review the teaching schedule?"

"Aftershave? Me?" Ambrose said, running his fingers through his beard and looking around the room. "Damn, where did that boy go?"

Jacob frowned at Paul's disappearance and Joe's forgetfulness. They had made plans to go out, and Jacob wasn't sure if he should feel slighted. He realized Pius and Joannicus had a lot to discuss so that they could both settle into their new lives. The two walked away, lost in the world of academia.

Father Jacob knocked on Paul's cell door before entering.

Paul looked up from his Lego building, giving Jacob an icy stare.

"What do you want? You can't punish me. I broke nothing, and I didn't light the incense. It was already burning."

"Yes, I can punish you for misuse of sacred objects. Rule 25 of the priest handbook."

Paul frowned. Jacob wondered if Paul would question him about the nonexistent handbook for priests.

"Fine, but I'm in my cell already," Paul said, stacking green Legos.

"Do not play with the chalices."

Paul's face crumbled as if Jacob had announced no play forever.

"Fine. I have some old chalices. You can pick one and play with it in your cell as long as you tell no one."

"Really?" Paul's face brightened. "That's a dumb punishment, just so you know."

Jacob shook his head. "Most people say thank you when they get what their heart desires."

Jacob sat down on the floor, his skirt billowing around him. "What are you building?"

Paul clicked his tongue. "It's Monte Cassino. See." Paul handed Jacob a floor plan of the ancient monastery of the founder of their order, Saint Benedict. "Father Abraham got me the plans. Isn't it wonderful?"

Jacob would have chosen the word *creepy*. Most children build houses and dragons. This is not normal. What did he expect? The kid was surrounded by talk of Jesus, God, and souls.

Jacob smiled. "Cool. What are you doing for dinner? I have this card, and it pays for a dinner for two. You interested?"

Paul's eyes narrowed as he looked at Jacob. "I'm not supposed to be alone with you."

"I am not the monk who hurt you," Jacob said, trying to sound stern. "Even if nobody else knows the truth."

Mischief twinkled in Paul's eyes. "Okay."

Jacob laughed at how easy it was to influence Paul. "Meet me in the back parking lot. In ten minutes, do not be followed."

How much trouble would he be in for taking Paul off the hilltop? Would they even notice that they were gone?

"No problem. I'll be there."

Jacob headed down the hall and noticed an ominous sign posted on Paul's door that read, 'Keep out! No monks allowed—that means you! Go away!'

When Jacob arrived in the parking lot, Paul sat waiting on the hood of the Ford.

"That did not take long."

"I got excommunicated from dinner. Abbot Gordon doesn't enjoy burping."

"The word you are looking for is *expelled*," Jacob said.

"What does that mean?"

Big words again. He needed to remember he was talking to a kid, not a confrère. He is an incorrigible, bratty, intelligent, and funny kid, but he needs guidance, some limits, and love.

Jacob smiled as Paul chatted. The car headed down the hill into the secular world.

"This is risky, Warrior," cautioned the Elder in his mind.

He agreed but knew it was the right choice.

CHAPTER 14

JACOB'S GOD

Psalm 45: 8
The Lord of hosts is with us.
The God of Jacob is our stronghold.

P aul and Father Jacob returned to the monastery through separate doors as the bells rang for evening prayer. Jacob took his place in the choir, noticing that Joannicus was absent. Sadness felt heavy upon him at having missed Joe's departure. Brother Ambrose snored softly on Jacob's right. Jacob figured the solitude of parish life would suit Joannicus. At least he knew Joannicus would be obedient and return for the weekly visit.

He'd make the farm part of the Juniors' routine. They may as well learn how to juggle work and school.

Prayer ended. Jacob turned off the lights in the church and walked past the sacristy. He heard voices and a shout as he headed to the dressing room.

"Leave me alone."

That was Paul's voice. Jacob caught his breath. Was Paul nearer to the church or the monastery? He headed right toward the monastery. There, in the hallway, he saw Paul and Father Pius. Even from a distance, Jacob could tell it was Pius.

"I'll not ask you again. What are you doing skulking around here?" Father Pius hissed, cornering Paul.

Jacob slowed to a walk. Paul attempted to move around Father Pius.

"Nothing. I want to go."

"What are you hiding?"

"Nothing," Paul said in a panicked voice.

"You're such a liar," Pius said, grabbing Paul's arm and shaking the boy. "Hand it over."

Paul handed Pius a book and crumpled to the floor. Father Pius opened the book and flipped through the pages. "Well, I wonder what Father Joannicus will say when he sees this."

"He won't say anything," Paul said, but his face betrayed his words.

"Father Jacob," Pius said, without taking his eyes off Paul.

"Problem?" Jacob asked, looking at Paul's huge brown eyes that smoldered with anger. Those eyes pleaded *Help me* all in one blink.

"Unsupervised children always are," Pius said with a crooked smile as he handed Jacob the book.

Jacob looked at the title: *While the Clock Ticked.* The cover depicted two boys tied up and gagged, fearful expressions, and a sinister man behind a grandfather clock. Why did Pius care what the boy was reading? Perhaps Pius wasn't aware that Joannicus had taught Paul to read early to keep him occupied.

"It is bedtime, so you'd best get into bed," Jacob said, giving Paul a reason to leave.

Paul nodded.

"Well, then off you go," Jacob said as he reached past Pius, pulling Paul out of the corner.

Paul ran, stumbling down the hallway into the monastery.

"I don't suppose reminding him to walk would help," Pius said, shaking his head.

"I think Ambrose broke the off switch."

Pius laughed and continued into the monastery.

Jacob finished his sacristan tasks, walked down the silent hall to a neglected bookshelf in the television room, and then headed to Paul's cell. Jacob knocked on the door. When Paul didn't answer, he entered the room. A loud bang startled him as he saw Paul dart toward the bed.

"Whoa, hold up."

Paul skidded to a stop.

"What the hell is all this?" Jacob clanged the sheep bells that dangled from the doorknob.

"A distraction. I didn't know it was you," Paul said, breathing hard.

"I brought your book back and the second book in the series. We have volumes of Hardy Boys mysteries in the second-floor TV room."

"Brother Ambrose gave it to me, but Father Jonah would disapprove because it's not real. He wants me to read real things, like the lives of the saints," Paul said, hiding the books under his mattress.

"Brother Ambrose can read?" Jacob asked, trying to avoid a negative comment about Butler's *Lives of the Saints*.

Paul climbed into bed. "Yes, he can read. You won't tell Father Jonah, will you?"

"For these and all your sins, you are forgiven," Jacob said, raising his right hand and blessing Paul. "It is just a book. Father Joannicus tells stories. Tell him it is just another story."

Paul rolled his eyes. "I won't need to. Father Pius will tell. He's mean."

Jacob sighed. "Not everyone is mean. He is not that bad. You need to give people a chance. Do not let what Father Pius said bug you."

Paul's brown eyes stared coldly at him.

Jacob frowned as he tucked the blankets around Paul. He stopped when he felt the cold metal.

"What the..." Jacob said, sucking the blood from his finger. "Give me those."

Paul handed Jacob the shears and then pulled the covers over his head.

"What is this doing in your bed? You better not give me some story about swords and the Rule of Saint Benedict."

"Protection." Paul's voice trembled as he peeked out from under the covers.

Jacob sat down on the bed, still sucking his finger. They stared at each other.

"All right, I get it. However, you cannot sleep with shears in your bed. Sleep in Father Joe's cell. No monk will go in there."

A cell was a monk's sanctuary—a place where he could be alone. Invitations to visit did not come.

Paul sat up. "If he wants to find me, he will. You don't get it. He's powerful."

"He is a monk and too busy to be stalking you. Nobody is that powerful. If you tell me who it is, I will stop him."

Paul flopped, defeated, onto his pillow. "I'm not stupid. I have talked enough, and he kept his promise."

Jacob realized he'd missed something. "Promise?"

"He told me if... never mind." Paul's face paled, and his eyes darted wildly around the room.

Jacob refrained from shaking Paul. "If it has already happened, then what more can happen?" *Tell me who; just tell me.*

Tears rimmed Paul's eyes. He hung his head as if defeated. "He said he would send Father Jonah away if I told anyone."

The child's logic made little sense. "But you have told no one."

"He thinks I have told you." Paul wiped a tear. "Now I'm stuck here alone."

"He did not send Joannicus away. I did." Jacob stumbled over his words, deciding in mid-sentence to take the blame.

"Father Jonah is gone. He can do anything." Paul's voice was harsh with emotions. "What if he makes all his promises come true?"

Paul hugged his knees to his chest. Jacob wanted to tell him to stop acting crazy, but he could not. He'd experienced this fear as a teenager, real or imagined. To sleep without fear when his stepfather was away on trips, he would push a heavy bureau against his door. Like Paul, he had been just a boy filled with fears, hopes, and exaggerations. It had saddened him to think his mother disliked him so much that she had threatened him with harm. He was sure she could never hurt him when he was awake, but anyone was vulnerable when asleep.

"Tomorrow, I will install a lock on your door, but only if you give me your solemn promise that if I need to enter, you will unlock it."

"How will I know it is you?"

Jacob bit his tongue. This had gone from a tropical storm to a hurricane. "Give me a password."

The concentration on Paul's face pinched tight.

Jacob disconnected the bells. He walked across the alcove into Joe's cell. He lifted the mattress, hauled it to Paul's room, and dropped it on the floor with a thud, careful not to crush Monte Cassino.

"The password is Psalm 45:8," Paul said. "The Lord of hosts is with us. The God of Jacob is our stronghold."

Jacob nodded, planning a lock with two extra keys: one he would always carry with him and one hidden in Joe's cell.

"Abbot Gordon won't like this," Paul said as Jacob unzipped his habit and draped it on the chair.

"Are you going to tell Abbot Gordon? I am not talking to him," Jacob said, slipping off his shoes. Exhaustion was draining him of fight and reason.

"I know. That makes him very sad."

Jacob grabbed a book from the bookshelf and sat on the makeshift bed, refusing to get into that discussion.

"Are you my *aassahke*?"

Jacob peered over the book. "What? No, I am not your clan uncle. Where did you hear that word?"

"School. Denny says he's Cheyenne, but he knows a lot about all the tribes. Not so much about Sioux."

"They like to be called Lakota, and Denny is Tsitsistas."

"Oh, Rhonda No Runs is Apsáalooke. She said you are *akbaaoochiahche*."

"She is mistaken. I am not a healer."

"That's funny because Brother Ambrose said you have *baaxpee*."

The monks were tolerant, but some still held onto misguided beliefs and history, and Paul didn't need that badge added to his faults. Nor did he need others worried he was converting Paul to Native beliefs.

"Ambrose has a big mouth. I am not holy. I do not have power. I cannot get you to shut up and go to sleep."

The boy's face glowed as he closed his eyes and became silent. Jacob turned off the light. He focused on the shadows dancing on the walls as the wind moved the branches outside. The pillow and blanket smelled faintly of Joannicus. Sadness settled around Jacob as he listened to the child shift in the bed beside him.

This was risky.

"It's one night. The door is open," the voice of his wife, Faith, chided.

Paul's breathing evened.

He could sneak out, but trust would be shattered if the boy woke up.

Sleep did not visit Jacob. Thousands of questions and just as many answers powwowed in his mind—*round and round*. The evil monk was still torturing Paul. How many bruises were from falling? How many were little reminders? What a power-hungry bastard this person was to pick on a kid!

The morning bells called the good and bad to pray. Jacob

welcomed the sound and followed Paul to the church. He took his place in the choir.

"Father Jacob." Ambrose's voice trickled its way through the fog of sleep.

Jacob pried his eyes open, realizing prayers had ended.

"Sleeping during prayers is not a fine example for our Juniors," Pius said.

The comment irritated him, even though he suspected it was in jest.

Jacob searched for Paul, but the church was empty.

"Father Jacob, might I suggest a rest? You don't look well," Ambrose said, scrutinizing him and nodding. "Go rest. I got things covered."

Jacob nodded and headed to his cell, making a mental list of the tasks that awaited him. He secured a lock without raising too much suspicion. He also said a prayer of thanks that his sleep had not been haunted by nightmares.

CHAPTER 15
HALLOWEEN

Psalm 57: 6
They are heedless as the adder that turns a deaf ear
lest it should catch the snake-charmer's voice.
The voice of the skillful dealer of spells.

F ather Jacob quickly fell into a routine that kept him as far away from Abbot Gordon as possible. Prayer, work, and keeping his eye on Paul made for a full day. Paul had his routine—prayer, school, farm, homework, prayer, and bed—yet something was missing. Paul was an exemplary monk. He was always at prayers and ready to help. Jacob found that disturbing.

The start of school meant both Juniors and Paul were busy. Jacob fixed himself a cup of coffee in the community room kitchenette. He sat at a table, watching the brown and yellow leaves dance on the patio. Ambrose would deliver pumpkins, corn stocks, and a bale of hay to the church this afternoon. Jacob had selected a cloth with fall leaves, bright yellow and orange, to make a display around the crucifix and candles. A thought struck him, and he laughed.

Father Pius entered the room and glanced around, giving Jacob a questioning look.

"I was thinking of Brother Mellitus and how delighted he would be if a mouse crawled out of the bale of hay during prayers."

Father Pius smiled, "Pandemonium, especially if it ran up someone's black robe."

"Besides April Fool's Day, Halloween was his favorite holiday," Jacob recalled that Brother Mellitus always found humor or made it, often at the most inappropriate times. For all his faults, Brother Mellitus stayed a member of the community, loved, hated, and tolerated, depending on the encounter one had with him.

Paul burst into the room and shouted, "It's perfect. Just like yours. Pockets and all, see."

Brother Moses appeared seconds later, wringing his hands, one of which was smooth and reddish from the burn he had sustained months ago. "This is not a good Halloween costume. Paul has never celebrated Halloween."

Paul spun like a dreidel, the cassock billowed, and his small scapular whipped around.

Father Jacob watched Pius open and close his mouth, then rubbed his goatee. Paul looked good in the black habit of a monk.

"Did Abbot Gordon approve this?" Moses said, turning to Jacob for an explanation. Jacob hadn't considered Moses would protest.

"I was not aware one needed approval to celebrate Halloween."

Pius shook his head. Jacob felt a tinge of guilt, for he hadn't consulted others. He had asked Paul.

"Is it wrong for kids to dress up as soldiers?" Jacob asked.

"Soldiers are secular; habits are religious. I find it offensive that a child is wearing it. He's not a reliable representative of Benedictine living," Pius said.

"If I dressed him as Friar Tuck, would you find that offensive?" Jacob asked, getting defensive.

"I'm not sure a fictional character is a fair comparison," Father Pius said, his voice laced with condemnation.

Oblivious to the adult's concerns, Paul announced, "I have four pockets."

Paul lifted the front of his scapular and revealed a breast pocket. "And if you count my pants pockets, I have four more, but it's kind of hard to reach those." Paul slid his hand into the slits of the cassock, trying to reach the back pocket of his jeans under the material.

"Pope robes and red shoes are out?" Jacob asked, thinking the fuss was rather petty.

"I'm not the only one who will protest this. What will Father Joannicus say?"

Jacob grimaced. Joe's disapproval of secular events had always unnerved Jacob. The world was secular. Parish time would show him that the two worlds were not diametrically opposed. Jacob reached out, putting a hand on Paul's shoulder to stop the twirling. He reached down to straighten the scapular so it hung evenly over Paul's shoulders, front and back.

Jacob knew Joannicus didn't abide by Halloween but was shocked to learn that Paul had never gone trick-or-treating. The college students and staff dressed up for the day. When he was a junior monk, Jacob had even attended celebrations, claiming he was going as the grim reaper.

"I could put my whole lunch in one," Paul said, his eyes dancing with delight. He placed his hands into the deep side pockets of the cassock.

"Do not. There are rules if you are wearing this," Jacob said. "Stop squirming. Act like a monk." The habit looked perfect.

Jacob wondered how long it would stay in that pressed state.

"Not a problem. I know what to do. I can bow and keep my hands under my scapular, not in my pockets. I can do this."

Jacob shook his head. "I was going to tell you to only wear it on Halloween."

"Can I wear it in my cell? Please," Paul interrupted. "I will keep it there, hang it in my closet like everyone else."

Jacob's heart melted. The joy on Paul's face made it impossible to say no. Brother Moses shook his head so hard Jacob worried he might strain his neck.

"It is okay," Jacob said, knowing there would be words of disapproval and knowing it was too late. "This is for one day. Think of it as free advertising for vocations."

"I have the protection now, don't I?" Paul asked, looking at the monks. "From vampires and werewolves."

Jacob snickered. "Now, Brother Paul, take your habit to your cell. It goes in your closet until the thirty-first."

"It's Father Paul," Paul said with authority. As the little monk left, Jacob was unsure of his decision.

"I'm surprised he didn't say *Abbot*," Pius said, tones of warning punctuating his words. His right hand wagged, and the ring on his pinkie winked. You shouldn't have done this, Jacob."

"He wants to be like us. It is just for one day."

Fathers Pius and Jacob watched as Brother Moses wagged his head and mumbled, "One day, one day," and left the room.

October 31st was cold, with a hint of snow in the air. Jacob sat in the darkened church before the morning bells.

"Today is the day, right?" whispered Paul, jarring Jacob from his meditation.

Jacob nodded and opened one eye, hoping Paul was not dressed in a habit. He wasn't.

Prayers began, and Jacob listened to the excited tapping of feet behind him.

After prayers, Jacob headed to breakfast, waiting with his other confrères in the hall for Abbot Gordon. Paul stood pressed against the wall outside the refectory as if wanting to become part of the brickwork. Wolfgang was shaggier than usual, hair and beard uncombed. The man sniffed the air like a hound dog on a hunt. Jacob inhaled. The air was heavy with the aroma of freshly baked cinnamon and pumpkin rolls. Paul slid down the wall toward Jacob. Brother Wolfgang grinned and scratched with vigor at his left ear while simultaneously thumping his foot on the ground. Brother Ambrose beamed, eyes twinkling with mischief.

Jacob had a sneaky feeling his confrères were up to no good.

"There is a full moon tonight," Brother Ambrose said, bouncing and catching the ball. Wolfgang followed the up-and-down movement with unnatural interest.

"Hey Paul, want to play fetch?" Brother Wolfgang asked, panting and tossing a rubber ball in Paul's direction. "I mean catch."

Plonk. The ball hit the wall and bounced before it rolled under the bench. Paul peeked around Father Jacob and shook his head.

Paul gripped Jacob's habit as they headed toward the refectory.

"He's a werewolf," Paul whispered. Jacob shook his head.

"You know that is not true."

"Why did Abbot Gordon give him the name Wolfgang?"

"If he were a werewolf, he would turn on the full moon every month."

Paul rolled his eyes. "His protection is wearing off. I read about it in a book."

Maybe Paul shouldn't be allowed to read everything.

They entered the refectory, and Jacob sat down, reflecting that Wolfgang shaved his face and head every year on All Saints' Day. Jacob shook his head as he stirred his coffee.

Werewolves? What else did these clowns have planned?

He had heard tales of Paul's confusion with fairies, trolls, vampires, and saints who could fly and walk on water. Fairy tales, miraculous events, and myths share many similarities.

Jacob dumped a third spoonful of sugar into his coffee. He watched Paul eating his bowl of oatmeal and smiled. It had been a while since he had seen Paul this excited.

Since Father Jacob's arrival, there had been an uneasy dance between them, as if Paul feared Jacob would beat the truth out of him. The truth would arrive only when Paul trusted him. Jacob noticed that the two visiting monks, Fathers Thaddeus and Urban, sat at the same table as Paul. Jacob noted that Paul rarely interacted with visitors, secular or monastic, now that Joe was no longer in charge of the guesthouse.

"Oh my God, oh my God," Paul shrieked, causing Father Pius to drop his roll. The boy backed away from the table, chair crashing to the floor as he darted across the room, climbing into Jacob's lap.

"Good Lord, child, what on earth is going on?" Jacob steadied his coffee cup, pleased that Paul had chosen him for safety in a room full of monks. Jacob hoped that Abbot Gordon was watching.

"He's a vampire, a real vampire. Look, see, his teeth are pointy. Don't let him suck all my blood. Father Jacob, please make some Jesus blood for him.

Jacob laughed. "Paul, vampires are not real."

"No, Father, give him the blood," insisted Paul, hiding his face in Jacob's chest. Laughs, tsks, and groans added to the broken silence. Jacob sent a pleading glance to Father Thaddeus, who grinned and removed the pointy teeth.

"Those teeth are fake," Jacob said.

Paul peeked out. Thaddeus smiled. The fake teeth were gone.

"It's not a funny joke," Paul said, breathing hard. "Can I eat at your table, Father?"

Jacob untangled the frightened child. Paul needed to head to school, but only with a protective escort of junior monks. Jacob was grateful they had volunteered and worried they might spend the time filling Paul's head with more visions of specters. Dressed in his farm overalls, a beaming Ambrose stood outside as Jacob exited the refectory.

"That was fun," the large man said. "Cool costume. Just keep it out of sight. I don't want the big debate about whether you are skirting on sacrilege by letting him wear it. It was a good choice. It's not like you let him play with chalices."

Jacob smiled, hoping he looked innocent.

Jacob and Paul returned to the monastery after ten o'clock. It had been a long night at Saint Clare's parish harvest festival. Paul ran into the darkened community room and opened the cabinets in the kitchenette. He hauled out a large bowl and emptied his candy into it.

"Hey, do not dump it all. I want the chocolate nut bars," Jacob said, carrying two homemade desserts that Paul had won playing the cakewalk. His own kids would have been fighting him for the select pieces. Rosie would have consumed most of the chocolate bars before they got home. Jacob chuckled. She was so much like her namesake, Brother Ambrose, holding on to life with both fists. That is how she entered the world.

"I'm too tired to pick them out. You do it," Paul said.

Two figures are sitting in a room—enough silliness. "Guys, come on, it is late. We had fun with the vampires, but ghostly specters in the night? What next, zombies?"

"I assure you, we are not," Father Pius said.

"Hi, Father Jonah," Paul said, putting the large bowl on the table in the community room. "How come you weren't at Saint Clare's? I was there. Did you see my cool costume? Brother Mark made it. It's real, like yours. Now I'm one of you. Charlie wore black, too."

Jacob's throat tightened. The black that Charlie wore was a witch's costume. Father Joannicus scanned Paul from hood to sandals. Jacob swallowed hard. Joannicus couldn't be mad now, could he? Jacob heard from Rebecca that Joannicus had tried to stop the harvest festival. She had told him to hide in the monastery and pray for his approval, which didn't matter. Jacob assumed Joannicus had left for the evening when he wasn't present at the event. Sadness filled him because a pastor needed to be a part of his community and attend events important to the people. Only then would the people attend events important to Joannicus.

"It's past your bedtime," Joannicus said, his voice sharp. "Don't forget to brush your teeth."

Paul didn't seem to notice Joe's disapproval. "Thanks, this day was awesome," he said as he headed to bed.

Joannicus watched Paul leave.

"Seriously, I don't understand how you could have allowed this. Our robes are not costumes."

"It is not the robe. It is the person wearing it," Jacob said, eyes narrowing at Pius. *Tattletale.* "Let me explain."

"You are a monk," Joannicus said. "And you know my disdain for mixing the secular with the sacred."

"But it was important to Paul. Did you not hear him say he is one of us?"

"He can't be one of us. He's a kid."

Yes, a kid, so why are you crushing his spirit? "You do not have to decide what Paul needs."

Shock registered on Joe's face. Jacob found it hard to accept that Joannicus was upset about one night out. Was this jealousy? Was Joannicus upset because Jacob was doing well with Paul? Sadness filled Jacob. Joannicus didn't realize how much Paul loved him, and not for one instant did Jacob suppose he had replaced Joannicus in Paul's heart.

"He did nothing disrespectful. This meant a lot to him."

"It's late," Joannicus said as he turned and left the room.

Jacob sighed.

"What did you expect? Father Joannicus is right," Father Pius said.

"You did not have to tell him or sit with him until we came home."

"He asked. I wasn't going to lie."

"You could have said Paul was at Saint Clare's. You did not need to mention the habit." He always suspected Pius was a stickler for rules but not a snitch, too.

"What good would that have done? He would have found out. Paul can't keep a secret."

Jacob snorted.

"Paul did not realize it was a secret. Like everyone else around him, he wanted to be a monk. I do not know why he wanted to be with us. I have not been impressed with anyone who wears the black. Sometimes, my confrères can be so holy, and other times, they appear ignorant oafs."

Father Pius gave Jacob the gaze a parent gives a petulant child. "I'm not the guilty one. Your slack ways are the issue here, as they were in the parish. Don't you think it is time for you to start living the Rule rather than just expecting others to?"

Words unbecoming to a monk wiggled on the tip of Jacob's tongue.

Careful, warned the Elder in his mind. *Deep breaths.* Jacob reached for the candy.

"Your ne'er-do-well ways have caused Joannicus difficulty. He is concerned about the attendance at Mass. Only two parishioners were present."

Jacob unwrapped a bar and shoved it into his mouth. He wondered who had attended. Could it have been Peanut Man and Grandma Wren? They had never missed a service, and just because he wasn't the pastor probably didn't matter to them. Peanut Man sat in the back of the church, shelling peanuts and leaving them in a bag in the last pew. Grandma Wren was a wiry, wrinkled woman who sat in her brightly colored shawl and belled moccasins in the front to be the first in the communion line. Jacob always knew when his sermons were running too long, her feet would jingle, saying, "*Recess time.*" Jacob saw them as the cornerstones of the church, not as the last two faithful.

"Perhaps Joannicus should talk with me. I could help. It was my parish."

"Was it? For it seems like the commandment to keep holy the

Sabbath means something different to you than it does to other priests."

"Sabbath. Well, keep holy something," Jacob snapped, resenting the judgment by this man who always appeared pious, like his name, but often fell short of the virtue. "It is about welcoming, not punishing. My Sunday saints and part-time parishioners are loyal and faithful. I welcome them back rather than make them suffer guilt for coming."

"It seems we see a pastor's duties differently. I was under the assumption that we both wanted Joannicus to succeed," Pius said. "Joannicus is wasting his talent and time. Perhaps your brother, our Father Vincent, would understand these people better."

Jacob's good mood drained. Those people were his people—God's people. Jacob bit his lower lip. Joannicus was a better fit. Vincent was more comfortable in his white world than being Apsáalooke. Jacob sat at the table, pulling the bowl of candy to himself. "Joannicus will be fine. It is his first time out. He will improve. I am sure you gave him expert advice."

Pius snorted and left the room as Jacob unwrapped another chocolate bar. *Maybe Paul was right. He is a mean monk.*

CHAPTER 16
TREATIES

Psalm 77:1
Give heed, my people, to my teaching:
turn your ear to the words of my mouth.

Father Jacob entered the conference room expecting to see his Juniors, but the room held only sunlight. He waited. They were to meet here, not recreate before prayers. Sitting down, he reflected on his newest Junior. Paul hung out with the Juniors and showed up at meetings. Jacob didn't mind, but he was sure Abbot Gordon would once he got wind of Paul's activities. He *can't blame me for this. I didn't ask Paul to join us.*

Paul's energy level and childish wisdom reminded Jacob of his children. He had enjoyed being a father. Jacob recalled how fearful Joannicus was when Brother Ambrose plopped Amber Rose Mackenzie in his lap. Too bad Paul hadn't arrived as a helpless infant. Maybe Joannicus would have bonded quicker with the boy.

Jacob remembered the first time he'd held his infant brother Tommy. The day he'd understood the fierce love his sister Rebecca had for him. The depth of that love astounded him. He had been overwhelmed by it when Faith handed him his first daughter, Katie. Those innocent eyes trusted him. The power, the responsibility, the awe, and the love that washed through him—he felt it every time Faith presented him with a baby. Jacob likened the experience to what Joannicus expressed when he became a monk: life-changing.

After twenty minutes, Jacob headed to the community room in search of his absent monks. He took a detour to the church and ran into Mrs. Carrington, the mother of Father Pius. She looked as polished as an agate; her hair was platinum, and she wore a peach-colored pantsuit. She paused and assessed him, and Jacob felt she would dismiss him, but to his surprise, she addressed him.

"Say, if you see Pius, tell him I'll be in the parlor. I miss Father Joannicus. He always had wonderful treats waiting when one arrived. I was sure glad when Paul showed me the secret stash of goodies. I was famished from my travels."

Jacob noticed she did not address him as Father or Brother and figured she felt angst at seeing his brown skin. He wondered if she knew her son was the new Guest Master. The little devil inside of him spoke. "Father Pius is in charge of the guesthouse now; perhaps if you mentioned that to him."

"Oh, I have. He sometimes chooses not to listen. He does what he wants. So now I'm telling you. I'm glad Paul's still around. Such a sweet little person; reminds me of Pius as a boy. So polite and hospitable," Mrs. Carrington said, as she smiled a weary smile and headed out of the church.

Jacob watched the woman, who had perfect posture, head to the guesthouse.

Jacob entered the community room and observed his Junior monks lined up with noses pressed to the wall.

"This is ridiculous," Father Pius said, his ears red with frustration. "Father Jacob, is this your idea of a joke?"

"What is going on?" Father Jacob asked, seeing Paul standing with the monks.

"This is a punishment," Father Pius said. "These Juniors are making a mockery of it."

"Formal protest," Brother Ryan said.

A smile played on Father Jacob's lips. If Brother Ryan was protesting, the reason had to be sound.

"Monks do not protest," Jacob said, amused at the sight of grown men being punished like errant boys.

"Don't you have guests to deal with?" Paul said, his voice huffy but softened by his arms.

Pius spoke with a controlled voice as his eyes smoldered. "This is not over, little boy."

Paul turned to glare at Father Pius, his face etched with indignation.

"How about an explanation?" Jacob asked, stepping toward Paul and turning him back to the wall.

"Paul did nothing wrong," Brother Ryan explained.

"Paul thinks he's Junior Guest Master," Pius said, crossing his arms under his scapular. "He attended to guests when he has no business doing so."

Usually, the Guest Master greeted and attended to visitors. Saint Benedict directed all to treat guests with kindness. Pius prided himself on fulfilling his responsibilities. Jacob guessed that Father Pius was teaching and unavailable when his mother arrived. Jacob doubted Paul knew who the guest was, but he did now.

"You weren't there. Guests are everyone's business," Paul said.

"Who put him in the corner?" Jacob asked, silently siding with Paul while placing a calming hand on the boy's shoulder.

"Abbot Gordon," Brother Ryan said. "But we disagree because Paul was just practicing hospitality. He shouldn't be punished for doing what the Rule says."

Abbot Gordon entered the room. "All is well, Father Jacob. No need to concern yourself."

Jacob turned around. "Yes, Father Abbot. But the Juniors are my responsibility."

Abbot Gordon glanced at the Juniors. A confused smile appeared on his face.

"It's unfair." Paul's muffled protest came from his folded arms.

"You need to exert more control over your Juniors. Paul has no business in the guesthouse," Father Pius said, cracking his knuckles and glaring at Jacob.

"If I had known they were your guests, I would have sent them away," Paul said.

Jacob turned, enveloping Paul. The child smelled musty, as if he hadn't changed his clothing in a month. Jacob hissed in Paul's ear, "Quit. Apologize. Now."

Paul's arms fell to his side as Jacob turned away from the wall.

"Sorry," Paul said, although Jacob could tell the apology was not sincere.

It's a start. Jacob headed out of the community room.

"What about us?" a Junior asked.

Jacob smiled. "Juniors, sometimes you have to succumb to the greater good. Suffer for injustice. I suggest you all finish your time, and tomorrow, we will discuss the grace received. Paul, mind your tongue. Practice humility with silence," Jacob said as he felt Abbot Gordon's gaze burn. He was not about to challenge Abbot Gordon even if he disagreed.

Jacob seethed and walked to the darkened church where the odor of beeswax lingered. The punishment made no sense. Why was Pius angry? Did he think Gordon's punishment was silly? Or was he upset at his mother for praising Paul? Jacob knew little about their relationship. He recognized an aloof stiffness between mother and son. Why was the Abbot disgruntled with him? He let the punishment stand. Abbot Gordon needed to understand that Jacob wasn't the problem—he was part of the solution, or at least wanted to be.

Father Jacob sat, jaw clenched, eyes closed. He guessed Paul argued and mouthed back when Pius confronted him, and Abbot Gordon stepped in, hoping to avoid a bigger issue. Jacob could see Pius insisting that Paul be corrected for stepping out of line. Pius was a rule follower and thrived on order.

The sounds of birds filtered through the open windows. *How do I teach Paul to stop and think before reacting?* Jacob listened to the footsteps as the bells rang, calling the monks to prayer.

The odor of staleness caused Jacob to open his eyes. The boy needed a bath. Hadn't anyone seen to that?

Paul poked Jacob's arm.

Jacob closed his eyes, ignoring the disgruntled child.

Paul growled.

"I am praying. I will talk to you later."

"No." Paul stomped his foot.

"Paul, not now."

"You're just a dumb old monk."

Father Jacob locked his jaw.

Don't engage, the Elder inside of him warned.

"Stop."

"I'm not one of your stupid Juniors," Paul said. "Why did you take his side?"

Jacob looked around the church. Monks had arrived, and he needed to end this moment with the least amount of attitude. *Should he tell him to sit down and shut up? He'd best stick with logic and the Rule, which he knows.*

"Once again, you assume too much. I know you are smart, so I expect more from you. Perhaps you need to read the prologue to the Rule again. Or do an instrument of good works, perhaps Number 30 in Chapter 4. Do no wrong to others and bear patiently the wrongs done to you."

Father Jacob shifted in his chair, focusing on the patterns of light on the carpet as the sun set. Paul moved away, slamming his books on the wooden seat behind Jacob. Someone tsked loudly. Jacob took several deep breaths, fiddled with his braid, and tucked it into his hood. *Let someone else deal with the angry child.*

The boy tested the adults around him far too much. That had to end. Prayers did not calm the frenzy brewing inside of Jacob.

"And who are you angry with?" the Elder asked.

Me, you old fool. Who else is here to instruct the child?

After prayers, Jacob walked outside in the twilight before heading to Paul's cell at a snail's pace. He wondered if Paul had locked his door. He turned the handle and entered the empty room. The odor of dirty laundry insulted Jacob's nose. Little boys didn't do laundry. He picked up and sniffed garments strewn around the room.

He had been shortsighted. Paul needed more than just a schedule.

"He is a child. Guide; do not direct," the Elder said.

The laundry was sorted. He straightened the papers on the desk, reviewing the grades and comments. Jacob noticed Paul neglected to have parental signatures on many things and missed several school activities. Picking up the pen, he signed the latest slip.

The door opened. Jacob turned and saw a damp Paul.

Good; he'd taken a shower.

"Before you start, listen. I do not want to taunt Abbot Gordon or provoke other monks. I am calling for a truce between you and me. You work with me, or I am done with you. Find someone else to torment," Jacob said.

Paul walked to his closet. His dark eyes glistened with anger. "Why did you take his side?"

Jacob shook his head and looked out the window as evening settled in. "Abbot Gordon may punish you when he sees fit. He is the Abbot."

"But I did nothing bad," shouted Paul.

Paul's anger was out of proportion to the incident.

"It seemed unfair; I agree. Perhaps Father Pius does not like to share his mom."

Paul snorted. "I'd share my mom if I had one to share."

The glowing red dot outside of Paul's window caught Jacob's eye. Bear. Brother Ambrose, outside smoking. Jacob turned his attention back to Paul.

"You need a caretaker. I am an excellent choice."

Skepticism filled Paul's face.

"Try me. I promise I am more reasonable than Father Joannicus, and I like having fun."

Paul's eyes narrowed.

"I have more imagination than Brother Ambrose, and I can play a mean game of checkers—certainly more challenging than playing with Brother Moses."

"I let him win half the time," Paul said.

"Yes, I am aware of that. That tells me you are a kind person. Do you know what changes for a Novice when he becomes a Junior?"

"Freedom?"

Jacob laughed. "Responsibility. You are now responsible for cleaning your cell and putting your clothes away. Also, it would help if you listened and trusted my advice occasionally."

"This is a treaty, isn't it?" Paul asked.

"This is not a treaty. Indians do not make treaties with whites. History has shown that Indians end up with the worse part of those deals."

"I know about treaties. We learned about them at school, and this sounds like a treaty, so I want something too," Paul said, dropping his dirty clothes on the floor.

The word "treaty" left an aftertaste. Jacob suspected he might regret this truce, but to win, one sometimes needed to compromise. Therefore, Jacob said, "Okay, what do you think you need?"

"I want you to play with me."

Jacob let his face crease with thought as he glared at the dirty clothes. Paul picked them up and put them into a laundry bag.

Play was a word with many meanings. What he understood was that Paul wanted positive adult attention.

He could do that. Jacob had observed that the community had ignored the invitation to take Paul to school events.

"Deal."

"I wanna go to a powwow. All the kids talk about it."

Jacob nodded. That made sense. The children at the school were from the local tribes. Powwows were as much a part of their lives as prayer was part of Paul's. Paul needed a little less prayer and more brief escapes into the world.

He could benefit from a little less prayer too.

"This year's powwow, it is a date."

Paul let out a loud whoop.

"Have you been to Yellowstone?"

"No, where is that?"

Jacob smiled and left the room; he heard the soft clink of the lock. He turned the corner and noticed an enormous shadow. Jacob marched past it, not wanting to hear Ambrose's advice. He didn't care if Brother Ambrose snitched on him. Abbot Gordon was wrong to order him to stay away from Paul. Jacob just needed time to prove it.

CHAPTER 17
NOT-SO-JUNIOR MONK

Psalm 22: 4-5
If I should walk in the valley of the shadow of death,
No evil would I fear.
You are there.

J acob opened his eyes. Lightning lit up his room. A boom of thunder rattled his windows. He groaned and rolled over, falling back to sleep. The movement of his covers and a hand caused him to jump and bang his head on the shelf above his bed.

"Holy crap," Jacob shouted over the thunder as he reached for a light switch. Darkness vanished, and Paul stood there clutching a tattered white tiger. Thunder boomed, and Paul dove toward Jacob.

"Whoa! Hold on."

"I don't like thunder!" Paul screamed.

The lightning flashed again as warning bells rang in Jacob's head. The lights flickered.

"Okay, but you cannot sleep here."

"Father Jonah let me sleep with him when the thunder talked."

Jacob climbed out of the bed, grabbed his jeans, and hopped on one foot into them. Father Joannicus must have been insane. "It is thunder. The storm will pass. It can be exciting."

Thunder rumbled like a logging truck as Paul let out a whimper.

"Shush, you will wake everyone up," Jacob said, panic crept into his voice. He did not want to explain it. "Follow me."

Paul clutched Jacob's arm like an old woman as they headed to the community room. Jacob tried to peel the child from him with little success. His own children had loved to watch the storms. Jacob recalled they would collect pillows and blankets and gather on the floor. A massive group of arms and legs cuddled together, squealing with delight when the house shook and the windows rattled.

"Want to watch the storm?"

"No."

"Cards? What do you want to play?"

"Cribbage."

Jacob shook his head. Not Slap Jack or Old Maid? Cribbage was not a game for a child.

"There is nothing to be afraid of. It is a fireworks show put on by God," Jacob said, slipping the deck of cards out of their box.

"What are fireworks?" Paul asked.

"Fourth of July, pretty lights, and big booms," Jacob said, finding it hard to believe the monks hadn't allowed that celebration. "Your godparents, Gracie and Patrick, took you to the fireworks shows, didn't they?"

Paul shook his head. "I don't like noise. How can you say this is fun?"

Jacob dealt the card. "It is. It is like a roller coaster ride, the anticipation, the rush of excitement as you plummet over the top."

"What are you talking about?"

"You have not gone on carnival rides at the county fair?"

Paul shook his head.

His confrères hadn't supplied Paul with anything but prayer and rules. The storm clamored on. After two games of cribbage, sleep overtook Paul. His head rested on the table. The sky flashed blue bolts, and rain pelted the windows. Jacob moved Paul to the sofa, covering him with a blanket.

Montana had thunderstorms, yet Joe had never mentioned Paul's fear or confessed that Paul slept with him. He supposed that was wise but risky.

"No, Father Joannicus is not one of them, you know this," Faith scolded. Stop being paranoid.

Jacob reflected on when he applied to St. Alberic's College. Father Hilary, Brother Mellitus, and Father Gordon decided on the recipient. Mellitus voted in favor, and the scholarship was his. He suspected Mellitus did so to spite Gordon. Was the old monk expecting a different future?

The coffee urn in the kitchenette hummed and moaned. The aroma called to him; Ambrose would arrive soon. Jacob yawned.

He couldn't miss a night of sleep.

Jacob chuckled. He recalled once falling asleep on the monastery patio after a long night with a colicky baby. Ambrose claimed they moved him indoors, and he slept while the monks recreated around him.

Keeping Paul away was a bad idea. Did Gordon know what Paul said? He was not the one. What was the truth? How would any of them know? A scared little boy's utterance could not be trusted.

"I follow my heart," Jacob said as he walked to the kitchenette, poured two cups of hot brew, and ladled sugar into one.

"Talking to yourself is a sure sign of sainthood," Brother Ambrose said as he entered the darkened room. Ah, you got stuck with the thunder watch."

"Yes. I have a question. Who is filling in for Father Joannicus in the physical care of Paul? Has Abbot Gordon assigned anyone to remind the boy about showers or to change his clothing?" Jacob asked, handing Ambrose a cup of coffee.

"Abbot Gordon is a great guide for adults, but not for kids. Besides, he had selected Father Hilary as Paul's caretaker, and Paul picked Father Joannicus. And if you haven't noticed, he has picked his next victim."

"I do not understand Abbot Gordon sometimes," Jacob said. "He is unbalanced."

"You have been away too long. It isn't him that is unstable. It is the community. Each of us is different, and we all have unique needs."

Jacob blew over the surface of his mug, causing the liquid to ripple. "Paul needs consistency."

"I agree, but it ain't easy. The Abbot's job is damn hard, too. I see how he frets and struggles with every decision he makes concerning us. He didn't assign you the Juniors to keep you busy and away from Paul. He knows you're a teacher, a leader, and a great parent."

Jacob shook his head, then sipped his coffee.

"How come Paul does not attend school functions?" Jacob asked.

Brother Ambrose slurped his coffee. "Are you asking what I think you're asking?"

Sometimes, Ambrose was as slow as molasses, and other times, his perceptiveness was like a bolt of lightning.

"I think it's a good plan. Abbot Gordon won't be happy. I'll cover for you. Run interference. Just keep me informed when these little ventures occur."

Jacob nodded. Ambrose ran a calloused hand over his short hair and then scratched his beard. "Promise me that the boy wears a helmet when you go tearing up the countryside."

Jacob smiled. His kids loved it when he took them on his motorbike.

"Great idea," Jacob said.

Ambrose laughed. "Boys and their toys."

CHAPTER 18

CONFESSIONS

Psalm 115: 10-11
I trusted, even when I said,
I am sorely afflicted,
And when I said in my alarm,
No man can be trusted.

Father Pius glanced at his pocket watch, which sat open on the lectern. Today, he taught Comparative Religions, an upper-division class with fewer students. Pius felt proud that his classes were well attended in just under a year.

He walked around the room, listening to the small group discussions. He moved toward the group, seeing Marianna, a coed student, as she sat next to Felix, playing with his scapular.

What was it with women who assumed flirting with a celibate man was safe? Over the years, Pius had often listened to Joannicus complain that college coeds were a challenge.

He wondered if women would be a problem at Saint Clare's parish. As the former pastor at Saint George, Pius had learned tricks to keep women at bay.

"Oh yes, Father, I would love to help. Be part of the altar society," they would gush. Yet Pius knew they only hoped to corner him in the sacristy, bumping and stroking, smelling like the perfume counter at Hart-Albin. The questions were always poisonous. "Do you like my dress, Father?"

Single mothers and divorcees were needy. The weepy woman in the tight, revealing sweater suggested the sins she wished to commit rather than those she had submitted to.

Pius didn't have problems with coeds because he spoke to them when they crossed the line. He was a monk, not a safe date. Brother Felix needed to learn that to survive. Perhaps he should speak to Jacob.

That appointment had been a surprise. One second, Jacob was a pastor, and the next, he was the Junior Master and living in the monastery. Joannicus had moved to Saint Clare's parish. Sometimes, he wondered if the Abbot was all there. Some of Abbot Gordon's decisions seemed whimsical and rash. He knew he shouldn't be judging.

Pius placed a firm hand on Felix's shoulder. "How's the discussion of Divine Intervention going?"

Felix tugged his scapular away. Message received. Every man needed help to avoid the near occasion of sin.

Marianna turned to the doorway where Father Jacob was standing. Pius heard the young woman sigh and sit up straighter. Pius shook his head. The girl needed a boyfriend. He had wondered why she had taken his class, and now he feared she was only there to snare a monk.

Jacob flashed Marianna a winning smile, and she blushed.

Pius announced, "Time to go. I have a meeting with Father Jacob."

A groan erupted from the group. Although class time was over, the students desired to linger. An inkling of pride surfaced as Pius tried hard not to gloat.

"Father Jacob." Marianna's voice was coated with interest as she lowered her eyelashes. "What classes are you teaching?"

Jacob laughed. "I teach classes to monks, so unless you are planning on changing your gender, you cannot attend."

She frowned as she left the room, walking too close to Jacob. "Too bad. I'm sure you would make a brilliant professor. Hope to see you around."

Pius gathered his lecture notes and headed down the hall with Jacob.

"Nice girl," Jacob said.

"Marianna isn't looking for a degree. One would be smart to avoid her."

"That is a harsh judgment. She is young."

"Marianna will lead men to sin. Men are a conquest to her. She's one of those women attracted to that which is unavailable."

Pius opened the door to his office and allowed Jacob to enter first, reflecting on the number of confessions he had seen over the years where friendships had gone sexual.

"You have settled in well," Jacob said, glancing around the office.

"Better than Joannicus," Pius said, having overheard that Father Joannicus found Saint Clare's parish lacking a strong Catholic influence. "I noticed that he's exempted from the weekly monastery visits."

"He will adjust. As for weekly visits, Abbot Gordon trusts Joannicus to be strong," Jacob said.

Pius found that thought offensive as he walked by the maroon Victorian chairs to his desk, where he placed his folder.

"Attendance is low."

Jacob sat down in the stiff-backed chair. "Then he needs to work on inspiring rather than correcting."

Father Pius disagreed. Joannicus inspired him, and he was sure students would experience the same. They all complained about the professor's absence. Pius straightened a book on his shelf. He missed Joannicus, too.

"Are you sure about this? Confessing in a house makes for awkward moments," Jacob said, shifting in the chair.

Father Pius had been the confessor for many of his confrères, and their past confessions sometimes caused Pius uncomfortable moments when disclosure and daily living were met. Listening to someone's faults and witnessing them repeat their sins was difficult.

Jacob settled back, pulled a stole from his habit pocket, and placed it around his neck. Father Pius sat and closed his eyes. Confession was never easy for him. Sin was not a petty thing, and conversion of one's life was a critical vow—one he struggled with. Pius believed in taking responsibility. Failure did not sit well with him. Father Pius knew his standards were high not only for himself but for others. Perhaps it came from growing up with a critical mother, never quite measuring up. Either way, he struggled with his faults, not finding them but forgiving them.

The muffled sounds of students and the squeaking of the old wooden floors faded. The leaky faucet dripped, making a soothing rhythmic sound.

Focus.

Pius began his confession with the sign of the cross. "In the name of the Father, the Son, and the Holy Spirit. My last confession was two months ago." His eyes opened, and he focused on the medieval art on his walls. "It happened again," he said, his voice edged with resignation. "Try as I may, I can't seem to control myself. It's like a roller coaster at some point. You realize the edge is near, and you can do nothing to stop the fall."

"What are you referring to? Women? Drink?" Jacob asked. "One does not have to carry the burden alone. Help is available."

Leg muscles tightened. How could Father Jacob think he could fall into the trap of lust? He'd be safe in the monastery if that were his sin.

The knuckles on his right hand snapped, and Pius hung his head.

Shame, like dust, settled on him. He had tried hard not to give into temptation, but the cheeky child had taunted him, like a snake in his Garden of Eden.

"I try to avoid him, but he's everywhere—in the church when I wish to be alone, in the community room causing a fuss, even at the farm whining incessantly. What bothers me, though, is the rudeness. He has no respect for others. When he steps over the line and then pushes, I snap."

"Are we talking about Paul?" Jacob asked.

The dripping faucet thumped a rhythm in time with his heart as silence punctuated the moment.

Pius looked up at Jacob.

"No, we're talking about Moses. Yes, we're talking about Paul."

The muscles in Jacob's neck twitched. "Just what are you doing to him?"

"I'm not doing anything to him," Pius said, his face flushed. "I struck Paul too hard. He has a bruise. I seem to let my temper get the best of me. I'm sorry. And I'm sure it won't happen again."

"Again?" Jacob's voice cracked, and his hands gripped the armrests of the wooden chair. "You're the one."

"Excuse me?" The room swirled with his soul in confusion. *The boy had told!*

"January, two years ago, Paul..."

Pius cracked the knuckles on his left hand. "We're not talking about two years ago." He had lost his temper that time, but he had been provoked.

Jacob folded his arms across his chest. "So, you confessed this to Abbot Gordon?"

He had told nobody. What was Jacob up to? "What I confessed and to whom is not what we're doing here," Pius said, his words clipped.

"I do not believe you," Jacob said, each word controlled.

Hairs on the back of his neck rose. Pius swallowed hard. "That was two years ago. I have changed."

"And yet Paul has a bruise. How many bruises are covered in lies told by you and Paul? This has to stop."

Jacob's hard stare showed rage and disgust.

"It has. I slipped up. I'm sorry. It'll not happen again," Pius said, surprised by Jacob's demeanor.

Jacob stood up and walked to the door, his back to Pius. He said, "No, I cannot do this."

Shock gripped Pius, sweat dripping down his neck, and his white priest collar threatened to strangle him. Before Mass, he needed to be cleansed. He picked Jacob because he figured this man would understand how hard it was to find balance and maintain control. He had children. He knew the frustration.

There were rumors that Jacob had been abused. Pius heard victims harbored emotions and often struggled with keeping control. A slow realization came upon Pius. Jacob hadn't dealt with the abuse of his past, neither as a victim nor as a potential abuser.

Pius watched as Jacob gripped the door handle. Why wasn't the door open? The man turned, a look of illness seizing his features.

"You have been hurting Paul. He is a child."

"He needs discipline."

"That job belongs to someone else," Jacob said.

"Joannicus is not here. I'm not here to confess to a spanking. I'm confessing my lack of control," Pius said, convinced that Jacob did not understand the sin he was confessing to. "If I were confessing to alcohol abuse, we wouldn't be discussing the brand of liquor. If I had sex, you wouldn't be asking me about the pleasure. Why are we even talking about Paul? Jacob, I know your past, but this is not your childhood played out again."

Jacob took a step closer. The look of a warrior faced Pius, causing him to stand and put the two burgundy Victorian chairs between them.

"You know nothing of my childhood," Jacob said, his voice mimicking a low growl.

"Vincent has spoken of it," Pius said, crunching his knuckles randomly on both hands.

Jacob narrowed his blue eyes. "Vincent knows little of the truth, which is how I want it to remain. Nobody needs the image of a monster for a father."

He was right. This odd reaction was from Jacob's past.

Jacob's half brother, Vincent, had spoken to Pius about his childhood memories—fights, explosive ones that echoed through the house and one's soul. He had thought Jacob would understand. He had misjudged.

"Please, forgive me," Jacob said, his voice soothing like the silence before the cyclone. "Sit."

"It is I who would like forgiveness," Pius said as he sat down, fearful of the sudden change.

"If you are sorry, then you will have the forgiveness you seek," Jacob said, tugging on the stole and pulling it from around his shoulders. "I am sorry, but I cannot give you absolution; not like this, not now."

"You must," Pius said, stunned, his vision narrowing. "I confessed my sorrow and conviction to change."

The *drip, drip, drip* of the leaky faucet echoed in the room.

"You do not understand the ramifications of your actions. You live in a community. When you see what your actions have done, then come see me."

"I have made amends, knowing one member's actions can harm everyone. Do not withhold forgiveness. It is your duty to absolve me," Pius said, attempting to keep his voice calm against the sense of injustice that rose inside.

Father Jacob stood, turned, and walked to the door. Then he paused.

"Show me. Make me believe," Jacob said, leaving the office and closing the door as Pius trembled in the empty room.

CHAPTER 19
SILENT SCREAMS

Psalm 78: 6-7
Pour out your rage on the kingdoms
They do not call on your name.
For they have devoured Jacob
and laid waste the land where he dwells.

Every curse word Jacob learned in English and Apsáalooke spewed from his mouth once he had closed the door to his cell. His habit flew as he threw it into the corner like a garment on fire. He sat down at his desk and pounded his fist.

"God damn it, God damn it."

Jacob's eyes fell on the crucifix over his bed. His muscles strained as he ripped the cross off the wall and tossed it into the trash can.

"That's what I think of your secret-holding rituals."

His absence from prayers would be noticed. He shoved his wooden desk against the door. They could knock, but he would not answer. He pulled the mattress off his bed, propping it against the chair. Jacob knelt as if to pray. Instead of words of thanksgiving, he let his fists talk as he hammered the dense material until his wrists and arms hurt. He pulled the kneaded mattress to the floor, curled up, and let a fitful sleep overtake him. But it did not last long. The bells for prayers beckoned him, causing his anger to stir again. *This is so wrong.*

He should scream it down the halls: *Pius is evil. He is the evil monk.* He should be able to tell Abbot Gordon. This was not his sin. This was not his burden—stupid Church, stupid laws, stupid Indian.

You can't, Joannicus said in his head.

"Just try to stop me," challenged Jacob, knowing that doing so meant discarding his life as a priest and everything the Church had taught him.

How could he live this life when it involved such evil?

He couldn't even think of words to describe the winnowing of his soul. A fury rose in him, like a bellow fanning the dying embers.

Scenes flashed in Jacob's mind. The excuses: *I was roughhousing, I ran into a door, I fell off my bike, I was riding the sheep.* Paul was a damn good liar.

He knew when he saw a bruise to put on his adult glasses, refusing to acknowledge what he felt in his gut.

He dug out an old coffee maker from the bottom drawer and made coffee. His phone rang. The clipped ringtone told him it was from within the house, not an outside line. Paul or Ambrose? He picked up the receiver.

"Go away. I'm sick."

He couldn't talk. He feared he would name the sinner, violating the Seal of the Confessional.

The aroma of freshly brewed coffee filled the cell, calming him.

Jacob poured himself a cup, ignoring the protest of his stomach against the bitter black fluid. Father Joannicus was confessor to Pius. Jacob was aware of that. Maybe Father Pius used confessors in an à la carte manner, picking one for each sin. Nobody is that conniving. Yet Pius had picked him to confess this so-called sin.

The coffee burned, scorching its way down to his stomach. Pius didn't see his actions as a sin. They were all good liars, able to stretch the truth and tell it in ways that softened the ugliness.

Father Jacob rummaged through his closet and found his breech-cloth. He tugged on his braid, letting his hair fall loose; Jacob transformed. The sun shone hotly into his cell. He climbed onto the counter by the window and sat, allowing his skin to burn.

He was in hell. *Let's make it complete.*

Someone knocked at his door. Later, someone tried the knob. Jacob smiled. He would not be disturbed. Soon, they would be more forceful, and if he continued to talk to himself, perhaps they would just send him away. He willed himself to sit and listen. Outside, voices drifted up through the open window.

Ambrose's admonishing voice announced, "Jacob had better 'Christian up' and stop this nonsense."

You are ignorant of the whole truth. He wished he could be like Ambrose. Shake his mane and let the cares of the world scatter.

His inner arguments, like medieval knights with lances ready, challenged each other again. They overwhelmed the voices far below.

You're a priest. Forgive and forget. You're a warrior. Take the coup and run. You're a father. Keep the kid safe. You're a beaten-down man. Take your dignity, and start over.

Meditation was useless. Prayers sounded like whining. He suffered like a helpless child. He was not a child waiting to be abused. He was a man, unable to protect the child waiting to be abused.

Bells rang, summoning the monks to Mass.

"I decline," Jacob said. He stiffly unfolded himself and scooted from the counter. From his closet, he pulled out and tied leather strips of bells to his ankles. He attached his porcupine headdress. He turned on the tape recorder to a deafening sound. The steady drumming shook the room. Jacob danced to the trilling chant of singers until he collapsed, sweating onto the beaten mattress. He reached over and pulled the plug from the wall.

Silence.

Jacob lay on the floor, listening to the war in his head. Accusation, reflection, the room grew shadows. Cool air filtered in through the open window. He listened to the bells for evening prayers. In the stillness, the chanting of the monks as they praised God rose and fell.

The evening darkened, the air chilled, and he faced the window. He watched the big orange moonrise as two owls called to each other. *Bilikaashee*, the owl, meant death. *Who would die, what would die?* The dull ache in his stomach reminded him he had not eaten. Carefully, he picked up his bells and headdress, putting them back into the closet that held his habits. He dressed in jeans and a black tee shirt and pushed the desk from the door. Outside of his door lay a tray of food. He moved it aside with his foot as he listened. Nothing but snoring echoed inside the hall.

Like a brave stalking prey, he clung to the shadows and walls, listening for sounds of life and movement. He walked undetected to the kitchen and raided the pantry. The walk in the cool night air chilled him. He paused and looked at the monastery—his home, his refuge. But was it? Who did they think they were fooling? The Warrior within challenged, *This is a cage to hide in.*

The owls hooted in agreement.

He wandered the parking lot. A blue Mustang sat arrogantly next to the old Ford Falcon. This blue gem belonged to Pius. A small tool shed stood at the far end of the parking lot. Jacob took out a screwdriver and hammer.

A rustling in the bushes caused Jacob to flatten himself and his food between the cloister wall and the juniper. Jacob held his breath, and a *xuahcee* sauntered by.

He wasn't even good enough to alarm a foraging skunk. A long time ago, when money was scarce, he had fallen to temptation and stole ripening food from the farm. Instead of being caught and punished, they invited him to dine and always sent leftovers.

How can such a group of misfits show both goodness and evil?

Jacob smiled to himself as he climbed into the Mustang. He shoved the screwdriver into the ignition and tapped it with a hammer. The car started, and Jacob drove away.

Hours later, a pickup truck pulled up to the monastery, and Jacob stepped out and waved to the driver. He needed a drink, so he walked to the brewery, glancing at the monastery's still-dark windows.

Jacob tried the door to the brewery.

Locked.

He ran his fingers over the wall, finding the loose brick. The key was cold to his touch. He settled for two six packs of Absolution Ale, enough to contemplate the graveness of sin. The sky was turning a light pink, so he quickened his pace, making it to his room with his stash as the morning bells clanked.

The day drifted between bottles of Absolution Ale and forgiveness. *I forgive you, mother, for not loving me.* Open a bottle. *I forgive you, Father Lucian, for keeping my secret.* Open a bottle. *I forgive you, God, for taking my family away.* Open two bottles. Lack of food and exhaustion, coated with alcohol, made the day drift from alertness to hazy moments when blissful unconsciousness won him over.

Jacob woke up with a dry and heavy tongue as if it had lain next to him as he slept. The open window leaked fresh air, making him realize he needed a shower, yet his brain said he needed firewater.

The moon was bright, and the night was clear as he found his habit. He pulled his hood up and headed to the cemetery. The grass was wet in front of the tombstones of his wife and children. He stretched his body between the stones, hoping the earth would swallow him.

"Faith, what should I do? I hate secrets. If only I had spoken the truth when we first met and disclosed the horrors of my youth. They believe the abused turn into abusers. Pius came to me because he hoped I understood the urge to hurt. He should be afraid of me. I need to end this cycle. Stop the abuse. Everyone here needs a good dose of reality. Nothing will change until they stop being blind and innocent or until I stop letting them be ignorant."

"Just love the boy." The words clung to him like the dew. That was Faith's answer.

Jacob sighed and then sang. When his voice became raspy, he thought of the liquor in the community room. He rose from the grave and made his way to the monastery, pausing occasionally, hearing twigs snap and bushes rustle. A *daxpitchee*, a bear, would be nice. *I would make a tasty snack*, he thought as he quickened his pace.

He entered the community room and cautiously moved to the large cabinet that held a variety of liquors. He opened the cabinet and smelled the familiar odor of tobacco. Ambrose. He moved to the sliding glass door and lowered the lock before returning to his search for whiskey. He loaded his side cassock pockets with bottles and slipped out of the room as someone tried to open the glass door.

Good monks are asleep, dreaming of saintly things, he said to the accusing guilt that chided him for locking a confrère out of the monastery.

Jacob paused at Paul's cell door. He gently tried the knob and smiled when he discovered the door was locked. He continued up the stairwell to the third floor. He heard a noise of shuffling feet and stopped. He was not alone. A figure, half-dressed, was wandering the hall. Father Cuthbert. Jacob coughed loudly as he approached the old monk.

"Restroom or cell, Father?" Jacob asked in a soft voice.

"My room is here somewhere," Cuthbert said, his head wobbling. Jacob guided the old monk down the hall to the elevator and discovered the abandoned wheelchair.

"Have a seat," Jacob said, inviting Cuthbert to sit. "We will have you tucked into bed in no time."

"You're such a good boy. You will make a fine monk. What's your name again?"

Jacob smiled. "Karl. Karl Mackenzie, Father." That had been his name before entering the monastery and being given a new name. He had more names than most, yet he wasn't sure that changing his name had ever changed him.

After securing Father Cuthbert in bed, Jacob made his way back to his cell and feasted on food while silencing the warring voices with alcohol.

Jacob opened his crusted eyes, disoriented, as a glare of sunlight pierced the darkness, followed by blackness and grunts of frustration. The closed curtains rippled. Jacob wondered if he was dreaming until he saw the skinny arm and leg coming out from under the heavy fabric.

Paul.

He should have closed the window.

Jacob groaned. "Holy Mother of God, Holy Virgin of virgins, Saint Michael, Saint Gabriel, Saint Raphael, all holy angels and archangels, all holy orders of blessed spirits, Saint John the Baptist, Saint Joseph, all holy patriarchs and prophets, Saint Peter, Saint Paul, Saint Andrew..."

Paul untangled himself from the drapes. The sunlight radiated around him like a transfiguration. Jacob closed his eyes. How could his confrères have allowed Paul to climb to the third floor? What if the boy had fallen?

Thank you, Lord, for keeping Paul safe.

"What are you mumbling?" Paul asked, out of breath.

"From anger, hatred, and all ill will, deliver us, oh Lord. From plague, famine, and war, deliver us, oh Lord. From everlasting death, deliver us, oh Lord. By the mystery of your Holy Incarnation, deliver us, oh Lord. By your coming, deliver us, oh Lord. By your birth, deliver us, oh Lord. By your baptism and holy fasting..."

"Deliver us, oh Lord," Paul said.

Jacob almost laughed as Paul picked up the staccato responses. The Rite of Exorcism required all present to respond.

Jacob squinted and guessed it was the afternoon of day three. He looked around, trying to recall yesterday. His cell had taken on the appearance of moving day without boxes, everything he owned strewn as if the FBI had entered searching for his soul. Paul jumped down from the counter to the floor.

"It stinks in here," Paul said, covering his nose with his hand. "Are you reciting the prayers for the dead? Because people think you are dead."

"That you spare us, we beg you to hear us. That you pardon us, we beg you to hear us. That you bring us to true penance, we beg you to hear us..." continued Jacob.

Paul opened the drapes, and the room flooded with light and dancing dust.

Jacob grimaced at the brightness. His head hurt as he wrestled his feet from the blankets. The room tilted.

"You stink. What is wrong with you?"

"I have the flu," Jacob said, his tongue thick and coated.

"Nobody else has it," Paul said.

"Well, good. My plan worked."

Paul walked across the room. Bottles clanged and tolled like church bells. Jacob stared at the fading green tint of a bruise that marked Paul's cheek. Jacob's stomach churned as a wave of adrenaline stirred in his veins. Damned Pius. Damn himself for not stopping this.

"Where did this come from?" Jacob asked, his hand trembling as he dabbed Paul's cheek.

Paul turned away. "I missed the ball."

"No; he hit you."

Paul's eyes got wide like a deer, unsure of the danger.

"I have the name. Stay away from him," Jacob said, running his fingers through his long-tangled hair. *This is never happening again.*

"How do you know?"

"Never mind how. I just do. I need to get ready."

"To do what?"

Jacob laughed. His throat hurt. He stumbled to the heavy desk that blocked the door and shoved it aside. There was no point in speaking the name aloud. He had a name. Paul would no longer be alone with Pius. The Warrior within vowed it.

Upon opening the door, Joannicus and Ambrose nearly fell inside.

"Good, you're alive," Ambrose said as he pushed past Jacob. "Time to rise and shine and cut this crap out."

"Agreed," Jacob said. "I need coffee, and you need to change the celebrant for Mass to me. Call Becca. I need a medicine woman."

Ambrose's face showed surprise. "Rebecca's here, but I think Father Pius was scheduled."

"He will not object," Jacob said in a knowing tone. "Take Paul with you."

Joannicus entered the room as Ambrose and Paul exited.

"What is going on? Why were you praying the Rite of Exorcism?"

"I have seen the devil. I needed help to send him back to hell."

Skepticism clouded Joe's eyes.

"The rules concerning confession were invented by a man who wanted to sin and not be punished." Jacob gripped the desk, steadying himself. "He came to me in confession. I cannot stop it, nor can I watch it continue. I do not expect you to have an answer. Our precious Jesus did not."

Joannicus sat down on the edge of the desk.

"Crap." He reached over and placed his hand on Jacob's sagging shoulder. "Seriously, I told you not to be a confessor in-house."

"Do you think I asked? Do you think I wanted this? He came to me under false pretense. He is wicked. Paul is right to say he is a bad man, evil," Jacob said, saliva dripping from his lips. "And I did not forgive him."

"You're a priest," Joannicus whispered. Jacob watched as the emotions of confusion and betrayal washed over Joannicus as if the Pope had just confirmed that Jesus was indeed married.

"He is not sorry." Jacob knew he would sin again.

"Don't set yourself up to be a judge. Don't lose your soul over his sin."

Jacob stood tall and grabbed his habit and bands of bells. "That will not happen. But he cannot have absolution until he is sorry."

"He can't be sorry unless he's forgiven. And I think you are mistaken about our Jesus."

Jacob frowned. He recalled the words, "Forgive them, Father. They know not what they do." The bells clinked as he headed to the showers. Forgiveness. Like that ever changed anything.

CHAPTER 20
POWWOW

Psalm 50: 3-4
Have mercy on me, God, in your kindness.
In your compassion, blot out my offence.
Oh, wash me more and more from my guilt
and cleanse me from my sin.

His sin wasn't that heinous.

Pius had spent the last few days confused. Disciplining a child wasn't a crime, and Paul had no broken bones. The Rule and Bible both warned against lax ways. Sweat dripped from his brow as he calmed his rage.

He needed to talk to Jacob.

The word from his confrères was that Jacob was sick. Pius thought otherwise. In the community, illness was passed along like notes in a classroom, and nobody else in the monastery was ill. He didn't see Jacob or the Abbot. Nobody had a believable explanation for the absences, and someone stole his car.

There was no celebrant as the bells for Mass rang. Pius stood with his fellow monks. Paul lingered in the hall.

He was about to order Paul to go to the church when he heard the soft tinkling of bells. He turned to see three women dressed in white buckskin as if ready for a jingle dress dance-off. They dipped past him in unison. He was aware of the myth but didn't believe a prayer dress could heal the afflicted. No one was ill or afflicted. Joannicus had been to the doctors. *Who needed an Indian medicine dance?*

Jacob.

Pius heard the drums beating. His scalp tingled, and his jaw tightened. The line moved as the thumping reverberated down the hall.

Okay, drums. I can handle this. It is not any odder than electric guitars at a folk Mass.

Pius stomped his way into the church. The Apsáalooke chanting began. A vowel-heavy wail pierced his ears.

This was Mass, not a Powwow.

He pulled the knuckles on his right hand. *Click, click,* and *click.* The monks and Pius glanced around, looking for Abbot Gordon. His absence was replaced with the entire Apsáalooke Nation. Were they Jacob's parishioners? No, his church was not large. Were they even Catholic? Pius rolled his shoulders as the weight of his robes made them ache. There were many Indians dressed in regalia, and others were barely covered. He had been to the opening ceremonies at gatherings and witnessed the spinning and bouncing of the fancy shawls on the women, the hypnotic two-step sway of their dance.

Surely, they will not make that noise all during Mass.

Paul darted across the church and pushed his way between the priests. To be next to Brother Ambrose, he took the seat meant for a monk.

Pius glared as he turned his head over his shoulder. Paul wrinkled his nose as he moved closer to Ambrose. Temptation was over-whelming as he watched the reason he was in trouble.

The noise stopped.

Oh, thank God, thought Pius, taking a deep breath to relax. The air was pungent, heavy with the smell of too many tanned hides. Just like Brother Ambrose, who spent his days in the barn, this group of crowded Crows had an odor.

Flashes of the past, high school drama, unpleasant moments with various tribal proud classmates, their superiority lorded over him. A sudden distaste for Jacob rose inside of him. Why wouldn't he give him absolution?

Neither of them were perfect men, but they were priests of the same faith.

People moved nervously in the silence. Rebecca and her squaw companions entered, singing in Apsáalooke to a lone drumbeat. She bounced to the rhythm of the drum, swaying, and her voice rang soothing and melodic. Pius closed his eyes. He could not watch her.

The drumbeat grew stronger and more forceful. Pius opened one eye and saw Jacob dressed in chasuble and green beaded stole, jingling as he walked. A headdress of feathers draped over his dark, unbraided hair.

He looked ludicrous.

Pius shook his head. The drum kept a steady beat, softer as Jacob chanted in Crow, not English. Pius wondered if Mass had begun. But it had—whatever Jacob said, the Apsáalooke Nation answered.

At one point, a few monastic members walked out. Pius looked at Father Joannicus, who seemed a little embarrassed, his cheeks tinged with pink as he sat attentively to the surrounding display.

Was this how Mass was said at Saint Clare's? Could Jacob be teaching a lesson to Father Joannicus? That seemed unlikely.

"I don't understand a word of this," Paul said.

That was loud and unnecessary. Pius turned and gave Paul a stern look.

Although he agreed with Paul, he couldn't bring himself to walk out of Mass. He was no longer anchored to the celebration. When do we stand, sit, or kneel?

Jacob stood in front of them after the reading of the gospel.

"It is all about forgiveness," Jacob said.

Something he was being denied, Pius fumed. His collar tightened around his neck.

"Life is nothing without forgiveness. Our faith is nothing without it."

Faith? Did Jacob even have faith? Father Pius looked around the church. What did Jacob believe in? His dislike for Jacob and all he stood for brought back the original thorn. Years ago, when Pius was a junior monk, the theology department had given Jacob a divinity degree scholarship.

This is a mockery of Catholicism and everything the community believes in.

Father Pius refocused on the homily.

"God forgave us our sin, sent his son, who forgave his killers. Are we sorry?"

Pius mopped his face.

Paul whispered to Ambrose. "What are we sorry for? I don't get it."

Paul's bruise stared at Pius.

Pius clenched hands in his lap. *He wants an apology, but that's not happening.*

Pius sat for a long time, immobilized.

"Father Jacob once gave me converted bread from dinner," Paul said.

Paul shut up.

Father Pius wouldn't be surprised if a group of Apsáalooke Elders came in with Jesus fry bread. Lines formed for communion. Paul gripped Ambrose's scapular as if it were a tail. Such disrespect, Paul knew better. Why was Ambrose allowing it?

Pius stood in line, his shoulders ached, and his head throbbed.

"Really?" Jacob asked as Pius stood before him to receive the host.

The trill of the wooden flute and the rattle of rain sticks, along with the continual bang of the drum, assaulted Pius.

How dare Jacob chastise him in public? The walls closed in as he blindly returned to his seat. He wouldn't beg for forgiveness. *If he doesn't give absolution, God will judge.*

Pius sat, gripping the armrest of his chair. He tried to pray, but the shrill sounds of the Apsáalooke language scraped at his soul. *Had anyone noticed Jacob's refusal?* With all the noise, Pius hoped it had gone unnoticed.

This is an outrage. This is not the Rez. They are a conquered people.

Pius rubbed his temples. His head throbbed with each thump of the drumstick.

God, make it stop.

Click, click, and *click* went three of his knuckles. Pius glanced at Joannicus. The man seemed so calm.

He wished he knew his secret. How Joannicus tolerated Jacob baffled him. He should have gone to confession with Joannicus. Then he wouldn't be sitting here in a state of sin.

Pius shook his head as he followed his confrères out of the church. The scholarship was the beginning. Jacob never wanted priesthood, and here he was a priest. Pius didn't believe God directly guided a man's life. He believed God left opportunities. One needed only to take them. Pius had to wonder what God wanted with Jacob.

"Was that an Indian?" Cuthbert asked, grabbing Pius's sleeve.

"Let go," hissed Pius.

Two novices stepped back and whispered to one another.

"What's he so grumpy about?"

"Someone stole his pony."

Paul stopped mid-dash. "He doesn't own a pony. We don't have a horse. Old Nellie died."

"Not a real pony—a car, a blue Mustang. They stole it right from the parking lot."

"Good," Paul said.

Pius glared, and the boy shrank back.

"Father Pius," Jacob said, standing extremely close to the pair.

"We need to talk," Pius said.

Jacob took off his headdress and handed it to Paul. He turned to face Pius, his blue eyes narrowed, his face stone like a photo of a warrior from an ancient history book.

"Yes, Father Pius. I have some things to catch up on. I will find you," Jacob said, his tone conveying a veiled evil. The subdued bells on Jacob's legs clinked under his habit as he walked away with Paul in tow.

Father Pius shivered.

CHAPTER 21
BROKEN CHALICES

Psalm 31: 1
Happy the man whose offense is forgiven,
whose sin is remitted.

Father Jacob felt the weight of his convictions as he walked to the recreation room. He still hadn't found the compassion to forgive Pius. In anger, he had taken the Mustang and hidden it, watching Pius suffer. Even though he could hear Mellitus cheering from the grave, the act didn't give him the revenge he wanted.

"It is your call, God. You pick the time for forgiveness," Jacob said in prayer.

Halfway to the community room, he met his half brother, Father Vincent Mackenzie.

Vincent stopped and asked, "Did you rearrange the sacristy?"

"No, why?" Jacob asked as they walked together.

"I was looking for my chalice. Not my travel one, but the crystal one."

The thought of the beautiful hand-blown glass, glistening when it held Jesus's blood, made Jacob frown. Envy licked at Jacob's soul. *It is just a chalice. We all have one.* A misshapen fruit bowl made of clay, but it was his. His wife's attempt at pottery. After her death, he'd found it among his possessions and decided it was the perfect size for a chalice.

"I have not moved it. Maybe a Junior did not realize it has a special place," Father Jacob said.

Jacob kept it away from the golden and silver ones in the sacristy because it was glass.

They entered the community room. Although the monks were playing checkers and chatting, Jacob detected a palpable tension. He scanned the room and found Paul sitting in a chair, guarding a lumpy cloth on the table before him.

Is that anger or fear on Paul's face?

"Excellent," Pius said, springing up from the table and snapping his book shut. "We have been waiting for you, both of you."

Jacob didn't rest easy despite knowing Paul's physical location. Dread filled Jacob. Those two were like metal and magnet.

"I don't care what the boy did. He's a boy. They do stupid things. He wouldn't annoy you so much if you left him alone," Vincent said as Jacob smirked.

As Jacob saw Pius's narrowing eyes, he cut the gloating short. His voice was soft and dangerous when he said, "You'll want to hear this."

The room became quiet. The fan hummed. The Warrior within Jacob said to be careful.

"Paul," Jacob prompted.

Paul's tears flowed. Jacob looked around the room for Brother Ambrose.

"Okay, I believe you are sorry," Jacob said, handing Paul a tissue.

Father Pius appeared content. What had Pius orchestrated now?

This little drama was an exaggeration meant to torture Paul. Except for the puffy eyes, Paul looked fine.

Something isn't right.

Paul wiped his wet face with his sleeve. "I'm very, very sorry."

Jacob still didn't know why.

Paul shook his head. Jacob looked at Pius. *See? This is sorry.* The repentance was wasted, for Pius seemed oblivious to the child's suffering.

"Enough play-acting," Pius said with a cheer that didn't fit the moment.

"I... I broke... I broke your..." Paul whispered. "They are both broken because your chalice fell on Father Vincent."

Jacob was in disbelief when he asked, "You broke my chalice?"

His clay chalice; his last possession from his old life.

Paul unfolded the cloth. There was a goblet of envy in chunks. Even in its shattered state, it looked beautiful. It was mixed with the brown earthenware that had once been Jacob's chalice—two chalices, two brothers' lives, mingled and broken. Jacob knew what had happened. His heavy clay had fallen on the delicate crystal.

"It was an accident. I'm sorry," Paul said as he clung to Jacob.

The half brothers stared at each other as if someone had announced they'd been chosen as Abbot.

"That's my chalice," Vincent said, his forehead creased, making him appear older than Jacob.

"You broke my chalice." Jacob repeated the words as if hearing them again might change the reality before him.

"You were playing in the sacristy again," Vincent said, his voice trembling.

"I'm sorry," Paul sobbed.

"Sorry? Sorry doesn't cut it," Vincent said, his voice rising an octave. "That was my chalice! A gift from my father. It came all the way from France."

Vincent grabbed Paul's arm. "How could you be so disobedient?"

Paul whimpered, Pius smirked, and Jacob looked around the

room. Nobody moved. The outside slider rolled on its wheels, and Ambrose's shadow blocked the daylight. Vincent reached for Paul's face. "Look at me when I speak to you, child. Stop that crying. I'll give you something to cry about. You'll be sorry you didn't listen."

Vincent, the reasonable man, evaporated. *It's just a vessel.* Could a man's chalice symbolize his priesthood, his honor, his most prized possession, a lover? Jacob didn't have time to contemplate the answer. Vincent's face went crimson with rage as he struck Paul. "I'll teach you a lesson you won't soon forget."

Paul wailed.

"Vincent, stop," Jacob shouted, breaking from the invisible bonds of familiar words from the past. Caught in a moment of outrage, Vincent did not heed him.

His heart pounding in his ears, silencing the fear that was mingled with rage, Jacob pulled Paul from Father Vincent and pushed the yelling child toward Ambrose. Turning, he faced his brother. Vincent's glazed eyes stared back at Jacob. Paul's crying and the cacophony of astonished monks filled the background. Vincent tried to push Jacob aside. The brothers struggled, arms and hands locked in a violent embrace. Vincent's angry words resounded in memories. Terence, Vincent, Pius, Judith, the smug faces of a mother and confrère. As they separated, Vincent raised a hand, and Jacob punched him. Vincent stumbled back and landed at the feet of the Abbot.

Blood gushed down Vincent's chin.

Jacob stepped back, arms raised as if to surrender. A swarm of monks closed off the distance between the men, helping Father Vincent to his feet.

Now they move.

"You hit me," Vincent said, his eyes wide with disbelief.

Was it Vincent's pride or the gleaming face of Pius that unhinged Jacob from his restrained self?

Oh crap. What had he done?

Father Jacob felt smothered in emotions and unable to penetrate the world. His arms and fists were still taut yet encased in marble, unable to move.

Paul broke free of Ambrose's embrace and raced toward Jacob.

"You've caused enough trouble. Sit," barked Brother Ambrose, removing Paul from Jacob.

Jacob stood immobilized as his confrères attended Vincent. Abbot Gordon and Father Pius stared at him, one with disappointment and one with a sneer of arrogance.

Ambrose's voice boomed over the excited and angry murmurs in the room. "You shouldn't have been playing with the chalices. Shame on you. We've taught you better than that. It's a misuse of a chalice. It would be like drinking the holy water. You don't drink the holy water, do you?"

Paul scowled at Ambrose. His cheeks turned red as the handprint blazed purple.

Paul hung his head. "It tastes just like regular water."

Brother Moses shuddered.

The tall, skinny porcelain pillar in the church's atrium had always looked odd to Jacob, unlike the little bowls by the doors that held holy water. The pillar was more like a fountain, with flowing water that echoed and bubbled. A vision of Paul using the flowing holy water fount as a drinking fountain filled Jacob's mind. Father Jacob discovered himself laughing. However, the laughter mingled with sorrow. Emotions like an infusion of caramel with chocolate swirled inside Jacob. His chalice was destroyed. The past became unhinged. His parents' words echoed in his ears. The blood of his brother, the gleaming face of Pius, blinded him. The horrified face of Paul mocked him with a future he didn't want to visit.

CHAPTER 22

JESUS MUG

Psalm 77: 65-66
Then the Lord awoke as if from sleep,
like a warrior overcome with wine.
He struck his foes from behind,
and put them to everlasting shame.

F ather Jacob waited outside the Abbot's office. The door was cracked open, yet he couldn't force himself to cross the threshold. As the bells rang for prayer, he raised his arm and knocked.

Jacob kept his head down as he walked to the church.

After prayers, he'd explain.

He didn't want to see the disdain in his confrère's eyes. Paul ran up to him, but Brother Ambrose shooed the boy away. Vincent and Abbot Gordon were absent from evening prayer. A moment of panic rose. Had he sent Vincent to the hospital? The voices of his fellow monks in prayer held no comfort, and the psalm that evening accused him.

"It is for you that I suffer taunts, that shame covers my face, that I have become a stranger to my brothers, an alien to my own mother's sons."

Blackness, the suffocating kind, encircled him.

After prayers, nobody lingered. He was left alone. In the morning he would go to the Abbot's office and accept the consequences for his action. There was no excuse for his behavior toward his brother. Tomorrow morning first thing to the Abbot's office, yet what words could excuse his actions?

This is what Saint Benedict meant when he spoke of a communal punishment, alone with your sin, thought Jacob as he walked to his cell. Worry settled within him. Would the police arrive? He had assaulted his own. Maybe, like so many things that happen behind closed doors, nobody called. He thought of when Brother Francis smashed his hand through the window during a drinking episode or when Father Simon had too many women visitors. They dealt with different things in the secular world. They sent people to jail.

The Elder inside him stared into his soul, asking, *Which world do you live in?*

"I live in the world that makes the right choices."

You have done what is right. You defended the weak, the Warrior responded.

Jacob touched the medicine bag that hung around his neck. *He was my brother and my tribe.*

Brother or not, he was not acting honorably, pointed out the Elder.

"Shut up," Jacob said aloud, banishing the Elder and Warrior within like the good and bad angels from his shoulders.

He didn't want to be that kind of warrior.

Jacob hung his habit on the hook next to the door and sat by the window, staring at the picturesque pastoral view of the farm and orchards. Vincent wasn't the only one surprised. He allowed his emotions to fight with his logic as he watched the darkness descend and his reflection appear before him.

Was it Vincent's words or expression, so much like his mother's, void of love, filled with rage? Was he then a warrior, touching his enemy but not killing him?

There was something wrong with a mother who sacrificed her son. Judith's actions were understandable, given her history. She was a victim. His arrival into this world after a beating by his biological father, Endow, had left Judith void of love for the child she bore early. Memories of that man's violence were as predictable as the sunrise. But to let someone beat your child... the action repulsed Jacob. Did he remind her so much of his biological father? Was she right? Was he like them?

He'd become what they'd predicted. How could anyone trust him after what he did? His soul would not accept that sentence. Learned violence. Abbot Gordon was right to watch him.

The Warrior within him shifted. *Stop riding sidesaddle. You did what was necessary. Who else moved to stop Vincent? Warriors are not* iisaxpuatachcheewishke. *Sheep follow; warriors lead.*

He should have beaten Pius if the future had been set.

Jacob laughed harshly as the sun cut the sky, bleeding into the dark.

He stood unfolded; his body ached as if he had been in a physical battle. His fingers fumbled to zip up his uncooperative habit. The Warrior and Elder had argued all night long, depriving him of sleep. These were excuses and justifications for a wrong action, making one a product of the past. *This is not who you are, nor does it make the choice right*—the wisdom of the Elders.

He walked down the hall to the church, debating whether to attend prayers. Shame wormed its way through him as he recalled the shock on Vincent's face.

Jacob's habit itched as he sat. There was a time when a monk who had offended the community by his actions would sit alone until they judged him to be penitent.

He couldn't do that. He needed them.

Jacob opened his prayer book and found a folded piece of paper. He held his breath. Was this the summons? The note contained perfect penmanship, the kind of writing that nuns send to you with requests for prayers or money, but this was from Paul—another apology. Paul wasn't the problem. The notes had to stop. *He* was the problem.

Jacob watched as Father Pius read the morning reading. He had become what he wanted to avoid.

Prayers ended, and for once, Jacob treasured the grand silence; nobody could ask him any questions. The voice of reason, Faith's voice, said, "You are not your father. It was just a lump of clay."

Jacob checked the door to the Abbot's office. It was closed. He watched members of the Senior Council enter and leave. They were discussing him. *No point in hanging on the knob*, Jacob thought. *It's not as if they can't find me.* He walked down the hall to the community room and sat. A silence like that observed during Lent encased the quiet monastery. Eyes avoided him. Paul had disappeared. Not one Junior had a need. The Warrior within him had no words for the dishonor of harming a brother. Jacob set his head on folded arms and slept.

A nightmare jerked him awake. Coffee—he needed coffee.

He rose and took his mug from the cupboard. Tucked inside, he found a scroll with another apology. The clock dinged a gentle reminder that Paul would soon be home.

A warrior would not let Pius fade into the chaos. What was in it for Pius? The man was perversely enjoying the discord. Had he set this up? Was this what it was like to beg for forgiveness? Why didn't Pius see his own actions as vile?

Jacob heard the voices of Pius and Joannicus in the hall. As they entered the community room, Jacob blurted out the question burning inside him.

"Where is my summons?"

Father Joannicus gave him a weary smile, the one he gave students who could not see the obvious.

"Seriously, does he need to? I think you know you've messed up. Besides, it seems you're not the only one making poor choices," Joannicus said.

"Don't forget, none of this would have happened if Paul hadn't been playing where he shouldn't have been," Father Pius added in a smooth, menacing tone. "It feels pretty bad to have something you treasured taken away."

Jacob ran his hand over the back of a velvet chair. Did Pius know? No, he couldn't; for he had told no one.

"Your car's not a chalice," Joannicus said, a note of disappointment in his voice. "I noticed you're the celebrant. I can take your turn."

"My chalice is available for you to use," Pius said. "I know my car is not a chalice, but it was still treasured."

"I'm sorry to hear about your loss. Thanks for the offers, but I have it covered. I considered using this coffee mug, my most treasured vessel." Jacob raised his mug before leaving as Father Pius laughed, and Father Joannicus looked worried.

Father Jacob put on a chasuble and alb and braided his hair. He stood looking at himself in the mirror, seeing a proper Catholic priest with no signs of a disobedient monk. This time, Mass was quiet. No drums, bells, or hymns. As he entered the church, behind the community, he saw the altar held twenty or more chalices that belonged to all his fellow priests. His eyes misted. Forgiveness hung in the air like the smell of baked bread. The community forgave him even if they didn't understand the root or the potential for violence. They would watch him for signs of anger. The funny thing was that when Jacob swung, he didn't experience anger. It was fear.

Jacob found yet another note in a childish scrawl when reading the Gospel. This time, Paul had become more creative in his continual apology, which was in fifteen languages, including Latin and Greek.

When it came time to speak his homily, he stood in front of the community, a strange mixture of men, some of whom he respected and some he distrusted. They were a conglomerate of talents and inadequacies held together by thin strands of hope and faith. Jacob had spent the afternoon sorting out the root of his reaction and call to violence. He wallowed in a deep sense of abandonment at losing one clump of dried clay. Most chalices went where the priest went. He and Vincent feared secular servers' clumsiness and kept their breakable chalices at the monastery, where everyone respected the sacred. He picked up the apology note and smiled before giving his shortest homily ever. "It is all about forgiveness."

After Mass, Jacob entered the sacristy, a room lined with cupboards and closets that held the cassocks and albs used for Mass. Jacob folded the albs, laid them in the drawers, and turned around to see Paul and Father Joannicus.

"Thank you," Jacob said, straightening his scapular. He suspected Joannicus had a lot to do with the rapid grace of forgiveness, which was necessary to allow this act of violence to be erased. He longed to know how much persuasion was exerted to convince Abbot Gordon.

"Once again, you are giving me credit for something I don't deserve," Joannicus said.

"You shouldn't have used your coffee cup. Abbot Gordon will take away your altar privileges," Paul announced.

"I washed it first and blessed it." Was his choice of chalice a worse crime than hitting his brother? It is funny what people find offensive.

"Why did you hit Father Vincent?" Paul asked, opening one of the closet doors and sticking his head into the incense-infused robes.

Paul inhaled the fragrant air before popping his head back and closing the closet.

"I do not know," Jacob said. There was truth in that answer.

Paul looked at him, confused. "I hit my best friend Denny once because he said I had no mother. It was dumb because I knew my mother was dead. It hurt when he said it. Is that what happened?"

The second closet opened, and Paul smashed his face into the scented robes.

"It's my fault, isn't it?" Paul asked. Joannicus gathered albs and sighed.

"You did not hit Father Vincent. I did."

Paul closed the closet door and stood with his back against it. "But you did it because he was hurting me?"

He'd done it because Pius was baiting a child.

A true warrior does not circle the wagons of the innocent to exact revenge. Jacob bit his lower lip, thinking if Pius had been hurting Paul at that moment, Pius would be in the hospital. Jacob would not have stopped at a bloody nose. He couldn't tell Paul that.

"It was still wrong," Jacob said. "We both made mistakes. We both sought forgiveness. You are forgiven. No more apologies."

Paul nodded. "Grandpa is coming tomorrow. Abbot Gordon and him will figure out what I can do to fix things and pay for Father Vincent's chalice."

The reference to Terence as a grandpa was unnerving to Jacob. "Why do you insist on calling my father grandpa? The man is not worthy."

Paul opened a third closet, but Father Joannicus stopped him.

"I call lots of people grand, like Father Jonah's parents and Abbot Gordon's mother. I like you and Father Vincent, so he is my grandpa."

Jacob noted that his mother, Judith, wasn't included in the family tree that Paul had constructed for himself.

Joannicus sent Paul on his way. "Where's the mug now?"

"I thought I would use it as my travel chalice, or perhaps I should just have Paul break this one too," Jacob said, wishing his pain hadn't leaked into his words.

"Seriously, you know you are pushing the limits of tolerance even for us Benedictines. I'm sorry about your chalice. I remember when Faith made it."

"A fruit bowl," Jacob said, his throat constricting, knowing it was more than that.

"It might have started out as a fruit bowl that cannot be replaced, but it held more significance. It was a portal to the past, and Paul destroyed it."

"Maybe it is time to let go of the past," Jacob sighed, undoing his braid and letting his long hair shake free.

The evening air hung dry as Jacob and Joannicus left the church, walking through the garden to the refectory.

Jacob stepped from flagstone to flagstone. "How is Vincent?"

Two birds landed on the birdbath, twittering, discussing the cleanliness of the water. Joannicus slowed. "He is confused, unsure why he acted the way he did or why you hit him."

"Everyone knows that our family history is composed of violence. We both messed up. I will talk to him. I do not want this to taint his relationship with our parents. It was my life, not his," Jacob said.

"Seriously, why not? The man was a monster." Joannicus kicked a stone off the path.

"Terence loves me. He is not a monster."

The two birds chased each other from wall to branch to birdbath rim.

"Seriously?" Joannicus said, stopping and giving Jacob a look of disbelief.

"Terence attended every powwow competition I ever entered. He read me bedtime stories. He adopted and took me in when my mother left."

"What are you talking about?"

"When I was about ten, Judith was carrying the twins, Vincent and Victoria. She left Terence and took my half-brothers and my sisters. She did not take me—Terence did. He gave me a place, a name, and an example of how to love."

"He mistreated you," Joannicus said as the birds splashed, carefree, in the birdbath.

"This is not a black-and-white matter, not an Apsáalooke and Catholic matter. It is a matter of the heart. For all his faults—and he has many—he cares."

"I'm sorry. I wish I could understand that you are so adamant that abuse is wrong, and yet you are so willing to forgive Terence."

"What side of Pryor Creek do you stand on?" asked the Warrior within. That was an excellent question. How could he defend Terence while condemning Vincent, Pius, and himself? "Are you Apsáalooke or white?"

Jacob knew he was not making sense.

"I can forgive Terence for his violence because it was with me. Some part of me needs a father. I may not like what he did, but he is still my father, the only one who loved me." Jacob sighed. Besides, revenge does not work.

His black habit lay heavy around his shoulders. The entire issue was complicated, like answering the question, which treaty do you uphold?

"Guilty, I am so guilty," Jacob said, stopping and picking the rosehips off the rosebush.

Joannicus picked a blossom and tossed it into the birdbath. "Do you feel guilty because Vincent's glass is broken or because you received joy at its demise? It was a little over the top, considering that your folks didn't give you a thing when you became a priest. I can't help the little tickle of happiness that Vincent's precious cup is gone."

Jacob snickered. "It was terribly insensitive of Vincent to accept it from Mom and Dad, knowing they had given me nothing. Do you think Vincent will forgive me?"

Joannicus pulled his hand out from under his scapular and

placed it on Jacob's arm as they entered the hall to the refectory. "He already has." He placed the first object on the altar.

Father Jacob turned, hearing Vincent's voice behind him, and encountered Abbot Gordon.

"Peace be with you, Father Jacob," Abbot Gordon said.

"And with you, Father Abbot." Jacob looked down, noticing a crack in the concrete under his feet. Abbot Gordon moved towards the head of the line as if nothing had happened. Jacob's face radiated heat as the cloak of humility draped over him. It was such a gentle reprimand—an acknowledgment, dismissal, and faith that Jacob would do better reverberated in his soul.

That was why he was the Abbot.

CHAPTER 23
STAYING

Psalm 122:4-5
Have mercy on us, Lord, have mercy.
We are filled with contempt.
Indeed, all too full is our soul
With the scorn of the rich,
With the proud man's disdain.

Father Jacob switched on the lights in the church and rearranged the flowers in front of the wooden statue of Saint Alberic, removing the faded blossoms from the greenery. Brother Ambrose's heavy breathing made him realize he was not alone. He saw Paul and Ambrose walking toward him.

"What is your father doing here?" Ambrose asked, his voice muffled by the bunches of flowers and greenery he carried.

"He wants to see me," Paul said.

Ambrose laid the greenery down.

"No, Little One, you did nothing he needs to be concerned with. I don't understand why he was told. He reminds me of a little pig who cried all the way home. We really don't need input into this matter," Ambrose said, shaking his massive body free of debris.

"Terence gave him the chalice. He and Vincent are close," Jacob said.

"I'd be happy if he brought two chalices. He has two priestly sons," Ambrose said, picking leaves from his beard.

"I do not need a new chalice, Rose. There are plenty of coffee mugs in the kitchen."

Paul stood and listened to their words.

"This is a monastic concern, not his problem. We are all grateful for his support; he has given us a lot."

Jacob cleared his throat and gave Ambrose his sternest look.

"I'll take no advice from him about raising a boy."

"Rose."

Ambrose threw his hand up in the air. "What?"

Jacob pointed to Paul, who looked from one monk to the other.

"Oh," Ambrose said, smacking his lips together. "So, what's the plan?"

"I got this, Rose. Come on, Paul," Jacob said, heading from the church to the monastery. Jacob had a secret that would end the money problem. They climbed the stairs in silence. The smell of beeswax candles greeted Jacob as they entered his cell. Jacob noticed his two rocks were now on the bottom shelf. "If you are hanging out in my cell, stop messing with my stuff."

"I wasn't."

Jacob turned. His scathing look cut short the child's formal protest. He knew Paul hid there, and he could not close off that sanctuary. Jacob dumped the contents of the second drawer onto his bed. He turned the drawer upside down. Taped to the bottom of the drawer were yellowed bank envelopes. The tape cracked and crumbled as Jacob pulled the packets off.

Paul opened an aged envelope, and money fell to the floor.

"Is this real?" Paul asked, gathering the bills. "You're not supposed to have this."

"I know, Father Joannicus."

Paul smiled, obviously taking the sarcasm as a compliment. "Why do you have this?"

"It is my just-in-case money."

"Just in case of what?" Paul asked. Suddenly gaining energy, Jacob stacked the six thousand dollars on the desk and found a clean piece of paper.

"I'm saving my allowance to buy a new chalice for Father Vincent," Paul continued as he fingered the piles of bills. "Only it's going to take me forever. Gracie doesn't give me much. Don't tell anyone that she gives me an allowance."

Allowance? Apparently, Paul's goodly godmother preferred to keep Abbot Gordon in the dark, too.

Jacob sat down at his desk and wrote a list of duties that Paul would perform to make retribution for his actions.

"You do not need to spend your allowance on a chalice. I am loaning you money."

"You don't have money to loan. It really belongs to the monastery."

"I am well aware of the Rule and possessions, thank you very much." He should let Paul teach the juniors about the Rule since he knew Chapter 33 well.

Jacob placed two fresh envelopes on the desk. "Here—put the money into two envelopes."

"Can we keep some money?" Paul asked, stuffing the envelopes.

"Sure, twenty for you, twenty for me," Jacob said, curious about what Paul wanted with money. Paul had money, but he wasn't aware of that fact.

Paul leaned over the list as Jacob wrote. "No, they won't let me do number three."

"I am the sacristan. If I say you can set up for Mass, then you can. If I say you can be an altar boy, you can. Besides, what better way for you to learn respect for holy objects than having to care for them? Do you agree with this arrangement?"

"Sure," Paul said. "But the date's wrong."

"No, I am late in writing the deal," Jacob said. "Let's go into the lion's den, Daniel."

Paul shook his head and sighed in exasperation, mumbling something about Terence being a pussycat, not a lion.

Jacob's chest constricted as they entered Gordon's office. He fingered the thick bundles in his pocket, as heavy as anvils.

When Jacob left the secular world, he consciously kept the insurance money so he could start again without burdening anyone. He often thought of turning it in but felt foolish for keeping it all these years. Now, if he left, he would start over in poverty.

"I found the money to pay for a new chalice for Father Vincent," Paul said boldly as they walked into the office. The three men, Abbot Gordon, Terence, and Vincent, stared at Paul and Jacob.

Abbot Gordon's eyes squinted as Paul handed him a crisp envelope. Jacob stared into the little courtyard outside the office. The bright pink and red flowers swayed in the breeze. The sun glistened on the highly polished desk as Abbot Gordon opened the envelope, spreading hundred-dollar bills on the warm surface.

"That is a lot of money," Vincent said, his voice filled with wonder.

Paul beamed at Jacob. "We made a treaty. I'll be working for Father Jacob until I'm fifty-two."

Jacob glanced at his father, who had a bemused smile. Jacob suspected they wanted an explanation but decided not to give one. He reached into his habit side pocket and withdrew the matching funds. Grinning, he set the bundle on the desktop.

"I meant to turn this in," he said sheepishly. "Come along, Paul, you are mine."

Jacob placed his hands on the boy's shoulders and exited the room to a stunned silence. Resolve washed over him like a condemned man heading to the gallows. Jacob sent Paul down the hill on a false errand while he smoked a cigarette and paced the sidewalk in front of the brewery. He had sealed his own coffin. The euphoria was almost liberating. He would stay now. A shadow darkened the sidewalk before him. Vincent's cheek was still greenish purple. His one brown eye stared at him.

"Where did this money come from?" Vincent asked.

Jacob detected a tone of worry. "It is mine. I did not steal it."

Vincent's non-swollen eye held steady.

"I wasn't aware that Faith made your chalice. I'm sorry. That must hurt seeing it broken."

Jacob crushed the cigarette under his sandaled foot. *Sometimes, monks' tongues wagged more than high school girls' tongues did at a prom.*

"Thanks. Sorry about your face."

"Yeah, I shouldn't let my temper get the best of me."

The wind shifted, and Jacob inhaled the odor of hops from the brewery.

"Sometimes we react and re-enact the past. When you yelled at Paul, I remembered being yelled at. When you did not stop, I lost it."

Vincent rubbed his arms. "Yeah, Mom yelled a lot when we were growing up. She mostly yelled at you."

"We are not close. I remind her of my biological father, Endow. Their relationship was not so great."

"I heard. I'm glad she and Dad found each other."

A cool breeze caressed Jacob's face. "Yes, everyone needs someone to love them."

Father Vincent ran a hand over the top of his head. The gesture reminded Jacob of Terence. "Why don't I remember the violence?"

Jacob's heart ached. He did not want to taint his brother's blissful childhood memories. The wind gusted, and their scapulars rose and fell around them.

This is not his burden. Jacob stood silent, hands digging into his pockets. Vincent's one eye pleaded with him.

"There are so many years between us. The family you grew up in differed from mine."

Careful, cautioned the Elder within him.

"But the violence? Is it true?"

The word *yes* hung on Jacob's lips like a first kiss. "Ask yourself where your reaction to Paul came from."

"But I don't remember."

Good. Bad things that cause flashbacks are not something to remember.

"My history is not your history. Do not let what happened to me ruin your relationship with our parents. Leave the past in the past." Terence said those words to him many times. Perhaps by speaking them aloud, they would become reality. "Vincent, we cannot change the past, but we can choose not to relive it. Make better choices when dealing with Paul and others. I will do the same."

The aroma of meat roasting danced by as Vincent hung his head. "I just wish you could see Mom and Dad like I do."

"Maybe with your help, I will someday," Jacob said, sure that he had just told the biggest lie of his life. He had long ago given up on motherly gestures of affection from Judith. His feelings for Terence were not so clear. He considered this man his father, not his stepfather. Terence had been there when he was sick and needed encouragement. Terence called him *son*, even though he was not white.

Yes, he was beaten, but he could hear Faith sigh. Even she never understood the complicated emotions that swirled inside him concerning the man he called father.

Both men watched as Terence shook hands with Abbot Gordon.

Jacob's stomach knotted as Terence approached. The wind shifted again, and the sweetness of tobacco wafted by.

"What is going on?" Terence asked, concern creasing his forehead. He looked old, not like the powerful man Jacob remembered from childhood.

"I am staying," Jacob said, hoping humor would distract his father.

"Honestly, son," Terence said. His expression filled Jacob with remorse. He didn't think he would ever be the son Terence needed.

Jacob studied the cracks and pits in the concrete walk where the ants raced aimlessly to an unknown destination. So often, Jacob listened to Terence's advice and did the opposite.

"Son, I'm worried about you. Abbot Gordon informs me you're having problems. I feared this day would come. I'm telling you this for your own good. If you can't deal with Paul, then let others do it. That goes for you, too, Vincent. There are many of you. In a marriage, the burden is on two. My advice to you is to be understanding. Children make mistakes."

Jacob swallowed hard. *So, his bruises were understanding?*

"He is forgiven."

Vincent nodded. "I overreacted. It was just a chalice. Paul didn't set out to break it."

Terence's hands reached out, and it took every ounce of courage within Jacob not to flinch as he clasped Jacob's and Vincent's shoulders. "Excellent. You can put this behind you. Get some professional help even. I'm acquainted with a few good counselors."

The fingers on Jacob's right hand dug into his palm as he let his father's words drip down on him like a melting icicle.

CHAPTER 24
SPOKEN EVIL

Psalm 54: 11
It is full of wickedness and evil;
it is full of sin.

Hours before sunrise, Jacob sat in the field, listening as the tall grass rustled with dryness. The monastery stood dark on the hill. Jacob tried not to think about the summons from Abbot Gordon that sat folded in the pocket of his jeans.

He didn't want to go.

Paul's breathing disturbed the silence. He gasped when he heard the cry of a field mouse caught in the owl's talons.

"That was so cool."

Jacob smiled. Owls were cool. Nothing beat a silent attack. Jacob rolled over and looked at the clear night sky blazed with stars. Paul did the same.

"I can name the consolations," Paul said.

"Put a *T* in that: *constellations. Stella* means stars," Jacob explained.

"*Sola* means solar system," Paul said.

"I will send you there if you do not stop."

"Stop what?"

"Being a smart-ass."

Paul loved to contradict. No doubt that resulted from living with a bunch of academic know-it-alls.

Or maybe it was just who he was. Jacob wondered about Paul's parents. They knew little about his mother and nothing about his father. He also compared Paul to the memories of his own kids, wondering how they would have turned out. Katie would have made a fine warrior. She was fearless. Elias was a scrapper. Amber Rose—Rosie—was a ball of energy and never one to be silent, much like her namesake, brother Ambrose. Almost Joanie was an infant when she died, so her personality was undeveloped, but he imagined she would be like Joannicus, a thinker.

"Hey," Paul said, bumping him.

Jacob drew in a deep breath. It was always hard to rise from the grave of memories.

"You need to improve on your table manners," Jacob said, reflecting on this afternoon. Paul had wiped his hands on his jeans instead of using the napkin next to him.

"You are always picking on me about something." Paul sighed. "I'm tired of playing Indian. Can we play saint instead?"

Jacob could see the bad habits of his confrères in Paul. "If you want to eat out in public, you will work on your manners. I am tired of playing saints. That is boring. We could play superheroes. I will be Batman."

"Who is that? I would rather be a saint. They could do things—like magic—but don't call it that."

"Batman can do stuff, too. He has special armor and other things that make him fly. You can be a saint. I will be a superhero."

185

"How's that gonna work?" Paul said, sarcasm rolling off each word.

Jacob sat up. "What? My superhero can beat your saint any day of the week."

"I know nothing about superheroes."

"Time to learn something new. Next on our reading list will be comic books." Jacob took off running toward the barn.

Paul was now eleven and odd, but his participation in school activities and being seen with an Apsáalooke warrior helped the other kids accept him. It was a silent truce. A no-Pius zone had formed between them. Nothing had happened in such a long time that Jacob considered giving Father Pius the absolution he so desired. The world had become calm. So why was Abbot Gordon summoning him? He hadn't broken any major rule.

They practiced shooting arrows into the bales until they heard the rumble of the truck heading toward the barn. Jacob and Paul dove into the loose hay. Brother Ambrose was early. They usually were back in the monastery, falling asleep an hour before Ambrose stirred. Hidden from view, they watched and listened, discovering that Brother Ambrose was not alone.

"Good of you to pitch in. I rarely have help," Ambrose said above the excited bleats of the lambs. Hildegard raised her head and thumped her tail but remained curled up. A night of frolicking in the fields meant morning sleep for her. Gregory the Great got up and stretched. The midnight play of boy and man was not his concern. He barked a greeting and followed Brother Ambrose as he released the sheep to the pasture.

"I couldn't sleep," Father Pius said. "And I hate to waste daylight. I think I have completed my whole summer syllabus."

"Wise, wise. I recommend a nap sometime today, or you will snooze through evening prayers," Ambrose advised.

"I thought I heard Jacob rustling around, but I haven't seen him."

Paul glared at Jacob as they lay listening to the men. The painted red lines on Paul's face made his scowl comical. Father Jacob stuck his tongue out at Paul. The deal was that midnight playdates would continue only if they stayed a secret.

"Yeah. Jacob's a restless soul. How are you two getting on?" Ambrose asked.

"We have come to an agreement. History can't be rewritten," Father Pius said, shrugging his shoulders.

"You tried to make a treaty with an Indian," Ambrose chuckled. "Not real bright of you. Many of them don't trust us to keep our word."

"We don't bring up the past," Pius said. "It does nothing for us to dwell on past sins."

Pius was a liar. As for past sins, they hung like a noose: a blue Mustang, a refusal to administer absolution, lies to the Abbot. So many sins.

Jacob recalled his years of monastic formation and Pius' continual protest of Jacob's Indian ways. Pius had worn his dislike like brake lights—a flash of red as a warning to be watchful. Had Abbot Gordon assigned Pius a parish to teach him tolerance? He hadn't learned that.

Jacob was baffled by the lack of tolerance because Pius had grown up in Montana, living, working, and praying in Indian country.

"I saw Paul up late the other night, yet he was at morning prayers, so I assumed it was a bladder run. He didn't seem cranky, so he must go to bed on time. We'd know if the boy was staying up all night," Ambrose stated as he handed Father Pius a shovel.

Paul placed his hand over his mouth, suppressing a giggle. Jacob wondered what was funny—the two of them not suspecting his midnight playdates or that Father Pius was about to shovel shit. Knowing that Pius was the bad monk gave Jacob insight into Paul's reactions to other monks. Jacob felt he had little influence over Father Pius but knew he could guide Paul.

Ambrose paused after pulling bags of grain from the shelves. The cats, Placid and Marcus, sprang into action as mice scattered from their morning meal. Jacob followed Ambrose's gaze and saw the abandoned bows and arrows. Ambrose retrieved the gear, examining them as if trying to figure out which tribe had attacked the barn.

"What the heck?" Pius said, mopping his forehead. "Paul's toys?"

"I think I'll hold onto these till he can learn to put them away," Ambrose said, glancing around the barn and scratching his head.

"You let him play Indian? That's got to be Jacob's influence."

Ambrose chuckled. "Yes, that's all, Jacob. Paul attends the Indian school, so he needs to know the culture. I'd love to show him hunting, but Abbot Gordon won't let me give him a gun. He would prefer I take him fishing."

"A wise decision," Pius said.

Ambrose picked up the pitchfork and deliberately poked the points through the hay. Jacob and Paul held their breath, eyes wide.

"I say there is mischief a foot," Ambrose said, setting the pitchfork aside. "Come help me with these sacks." Ambrose continued to stare in the general direction of the hidden duo.

Jacob and Paul headed to the monastery when the two monks exited the barn.

"You go to morning prayers?" Jacob asked, impressed. Jacob woke enough to mutter his apologies at the summoning of the bells, then slipped back into blissful sleep until around nine.

"Yes, I noticed you're always absent," Paul said in a rather authoritative voice.

That is what Abbot Gordon wants to talk about.

Jacob laughed. In the last few months, Paul's bossy attitude had become almost an endearing trait. "Do not forget to wash your face. We do not want others finding out."

Paul nodded as they slipped through a side door of the monastery. Paul hugged the walls of the first floor as he stealthily made his way to his cell. Jacob climbed the stairs to the third floor and walked past the glow of lights under the doors as he made his way to his bed.

. . .

Jacob sat in the church with his eyes closed. He listened to the birds singing and the buzz of a plane in the distance as warm, heavy air rolled over his bare feet. He heard footsteps approach and recede. He kept his eyes shut. The rhythm was not Paul's footsteps. It was a summons, but the deliverer did not disturb the praying monk. He had that monk fooled. Often, he sat in the church, but prayer was not on his lips. The act of worship had become the hull of a boat without a sail. He would have dived overboard if it weren't for the set routine. Instead, he gripped the sides, peering over the edge for a safe harbor. He was a man with secrets.

He rose and entered the atrium. On his sandals lay a note, another request. Jacob headed down the hall to Gordon's office. Incense was replaced with the odor of burnt toast from the community room kitchenette. He knocked on the open door, walked in, and glanced at the bookcase that held a balance of history and religion.

"The Lord be with you, Father Jacob," Abbot Gordon said, stepping into the office from the private patio outside.

"And with you, Father Abbot," Jacob said, wondering if he should sit or stand.

"It has been a while since we have talked," Abbot Gordon said, gesturing to the little living room space beyond the formal desk.

Jacob followed Gordon and sat down in the velvet chair. His clerical collar rubbed his neck.

A bee hummed as it moved from flower to flower outside the office window. They sat in silence.

"So, how are you?" Abbot Gordon asked.

"Balanced."

Abbot Gordon chuckled. "Are you overburdened with Paul and the Juniors?"

"No."

"Prayer and monastic living?"

"Good."

Abbot Gordon steepled his fingers and drew in a breath. "I can tell that Paul enjoys and thrives, pretending he's a junior monk."

"I do not make him follow what the Juniors do. He chooses to be with us."

Gordon smiled. "Leadership is difficult. There are so many personalities and needs, and each one is important. Deciding what to do sometimes takes more than faith and prayer."

Jacob bit his tongue. *Neither is being a disciple.*

"I accept Paul needs you and is safe with you. Your parental skills seem sharper than most. The last two years have been uneventful."

"This is a good thing."

The message rang like the bells for prayers. *You aren't the monk. Whoever it is has learned a lesson.*

Jacob had fathered children and raised them for as long as God had allowed.

"Thank you for the report about Paul and school. Have there been any volunteers for activities?"

"Ambrose and Moses like to attend. Ambrose tends to wind the kids up, so I need to be careful which functions he goes to."

Abbot Gordon nodded. "I have one small request."

Here it comes.

"I ask that you balance Paul's education—a little secular and a little monastic."

Jacob couldn't resist, and the words tumbled out of his mouth. "You want me to take him gun shooting, then?"

A stern but gentle expression crossed Abbot Gordon's face. He shook his head. "When he's older."

"We cannot wait too much longer. All his classmates are doing it," Jacob said. The reality of growing up in Montana meant guns; not just the excitement of shooting them but the dangers of using them.

"You jest, but soon enough, he will tell us everyone is doing it."

Jacob hoped he would be back at Saint Clare's when those words tumbled out of Paul's mouth. Teenagers were not his favorite people, with their wild emotional swings and propensity to test authority and refuse advice.

A wave of relief washed over Jacob. He didn't have to avoid Abbot Gordon now.

Abbot Gordon rose and tucked his arms under his scapular. Jacob assumed it was a signal to leave. As he approached the door, Abbot Gordon said, "I have put extra funds in Paul's discretionary account. Equip Paul with the head and arm gear necessary for those activities."

Jacob paused. How did Abbot Gordon know about "those" activities—motorcycling, skiing, and archery?

Abbot Gordon had more understanding of the needs of an eleven-year-old than Jacob had given him credit for.

The next day, Jacob worked in the sacristy. The morning dragged on. He put the broom away, untied his scapular from around his waist, and headed down the hallway that led to the monastery. He stopped, noticing that the chapel doors were closed. Jacob listened at the door. Nothing, no rustling of paper or cloth, no clinking of metal, no murmuring of prayers. He opened the door. He found nothing out of the ordinary. The crucifix was still there, the light was off, the alb folded, and the prayer books stacked. Jacob paused and listened at each door before opening them. As he approached the last door, he noticed a glow of light, then darkness. He waited. No monk emerged. Jacob slid open the door and saw Paul sitting on the kneeler.

"What are you doing?"

"Reading."

"In the dark?" Why wasn't Paul at the farm? He had assigned Paul to be with the Juniors that afternoon. "What are you really doing?"

"Hiding."

Jacob's heart thundered. Pius had to be at the farm. Paul still believed Father Pius had power. Jacob understood Paul's reluctance.

"Are you okay?" Jacob asked, scanning Paul's face.

Paul stood and closed his book. "Yes."

"You know that lying to a priest is a sin?"

Paul tossed his head with the added gesture of rolling his eyes.

"Why are you hiding? What happened?"

"I think someone will be mad at me."

"Because?"

Paul inched toward the opening. Jacob grimaced. He wished he could just say the name and dispel the magical hold.

That was when Jacob was a child—before the sight of a bruise became common. The adults talked about it in hushed voices and heated words. Jacob had watched, even eavesdropping on these conversations. He learned the reasons for their silence: money, power, fear, and loyalty. His stepfather, Terence, poured money into the church and took on a ready-made family. Where would Jacob and his siblings be if the conspiring adults called the authorities? *Fatherless.* It was better to endure bruises than poverty, drinking, and adversity.

Do not confront, the Elder said. *Keep the peace.*

Yes, that was what he would do. Join the circle of silence.

That is what Jacob called it—the excuses. As a boy, he had become skilled at making excuses for them all. Once a nun confronted him about his bruises, he told her to keep quiet. "Don't take away the only family I have," he'd begged her. She had protested. He boldly stared at her, asking if she would adopt him. She couldn't—she wouldn't. From that day forward, she, too, joined the circle of silence.

"Just continue to read in my cell," Jacob said. "Just stay out of my stuff."

"You don't got anything in there. It looks like a guest cell instead of a real monk's cell."

"Do not be nasty. I have two rocks. What more do I need?" Jacob asked. "Who are you avoiding? Let me guess."

Paul glared at Jacob. "Shut up. Don't say another word."

"If Father Pius is at the farm, you are safe up here."

Paul pushed past Jacob and ran to the monastery.

If Paul would say the name, would the future change? Could Pius be removed, given help, and forgiven by society as well as his confrères? He could pulverize the man. His biological father had beaten his mother. His stepfather had beaten him, and he could beat the man who hurt Paul and prove that he was his father's son. Logical as it was. That only made him a monster. What good does speaking the evil do? Jacob's childhood confessions to Father Lucian always began with, "Bless me, Father, for I have sinned; it has been one week since my last confession. My father beat me this week."

Then the old monk would say, "Child, don't speak so brazenly of evil."

But you are an adult, so speak up, the Warrior within advised.

CHAPTER 25
THE BEATING

Psalm 117: 53
I am seized with indignation at the wicked
who forsake your law.

J acob wiped the fingerprints off the stained glass window in the church and listened to the rattling of the lock that kept the wine cellar secure. It had to be Father Felix. Jacob had changed the lock when he had discovered Felix's fondness for sacramental wine. He ambled to the sacristy and opened the door. It was Paul.

"Why did you change the lock?" Paul demanded.

"What do you need in the wine cellar? Did Father Felix send you?" countered Jacob.

"I need ice," Paul said as Jacob turned on the lights.

Jacob's muscles tensed. Blood dripped from the boy's nose,

staining his shirt. A red bruise surrounding the crescent-shaped cut on Paul's face screamed at him.

Again.

Jacob's stomach churned, driven by the gale force of his heart pulsing in his chest. He grabbed Paul's arm.

"Come on."

"Where are we going?" Paul asked, his voice high-pitched with fear.

"To end this once and for all."

The force it took to move a reluctant eleven-year-old was greater than for a stubborn five-year-old.

"You don't even know what happened."

Jacob stopped, knowing that an explanation was a waste of time. "Okay, tell me what happened?"

"I'll tell you in confession."

"Hell, no. We both know what happened. Say the name so I can confront the bastard."

"You're going to get us killed," Paul shouted as Jacob continued to pull the boy down the hall.

"He will not kill you, and he certainly is not going to kill me," Jacob said, wondering if that was true. His mother, Judith, had threatened to kill him many times, though mostly she was just verbalizing her desire. Did he know that as a kid?

Jacob stopped in the hallway outside the community room.

"Do you want this to stop?"

Paul wiped the blood from his nose with his sleeve. "Yes."

"Then trust me. This is the only way."

"Please, Father Jacob, you are going to make things worse," Paul said.

Jacob saw Abbot Gordon and two monks appear from the office and head toward him. Jacob was done arguing, at least with the boy. He gave Paul a firm push into the community room.

"Father Jacob," Abbot Gordon shouted. "What are you doing?"

"Getting Paul some ice," Jacob said in a steady voice as he put distance between Abbot Gordon and himself. He would not be stopped. Jacob took his anger out on the ice tray and banged it loudly on the counter. Abbot Gordon approached Paul and frowned as he examined the boy's face, gently embracing him in a comforting hug. Paul's lower lip quivered.

Don't stop now.

Jacob scanned the room, finding Brother Ambrose and Father Pius—his victim and prey.

"Brother Ambrose, I have a bone to pick with you," Jacob said, his voice clear and clipped.

Ambrose crinkled his eyes, and his wooly brows formed a straight line.

"What happened at the farm?" Jacob handed Paul the ice pack. "He is bleeding, for God's sake. Did you backhand him?"

Gasps filled the otherwise silent room. Jacob estimated a third of the monks were present, enough to cause a stir.

Ambrose scowled. "Whoa, Nellie, it wasn't like that. What the hell are you accusing me of?"

Paul let out a yelp. "He did nothing."

"I can see that," Jacob said. "This should never have happened."

"Get a grip, Jacob. Things got a little out of hand. It was stopped," Ambrose said, his voice unusually calm for being accused of abuse.

Jacob stepped close to Ambrose, close enough to smell the barn-yard animals. Paul wiggled his way between them. The fresh hay scent wafted from the boy's hair.

"Out of hand? Someone struck Paul." Jacob's body tingled.

"Yes. I stopped it. He lost his temper. I stopped it."

Jacob met his gaze, wishing that Ambrose could read his mind. *You know. Say the name, and everyone will know.*

"No more excuses and promises. This cannot continue or happen again. We are better than that." Jacob's voice rang like thunder.

He had their attention. Pius stood frozen. Was he sorry yet? No, his face was calm, and his posture relaxed.

"Excuse me. Are you telling me other bruises were done by some-one, not by 'accidents,' as someone told me?" Ambrose said, his eyes opening wide as he looked at Paul in disbelief.

"Sorry," Paul said to Brother Ambrose as he grasped Jacob's sleeve. "Don't tell, please."

Jacob frowned. He placed his hands on Paul's shoulders, bent to eye level. "It has to stop. This is the only way."

The look on Ambrose's face was one of concentration. "I suspected you."

"I know, and I forgive you."

"It was never you, was it?"

"No, it was not me. But to be fair, I thought it was you," Jacob said.

They were part of the circle of silence, ordered to keep a secret.

"Jacob, you know I'd never hurt the boy," Ambrose said, hanging his head.

"This happens when we keep secrets, Rose."

The disappointment on Ambrose's face stung Jacob as if someone had slapped him.

"Crap," Ambrose continued, as his large, calloused hand smacked his forehead. Pius took a step toward the exit door.

"That will be quite enough, Father Jacob," Abbot Gordon said, his face turning a deep red. Jacob forced his gaze away from Ambrose.

"I am not done," Jacob said.

"To my office," Gordon said, heading alone to the door. His words were not enough to make Jacob drop the gauntlet and retreat.

Obedience. Jacob resisted the pull to follow Abbot Gordon.

Paul closed his eyes as if the gesture would banish the surrounding scene. Ambrose stared at Paul and Jacob. He collapsed into his seat and pulled Paul into his massive lap, hugging the boy.

"Father Pius, shame on you. You are a bad man," Ambrose said.

Eyes turned toward Father Pius as a murmur floated across the room. Arrogance seemed to drain from the man. His shoulders slumped, and he cracked his knuckles as if marking the number of times he had hit Paul.

Abbot Gordon moved back into the room. Jacob crossed the room to where Pius stood.

"Are you sorry now?" Jacob asked as the man intently studied the carpet's nonexistent pattern. Pius's cheeks flamed scarlet.

Jacob leaned close and heard the labored breath and the hard swallow.

"I absolve you, in the name of the Father and the Son and the Holy Spirit. For your penance, say a rosary and go in peace," Jacob whispered.

A sense of relief washed over Jacob, so fleeting that he almost didn't notice it. There was no joy of absolution. He still wanted to crush his spirit.

Abbot Gordon crossed the room and stood beside Pius, whose hands fell limp to his sides. Jacob scowled as he read the intention in the eyes of Abbot Gordon. Sympathy. Pius didn't deserve sympathy. Pius ought to have the community's wrath for his past and present actions.

"Thank you for bringing this to our attention, Father Jacob," Abbot Gordon said in a controlled voice as if he were reporting a leaky faucet.

Paul was strangely silent. Ambrose continued to hug the boy. A low murmur buzzed in the room like a lone fly. Earthquake Jacob had hit a nine on the Richter scale. There would be damage, but Paul was safe. The community would protect him. Abbot Gordon placed a hand on Father Pius and led him from the room like a dazed soldier coming off the battlefield.

"Father Jacob, follow me," Abbot Gordon called.

What? He had done nothing wrong. He had fixed the problem by ending the evil in the darkness. The desire to be a good monk slammed against his justification. This was not his sin. He'd kept the secret for too long. *We can't fight evil when we can't face it. No.*

Like the peace before a tsunami, Jacob felt a silent rage, and he knew he could not hold it. Jacob stared at the stunned faces in the room.

Why are they so complacent?

Jacob unbuttoned his cowl and scapular with trembling fingers, then unzipped his habit, leaving a mound of black cloth on the floor.

"I quit."

The room was silent except for the snapping of knuckles.

Jacob made his way to the parking lot. He stopped, realizing he had no car. He remembered his motorbike was at the farm. He looked back, wondering if he should grab more clothes. Once at the farm, he pulled his cycle from the shed, turned, and jumped.

"Don't leave," Paul said.

The plea stabbed Jacob in his soul, which at that moment was breaking.

"Take me with you."

"Not a good idea," Jacob said.

"You made them go crazy. Ambrose yelled at Father Pius. Others are talking and demanding. Stay. Fix this."

Jacob knelt in front of the boy. "I fixed it. You are now safe. Father Pius won't try to hurt you again. You have an army of monks on your side now."

"No. When Jenny told the teacher that Billy was pinching her, we all had to pinch Billy." Paul stopped, and his lower lip protruded, quivering.

Jacob shook his head as he thought little of Billy's punishment. "And then what?"

"Jenny is not at school."

"Well, maybe she's sick, or her parents moved. How long ago was this?"

"I don't know. I just think she's dead. Once, I told Abbot Gordon that Father Pius had hit me with a wet towel. He asked me so many questions. Like, what was I doing? What was Father doing? What did

I say? How did I say it? I felt like I had done something wrong. Father Pius only gets meaner."

Jacob thought about the ruler that Pius had annoyingly tapped when he gave a talk to the Juniors. Paul had been there that day. Jacob also realized that the thin branch Pius played with during the barbecue the other day was a subtle form of torture. Witnessed innocent habits and gestures took on new meanings.

Jacob exhaled and handed Paul a helmet, wondering how he would fix this additional problem. *How long will it be before they notice Paul missing?*

Would they think he had kidnapped Paul? He couldn't kidnap a kid that belonged to everyone. Would they come looking for them?

Jacob and Paul rode an hour to the Reservation and entered a tipi. The inside was a mix of modern and ancient. Colorful plastic bins held blankets and furs, and low wooden chairs formed a circle around a fire pit. The floor was dirt and flagstone, for this was a permanent spot, an Indian Hotel Eight. A large dream catcher hung on the wall alongside a family photo.

Paul looked at the picture. "Who are these people?"

"Family. This is my family's shared space." Jacob closed the entrance flap and pushed a raven's wing outside, signifying that today someone was inside.

Jacob built a fire as evening settled in. The flames rose, and the wood snapped.

"How long are we staying here?" Paul asked. "I'm cold. What's there to eat?"

"There is food in the cooler."

Paul pulled out a leather-like strip and sniffed it.

"Venison. Eat it. No complaining, or I'll call Ambrose."

Jacob stood up and opened a wooden box. "There is beef stew or chili. Which do you want?"

"We were having roasted chicken at home."

"Fine, go home."

"Aren't you coming with me?"

"I just left. I am pissed at them. I do not want to go home."

"Oh," Paul said as he chewed the dried meat. "Sounds like you are mad at me."

He was. Would this have happened if Paul told?

Don't blame the boy. Just admit it. Have you ever embraced the life fully? the Elder within hissed.

Jacob poured stew into the pot and set it near the fire. He then pulled out several furs and put them on the air mattresses.

"Air mattresses? I thought Indians slept on the ground."

"Do not be stupid. We make use of anything the white men discard," Jacob snapped, regretting his quip as it left his lips. His eyes glanced at the blue Mustang's license plate that hung from a pole like a trophy.

"Sorry," Paul muttered, getting up and filling two cups with water from the large jug that stood at the entrance to the tipi.

Jacob dished up the stew, and they ate in monastic silence.

What had he done? What was he going to do? No money and no place to stay. And a boy.

You have done what is right, the Warrior within said.

Just because it was right did not make it the right thing to do.

Protecting the boy is right, argued the Warrior.

And leaving? That was impulsive, whispered the Elder.

But right. "I am sorry too," Jacob said, breaking the silence and banishing the Indian spirit guides.

"Brother Ambrose says sometimes you have to nap and get over it," Paul said.

Jacob watched as Paul poked at the fire. Everything he loved self-destructed.

They went to bed without engaging in formal prayer. In the early morning, the sky rumbled with thunder, and lightning flashed as the teepee groaned with the wind. Paul woke up and moved closer to Jacob, waking him from a troubled sleep. Little streams creased the earth, signaling a warning that there was too much water to be absorbed.

Much like the community and your announcement, the Elder whispered between thunderclaps.

Jacob rose, and Paul cringed. A voice called in Apsáalooke outside the tent, warning them of flooding. It was time to leave.

The rain dumped onto the parched ground, soaking them as they headed down the highway on the motorbike.

CHAPTER 26

WHAT NOW?

Psalm 7: 16
He digs a pitfall, digs it deep,
And in the trap he has made, he will fall.

W hen he parked next to a large rose bush, the rain had slowed to a steady, miserable drizzle. Jacob beckoned Paul to follow him along the overgrown flagstone path and up the steps to the porch of the large white farmhouse. Paul's tennis shoes made a squishing sound as he followed Jacob around the back to a mudroom off the kitchen. Jacob tapped lightly on the window from the back porch. His stepfather, Terence, looked up and nodded. The aroma of fried bacon filled the air as they entered the kitchen.

"Look what the cat drug in," Judith, his mother, said, turning and glancing at them.

"Got caught in the storm?" Terence asked, sipping coffee from a 'world's best dad' mug.

"You could say that," Jacob said as Paul shivered beside him.

"You're dripping on the floor," Judith said, her dark brown eyes narrowing as she stopped cooking. Paul hopped to the rug in front of the sink, leaving little puddles behind him.

Judith stepped forward. Paul was almost as tall as her. She visually examined Paul and glared at Jacob.

"Who hit you?"

Paul grimaced, his teeth chattering, "Father Pius."

Jacob sighed. *Good for you.*

"Why?" Judith asked.

"How the hell do I know?" Paul muttered, holding Judith's gaze.

"We came only to get dry," Jacob said, anger rising inside him. She had never asked that of him.

"Impertinent boy," Judith said as she turned back to the stove. Her short black hair showed no hint of gray, at least none that Jacob could detect from this distance.

"Good idea. You look soaked to the bone," Terence said. "You're welcome to stay for breakfast."

Judith snorted. "Polite people call first."

White people call and make plans. Jacob led Paul from the kitchen down the hall to the stairway.

"What does impertinent mean?" Paul asked as he followed Jacob through the farmhouse.

"Wise," Jacob said as they walked down a hall of doors.

"You have lots of rooms," Paul said.

"I have a big family. Rebecca, my sister, Sister Marie, Terry, David, Tommie, our Father Vincent, and my baby sister Vicki," Jacob said.

He hadn't been upstairs in years, and the ghosts of childhood darted around the hall with slamming doors of hormonal teenage girls and mischievous little boys.

Jacob opened a door that led to the attic. The ceiling slanted, forcing the tall man to walk in the center. The room held dream catchers dangling from the ceiling, crosses, feathers, and posters of dancers in full Apsáalooke regalia. His bedroom remained a museum to Apsáalooke culture. Jacob opened the drawers, pulling out a pair of jeans and a T-shirt.

"Is this your room?" Paul asked, touching the various objects with a sacred respect.

"Yep, when I was a kid, I would watch the moon rise from that window."

"Where's Jesus?"

Jacob pointed to the wall opposite the window, where a milky white crucifix hung. It glowed in the dark but faded at night.

Jacob changed into dry clothing. A knock on the door caused him to jump. Opening the door, he saw Terence with a set of boy-sized clothing.

"Paul, go shower," Jacob said.

Paul grabbed the dry clothes and took off. Jacob imagined his mother complaining about thunder on the stairs.

Terence turned toward Jacob and leaned on the doorframe as if crossing the threshold would require payment. "So, son, what brings you home?"

"The rain," Jacob said.

"What happened?"

He wasn't staying, so Judith didn't need to fuss. Over the years, his stepfather had mellowed, and his mother's tongue had grown bold.

"You're welcome to stay for as long as you need to," Terence said.

"And Mother?"

"Your mother will accept. You're my son. You can stay."

"Stepson," Jacob said in almost a whisper, his mouth going dry as the word bubbled up.

Terence shook his head. "Is Paul any less important to you than your own children were? You care about the boy. You wouldn't be here if you didn't."

"Thanks," Jacob said.

Damn, how could he spit in the face of kindness? One night wouldn't kill them.

Silence hung between them.

"Vincent called," Terence said. "He said you quit?"

Vincent the monastic crier.

Why didn't the Abbot call? Why did he let Jacob leave? He was one of their own. Wasn't he the shepherd? Perhaps he was the proverbial black sheep.

Jacob looked out the window of his childhood.

"Yes, I quit. I thought they were men of God, better than the rest of us."

"They are human," Terence said. "Son, we all make mistakes. You should call them and tell them the boy is with you. You wouldn't want to add kidnapping to the equation."

"He belongs to all of us," Jacob muttered. "I will send the boy home soon."

"Yes, but home is the monastery. Call them and tell them Paul is with you."

"I guess they deserve that much. I do not want to talk to them. They are not the men I thought they were," Jacob said.

"Then have the boy call." Terence turned to leave and stopped. "I read somewhere that as long as a child has one person who cares, they turn out okay. Paul has a lot of someones."

"They hurt him."

"One man out of forty. And he's safe now, correct?"

Paul was safe. After Jacob's announcement, nobody would dare hurt him, and they would scrutinize every act of discipline.

"Yes," Jacob said, wondering why that didn't make his soul joyous.

By afternoon, Jacob had helped his stepfather repair the stair rail and the squeaky washroom fan. Jacob then had Paul call the monastery, but the conversation didn't go well.

"We are on a field trip," Paul said. "No, seriously, I'm good. What are you doing with Father Pius?"

Paul's jaw tightened, and Jacob knew Father Pius remained at the monastery. He needed to convince Paul that Pius was no longer a threat.

Did he even believe that?

Dinner moved slowly. Paul's manners were impeccable, and his appetite ravenous, taking seconds of the meatloaf and biscuits. Together, they cleaned the kitchen and then watched a television show. Close to nine o'clock, Paul rose and grabbed Jacob's sleeve.

"Let's go. I'm not sleeping in that room alone."

"Aren't you a little old to have bed partners?" Judith said.

"Nope. Besides, we haven't said vespers, and this is a sleepover," Paul stated, unabashed by the woman's sharp tone.

Jacob rose and followed Paul to his bedroom.

"I like those nets. Can you make me one?"

"Dream catchers. I can teach you how to make one tomorrow."

"Are you going to keep my cell open even after I grow up?" Paul asked, settling into the bed.

"Always," Jacob said.

"Good. Now, please put that Jesus away. He creeps me out."

Jacob took the glowing crucifix down and laid it in the dresser drawer.

"I kind of liked his glow," Jacob said.

"You're kind of odd. Abbot Gordon is worried," Paul said. "Are we going to go home?"

"You are," Jacob said.

"Not without you."

Jacob fluffed his pillow. "Why do I have to be there? Father Pius will never again try to hurt you. The community will stop him."

"Why didn't they send him away? I don't want him there."

Because they are stupid and believe that God takes care of everything.

"I do not know. Ask Abbot Gordon when you get home."

Paul yawned. "I don't want to go unless you're coming with me."

"You do not need me there."

"I do. What if Father Pius corners me and drags me to my cell, and tries to kill me?"

My God, where did that come from?

"He will not do that."

"He could."

"Pius has a temper. He is not a murderer." Jacob sighed and tried a fresh approach. "Do you like Father Pius?"

The springs on the old bed groaned with Paul's emphatic *no*.

"Then you owe him nothing more than the polite respect you would give a visiting monk. If he tries to drag you anywhere, you fight him off like a cougar, wolf, or bear. Now, stop being so dramatic. Have a little faith in the others. They care about you."

"What about you?"

Jacob took a deep breath. "Yes, I love you. Now go to sleep."

"All right, but we need to go home. Whenever I get upset, Brother Ambrose gives me a time-out and says, 'Get over it.' You need to get over it."

Thank you, Rose. Jacob lay on the floor, staring at the space where Jesus should have hung. Jacob had received it from Sister Jude for knowing all the Ten Commandments and the Beatitudes. He realized that the blending of his faith hadn't worked well. The finality of his actions reminded him of the days he had spent holding his dying family in his arms. The familiar words rang in his soul like the bells of the monastery.

What to do now?

When his family had died, the monastery took him in. The numbness of grief kept him there. As time moved on, he stayed.

The Warrior within laughed. *Liar, you did not decide until you gave the Abbot that money. That was a foolish, impulsive move. Now, what are you going to do?*

Wrong; he had decided long before that long before Paul.

Jacob listened to Paul's steady breathing. This one was alive. Jacob rose, took Jesus out of the drawer, and crawled back into bed.

Why are you playing with me? You let me heal at the monastery with those men and their kindness, and then you dropped Paul in my lap. Now that I love him, will you take him away?

Jacob's heart ached for his own children like a phantom limb.

He had never wanted much. He prayed only the proverbial, "Thy will be done." His life was a smorgasbord of opportunities, just as one gathers berries from the bushes. If it was ripe, he snatched it up.

Maybe he wasn't a warrior. He made Pius pay for his actions, but he didn't feel vindicated.

The furnace groaned, and warm air fluttered the feathers of the dream catcher.

What are you afraid of? the Elder whispered.

CHAPTER 27
FRONT DOOR

Psalm 53:13-14
If this had been done by any enemy,
I could bear his taunts.
If a rival had risen against me.
I could hide from him.
But it is you, my own companion,
My intimate friend.

After breakfast, Jacob announced it was time for a ride. Paul questioned him and demanded to know where. Thankfully, the wind, the helmet, and the roar of the motorbike cut most of the conversation. Jacob refused to tell him they were going to Saint Clare's parish church. As they approached, Paul protested, refusing to leave the bike.

"Suit yourself, but Mrs. Old Coyote makes fry bread on Friday. Your loss."

Paul leaped from the black Triumph and headed to the parish office, and Jacob went to the rectory. Jacob entered through the back door. He had never used the front door. *Had anyone ever used the front door?* The once familiar space now looked like a larger version of Joe's monastic cell. Books and file folders were stacked high on the counter and chairs. The table was pushed against the wall where the crucifix hung. He could picture Joannicus eating with Christ in monastic silence.

Jacob put a kettle of water on the stove. Who would arrive first? Rebecca or Joannicus? He sat at the counter and moved the stacks of papers to the side.

The back door opened.

"Before you say anything," Jacob said, seeing Joannicus, "Yes, it is true I quit."

"We all say stupid things," Joannicus said, opening the cabinet and setting down a sugar bowl.

"I was not kidding," Jacob said.

"Seriously, everyone takes a sabbatical from time to time."

"I said I quit."

"They heard sabbatical."

The kettle blew hot steam as it whistled.

Calm yourself.

Jacob covered his face with his hands. They heard what they wanted. The whistle slowed as Joannicus lifted the pot and poured.

"It's noon. We really need to pray," Joannicus said as he sat at the counter.

Jacob frowned as he took a tea bag and placed it in the steaming cup. It floated stubbornly on the water's surface. He scooped sugar, and still, the tea bag stayed afloat. Jacob jerked the string, causing the white granules to slide and dissolve into the coppery liquid. His hands cradled the cup as he bowed his head and breathed in the steam. Joannicus prayed aloud.

Prayer. What had prayer done for him? As a boy, he believed

prayer was magic. *Pray and receive.* Wasn't that what the Bible said? Only like magic, prayer had a price.

Jacob prayed in his heart. *Great Spirit, Wakan Tanka, Maker of Everything, Mother Earth, Yahweh, God, whatever the hell you are calling yourself these days, what do you want?*

He had paid the ultimate price, giving his life and soul to becoming a monk. What more could he give? He had tried to love and be loved to experience the great love prophets and saints spoke of.

"Amen," Joannicus said, ending his prayer. Jacob opened his eyes and sipped his tea. They sat in silence like a Good Friday Vigil.

He prayed, and silence answered. Had he not loved enough?

"Seriously, what are your plans?" Joannicus asked.

"I do not know."

"You're welcome to stay here."

Jacob laughed. "No thanks."

Relief filled Joe's face as he looked directly at Jacob. "You ruined a man's life."

Is he kidding?

"He hurt Paul."

"Two wrongs don't make a right."

"I did nothing wrong. I saved Paul."

"At the cost of one man's dignity," Joannicus stated as he placed biscuits on the plate. "You told me Pius came to you for help."

"He asked for forgiveness, not for help. He did not want to take ownership of his actions."

"You left him in the lion's pit," Joannicus said, his face pinched as if he had drunk strong coffee.

Anger bubbled inside of Jacob. "I gave him absolution. I did not leave him wallowing in sin. Now Paul is safe."

"Did you give him forgiveness? All I see is shame. Disgrace on him, on the community," Joannicus said, stirring his tea with a rhythmic clink of his spoon against the side.

"Are we talking about Pius or you?"

The stirring stopped. "I'm part of the community, as are you and Paul."

"You are right. We should all be ashamed for not stopping Pius sooner."

Joannicus sipped his tea. "Your leaving will hurt Paul. I don't see how that fits your desire to protect him."

Jacob stared into his teacup. "I was protecting him from Pius. I did that. He will find another mentor. My dad said it only takes one special person, and we both know Paul has many."

"Your dad? Seriously, you're taking advice from Terence. He abused you longer than Pius abused Paul and more severely, and yet you can live with him, but not Pius. I don't understand."

Jacob couldn't explain other than to say that his actions were steeped in emotion. He was forcing him to leave. The facts collided with his feelings. He couldn't live with people who ignored the truth. Sadness consumed him, for Joannicus assumed this leaving was easy. It was not. He never fit in. This was difficult.

As if a window were open, the air between them grew cold.

"You know you can't divorce God any more than you can stop being Apsáalooke," Joannicus said, banging his cup on the counter.

"I dislike the way God treats me."

"Seriously, maybe you should look at how you treat him," Joannicus said.

A gust of rage bellowed inside of Jacob, and he gripped the cup handle. *Curb your tongue, Warrior; don't burn the only bridge you have back.*

"I hoped you would understand."

"Did you understand Pius? You can't turn your back on God, Paul, and the community. None of us has turned their back on you. I don't understand how you can forgive your stepfather but not Pius. I think you're a hypocrite. That's what I understand."

Paul's voice floated into the room through an opened window.

A deep sadness filled Joe's eyes. "If you aren't coming back to the monastery with us, I suggest you leave before Paul comes in."

Jacob nodded as he used the front door.

CHAPTER 28
GREENHOPPER

Psalm 21:15
Like water I am poured out,
disjointed are all my bones.
My heart has become like wax,
it is melted within my breast.

The raven in the branch overhead cackled. Jacob started his motorcycle and rolled down the driveway. In his side mirror, he watched Paul run after him, thankful that the motor of his Triumph drowned out any shouts.

Betrayal.

Jacob headed in the general direction of the Rez. He stopped at the Snake Eye Saloon. Although it was early afternoon, the smoky room was filled with regulars. A handful of bikers shot pool and made noise around two pitchers of Budweiser. Unemployed field hands sat in twos and threes at tables, arguing about which direction to migrate next. Three women sat at the bar checking out the slim selection of future prospects. A few stools away sat a grizzled ranch hand who glared at Jacob. The women stole a glance of their own at Jacob as he came up beside them to order.

Jacob sat at the counter, pushing the peanut shells to the side as he smiled at the women.

"Absolution Ale."

Maybe he would get lucky. He was a good husband once and a good listener, too. He would need a job. He should apply. Barkeep or confessor—it was the same.

"What's your sin?" the bartender asked, placing the water-stained mug in front of him.

"*Peccata mortalia,* I wish to absolve," Jacob said as Paul's face loomed large and sad in his mind.

"You're speaking Indian gibberish. Talk English, you heathen," the man to his left sputtered.

"That's Latin, you moron. It means mortal sin," the woman next to him said as she leaned over in Jacob's direction. Her compressed cleavage threatened to flow from her tight blouse. Jacob looked away, realizing he was staring.

"An Indian with a soul."

The drunk's comment drew a few chuckles. Jacob downed the beer as if he'd wandered forty days in the desert.

When he ordered his third bottle, the bartender asked, "You got money to pay for that?"

"Yeah, Uncle Sam paid me this week," Jacob said. It sounded like a motor traveling around the room, but the low growl made Jacob realize that not all liked his humor.

"So now he's a comedian."

Jacob also noticed that aside from the three silent Indians in the corner, white men surrounded him. He ordered another beer.

· · ·

Jacob groaned as he shifted his weight on the narrow, hard bed. He looked at the peeling paint. This was not his kind of cell. A monastic one was much more comfortable. His head hurt; his ribs hurt. The taste of blood tainted his spittle. He staggered to the rust-stained sink. He splashed his face with water. Blood and dirt from his hands swirled a murky brown. Was it his blood or someone else's?

He remembered the lights and the two officers who pulled him over. He wondered if someone reported Paul's absence as a kidnapping. Had he said that? Yes, he'd been drinking. Was he drunk? He was an Indian off the Rez. He was drunk. That was all he recalled. The price one paid for tangling with the laws of white men.

Treachery.

Nobody understands an Indian, the Warrior within said.

Oh, shut the hell up.

Jacob cupped his hands and drank the water flowing out of the tap. His head throbbed, stomach clenched, and he turned to the steel latrine and puked.

Listen up, Warrior. Your advice has made life more complicated. He stood up for the weak and made the righteous decision, and it cost him his friends and his heart.

Disloyal.

A stabbing pain caused him to grip his side. He breathed in and used the wall for support. The room teetered. The bed looked a hundred miles away.

Jacob made a mad dash to the hard bed. The mattress reeked of mold, and his stomach protested, folding him in the middle.

He shouldn't have walked out. That was rash and impulsive. If Paul and Joannicus feel betrayed, how must the community feel? He could never go back. He claimed he loved them, yet he walked away. Joannicus was right; two wrongs added up to disaster.

Hypocrite.

The jingle of keys alerted him that someone was coming. The aroma of French fries stirred his stomach, and he rushed to the toilet, fighting the urge to puke.

A tall native officer dressed in olive green appeared carrying a white bag. He unlocked the door and set the bag on the bed.

"Thought you might be hungry," the young officer said.

Jacob looked at him with his one un-swollen eye. The man looked familiar. Did he know his family? The tag on his shirt said Greenhopper.

"Thanks. You were one of the helpful ones," Jacob said, as a half memory came back, a group of drunken men with alcohol burning in their veins, the parking lot. He didn't explain himself well by admitting to kidnapping a white child.

"Yeah, that was off duty. But you are Native, and they hired me to take care of the Native problem," the officer said in a hushed tone. The officer avoided looking at Jacob, and his manner showed embarrassed nervousness. Jacob realized what was happening. His blue eyes frightened the man.

He wasn't a sacred object.

Jacob's eyes commanded respect among his people. It meant that white recessive genes appeared in the bloodline of Apsáalooke. His first white ancestry was the one they honored with stories. A French fur trader in the late 1700s, Cold Feet lived with his three-times grandmother, Sings in the Night. The second recessive gene came from his father's side of the family, and nobody ever mentioned that liaison. That family branch claimed pride and purity. What a shock it was when he arrived with blue eyes.

"Any chance of me leaving?" Jacob asked, thinking he could use that blue-eye respect. "Call this a sleepover?"

Officer Greenhopper backed out of the cell as Jacob stood leaning on the wall, his head resting like a pillow. He would not press charges since he was sure he shot off his mouth. Given the amount of alcohol he consumed, that was a good guess. Jacob noted he was alone in the cell, and the white boys who engaged him in battle were nowhere in sight.

"Yes, and no. The kidnapping thing had to be investigated, but once we saw your ID, we figured it wasn't true. Nobody wants to tangle with the religious," Officer Greenhopper said. "Neither side. So, you might be here a while."

"You can toss my ID and put me down as Jack Daniels, the drunken Indian. I need to get home. How about a second chance?"

"You're kinda funny when you're sober," Officer Greenhopper said as he moved down the hall. Jacob hoped that meant he could leave before his injuries healed and he got fat on fast food.

Sitting on the bed beside the smelly sack, he thought about a second chance. *That is what we all want.*

You got a second chance, the Elder in his mind said.

Terence adopted him at age eight and loved him as a son.

Love with a barbed hook.

Joannicus was right. He forgave Terence as much as anyone could. The years of anger, the secret plots of revenge, were gone. Terence was not the man of Jacob's childhood. He didn't hate him. It was just hard to trust him completely.

Would Paul's perception of Pius ever change?

He was a fraud.

Hell, they were all hypocrites. They worshipped a God of love and justified their actions of violence with his name.

The sound of heels on the cement and a sweet scent wafted into the cell, mingling with the powerful odor of greasy food. Jacob's stomach cramped. Jacob looked to see a beautiful woman. She wore a gray suit and a turquoise blouse. A matching turquoise feather hung from her straight black hair.

"Karl?"

He looked closer at her. "Debra?" Jacob recognized her as Debra Sees the Ground. The six sisters he'd dated and kissed when he was Karl, before marriage and the monastery. She'd married Kenneth Beaumont, a long-standing tribal family. He'd heard she went to college and got a degree. A surge of pride ran through him.

"Fuck."

"Pass—maybe on your next visit. You were always horny. Did

they do this?" Her black hair swung as she tossed her head toward the guards. She didn't seem surprised.

Did he look that bad? The relationship between law enforcement and Apsáalooke often depended on the time of day, intoxication levels, where they caught you, and luck.

"Barroom brawl. You know me, always one to correct an error," Jacob shouted, hoping his captors would hear he held no ill will toward them. He was unsure if the locals or the police had thrown the last punch.

"I thought I was here to negotiate the release of a priest." Debra flipped through her notebook, looking for a name.

"That is me when I am good." The room pulsed like a drum.

Debra closed her book and shook her head. "You're still funny, Karl. I'm searching for a priest. Jacob Mackenzie. I heard one of your brothers took the black robe. Didn't you have a brother, Vance, or something?"

Jacob laughed and winced. "You mean Vincent? He kept his name, and I am Father Jacob."

She looked at him in silence. She had heard the stories. Indians told many stories.

"Okay then, long story short, sign a stupid paper of lies, and you're out of here."

"What are the charges?"

"Didn't they tell you? How about reading you your rights?"

"Sweetness, I was drunk. I do not remember anything." Jacob spoke in a firm voice that echoed down the hall.

"Well, this says you were disorderly and resistive, the usual charges for an Indian. I will pay them off. Your dad gave me some cash and a threat. He does their taxes." She grinned.

A slow realization came upon Jacob. They didn't want to hold him if he was a priest. Three big entities ruled this corner of the state: ranchers, Indians, and the Catholic Church. One had money, one possessed power, and the Indians outnumbered them all.

A riotous noise from down the hall drew their attention.

"Bastard, you let me in now, or I'll make you wish you'd joined the border patrol. Douglas, I'm warning you, I know your grandmother..."

Debra and Jacob looked at each other.

"Rebecca," they said in unison.

The door banged open. A sheepish-looking Greenhopper stepped aside, and Jacob's sister Rebecca, with her husband Todd, entered the hall. She immediately opened the door with a set of keys. The metal hinge groaned as she tossed the keys back to Greenhopper, who almost dropped them.

Nobody stands in the way of Rebecca on the warpath, thought Jacob.

Rebecca stopped. Her mouth was pressed into a hard line, making her cheekbones more prominent.

Jacob felt himself relax, even as his head throbbed. He would be out any second now without Terence's money.

Rebecca crossed her arms. "I will kill, plunder, and decimate." Those words were from a history book they had read in school; one that purportedly described what the Indians did to the settlers crossing the plains. Lies; all white lies. For Rebecca, it meant white heads would roll.

Rebecca turned and saw Debra. Her face softened, and the anger vanished.

"Hey Deb, how's that boy of yours?"

"Doing great, thanks. And Chickadee will be in the Jingle Dance this year. First time walking alone."

"I remember the first time we danced without our momma strings. They grow up so fast," Rebecca said.

Jacob wondered if he should ask for tea so the women could catch up.

"What are you doing here?" Rebecca asked.

"Your dad wanted to make sure that Karl, I mean Jacob, got treated fairly."

Rebecca placed her hands on her hips, and her gaze wandered

from Debra to Jacob and back. Jacob watched her mind work. Her face hardened with realization.

"We say he was drunk," Debra said. "I got money."

Jacob closed his eyes.

Rebecca snorted. "I don't know what you are talking about. It was a 'sleep it off,' nothing else, no deals or bribes. Keep the money, Deb. Put it in Chickadee's college fund."

She grabbed the paper from Debra's hand. Without even reading the words, she ripped it into small squares. Turning to Douglas Greenhopper, Rebecca grabbed his hand and deposited the scraps. Jacob peered down the hall at the two white officers. One with a shiner glared at him. Jacob wondered if that was his doing.

"Rebecca, you can't just pretend," Doug Greenhopper said, then stopped.

"I don't see the press outside or the FBI. It is simple, Douglas. This never happened."

She turned to the officers. "Tell your buddies Indian Country is all around them."

"Let's go," Rebecca said to Jacob, her eyes smoldered. Her husband Todd stood silent like a warrior watching the wagon train cross the plains. He nodded to Greenhopper and followed his wife out. Jacob and Debra glanced at each other and exited, leaving the officers alone in the hallway.

Once outside the station, Debra said, "You should work for me."

Rebecca's lips formed a tight smile. "I can only keep one safe. Indians need to realize they are putting themselves in harm's way off the Rez, especially if they are alone."

Debra nodded and flashed Jacob a look of 'you're in trouble now' before she left.

Rebecca stopped, eyeing Jacob as they approached her car. Her gaze was one of disappointment. The bright sun stung his eye, and he still felt unsteady, but the chill breeze from the snowy mountains helped clear his head a little. She had a right to be unhappy. Once again, she came to rescue him. Jacob's cheeks burned, and he lowered his eyes.

"What are you doing? Rose told me you walked out." Rebecca hesitated. "After accusing Father Pius, and I'll forget that name after saying it, of abusing Paul."

"It is true. I quit."

Rebecca's eyes narrowed. "Why? That's stupid."

"I failed to keep Paul safe," Jacob said as if it were perfectly logical.

"You weren't there to do that," Rebecca said as Todd stepped close to her. "Is he safe now?"

"Yes. He is safe," Jacob said. He watched her face contorted with words she forced herself to swallow.

"So now what?" Rebecca said as she leaned into Todd as if for support. Her jaw jutted forward. Jacob acknowledged she didn't believe him. The past, their childhood, had damaged her faith in the world. The small wrinkles around her eyes deepened.

"I'm working on a plan," Jacob said, trying to sound self-assured.

"It better not involve drinking. I won't rescue you again. Don't you get it? They took everything and tried to destroy us, and their booze is how they keep us down. I keep wanting to believe you're smarter than them. I'll side with Mom if there's a next time." She handed him the keys to his motorcycle.

Ouch. That hurt. She rarely sided with Judith about anything that involved him. Once, when Judith and Terence broke up for six months, Rebecca didn't protest when Judith sent him to live with Terence. He hadn't protested, either. He wanted to stay with his step-father. Jacob's heart swelled. He realized all he had put her through; still, she loved him. Her eyes brimming with tears, he perceived she was setting him free to stand or fall on his merit, no longer attached to momma strings.

"Everything will be fine, Becca," Jacob said, his voice tight with emotion.

CHAPTER 29
HOME SWEET HOME

Psalm 123: 2-3
If the Lord had not been on our side,
When men rose against us,
Then would they have swallowed us alive
When their anger was kindled.

Father Pius picked up Paul's voice long before he stood at Abbot Gordon's open office door. At Abbot Gordon's request, they met every week to discuss what the community could do to help him.

Paul's voice was angry. He could barely make out the words, but the name Jacob was clear.

Pius cracked his knuckles. It was past the hour he was to meet with Abbot Gordon. Yet he could not bring himself to knock.

"Why do you let him be bad?" Paul asked in a strained voice.

The irony was not lost on Pius. He said that to his confrères many times over the years concerning Paul. But Jacob is not a child. He knows his vows of stability, *Conversatio Morum*, and obedience. Stability was the only vow Jacob excelled in, and now he ignored that.

"He can't just walk out," Paul said.

The boy was right. There were rules, which did not include dropping your habit on the community room floor. Jacob hadn't even talked to Abbot Gordon. Papers had to be drawn up. Money contracts paid. Then there was the dispensation, the release from Rome of his priestly duties. Jacob was a priest, after all.

Father Pius had heard the Senior Council's advice to give Jacob time to reassess. That seemed fair. This was never a vocation for him. Jacob appeared agitated and stressed. Pius remembered how the monastery took him in after his family's death. After a year of grieving, he asked to be admitted—vocation by default.

Paul stomped out. Pius stepped aside.

"It's all your fault. I wish you'd just drop dead," Paul said.

He wished that too when his confrère avoided him in the hall or at recreation.

Father Joannicus appeared at the door, calling after Paul to apologize.

Pius waved a dismissive hand.

"No, seriously," Joannicus said. "He can be angry, but he still must treat you with respect."

Father Pius raised an eyebrow and then looked away. He found it hard to be around Joannicus. Father Joannicus had been silent these last few months. Gone was the familiarity. Yet now, Joannicus was talking to him like a confrère.

Don't let this opportunity slip by. Mend the fences. He couldn't live without a community.

Abbot Gordon appeared in the doorway behind Father Joannicus.

"Father Pius, could we postpone our meeting until after dinner?"

Pius nodded as Joannicus stepped past them into the hall, hesitating. Pius tried to keep silent, worried that his advice would be unwelcome. He clenched his teeth and cracked the knuckles on his right hand.

Joannicus sighed.

"Let Paul calm down," Pius suggested, for he learned from dealing with agitated female parishioners that, often with such anger, reason vanished.

"I'll talk to the boy," Abbot Gordon said and retreated into his office. Paul's display of emotions seemed to have shaken both men. One boy dictated the day.

"Come," Joannicus said. "We should talk."

Father Pius cracked his knuckles as he held his breath. He had been dreading this moment. From the minute Jacob and Paul left the monastery, Pius felt his world crumble. It was as if he had made his foundation on a sandy beach rather than a solid rock.

The error of his ways shone like a lone Easter candle in a dark-ened church. How easy it was to move from good monk to bad. All his teaching and study of the Rule caused him to wince when he looked at himself.

Why had he tried to parent? He had no skill in child-rearing. He lost his path, or at the very least, let it become overgrown.

What would they do with him? For the last six months, he had asked that question. The process was slow. He was sure they would ask him to leave. The Senior Council had held meetings. Looks from his confrères only added to his misery. What shocked him most was the wide array of emotions that came to him from his fellow monks when they came one by one to speak with him. The Abbot had ordered him not to argue or defend his actions and to listen to his fellow monks. Listen, he did. They were monks, so they forgave him, but some forgiveness seemed false. Those who were sincere caused Pius to wince in the glare of his mistakes.

"Father Pius?" called Joannicus, shaking him from his reverie. They walked out of the monastery, down the paved path surrounded by a garden.

"I apologize. I've taken too long to talk with you."

Pius exhaled. The man was apologizing to him. He was the sinner, not Joannicus.

"I needed to sort out my feelings, to examine your actions. Seriously, I despise them," Joannicus said, his eyes narrowing as if caught in a glare. Fear gripped Father Pius.

"But I perceive you as a person who strives to make good choices, so I can't sit in judgment. God knows I have made my share of mistakes with Paul. We weren't prepared to raise a child. I forgive you and have faith that you will not make this mistake again. With God's help, I know you won't."

Joannicus paused and faced Pius. He should have avoided that child. Look what his attempts to correct cost him. Pius looked away.

"Everything has changed between us," Pius said, his throat constricted.

"Yes, in a way. Your actions were wrong, and they have caused damage that might not be repairable. Seriously, you may never have a positive relationship with Paul, but you're a good man."

The snapping of Scotch Broom seedpods in the midday heat filled the silence. Pius clutched his rosary in his pocketed hand. The crucifix dug into his palm.

Father Pius opened his mouth, wanting to say the relationship that mattered was not with Paul.

"I may as well tell you that Abbot Gordon and the Senior Council have agreed that we need education to raise Paul, and I guess it is called socialization. Corporations are learning it to help their employees," Joannicus said, his brow creased as if he had witnessed something distasteful. "Seriously, Ms. Carr is lining up workshops."

A ruddy flush tinged Joe's face as he brushed off a bench with his scapular before sitting in the dappled shade.

It was the woman who bothered Joannicus, Pius thought as he filed the information away. It was the social worker who made Paul's placement a reason to hang around the monks.

"Paul doesn't forgive quickly," Pius said.

Joannicus smiled a thin-lipped smile. "Even Jacob has forgiven his stepfather, Terence, so I hope for Paul."

"But Jacob can't seem to forgive us," Pius said, considering how lucky Jacob was not to be at the monastery and subjected to endless counsel. If they ended up having to catch each other in a trust-building exercise, Pius believed he would be flat on the floor.

"Father Jacob forgets where the light switch is and spends too much time in the darkness of his soul, a dangerous practice for anyone."

Father Pius sat folding the long rectangle material of his scapular into his lap so it would not dangle on the ground. "I don't understand why he walked out. He got what he wanted—a confession from me and suffering."

"You are only a small piece of the puzzle; perhaps the catalyst. Seriously, I don't understand either, but Jacob still grieves over the loss of his family."

"That was so many years ago. Does he not understand that they are with God?"

Joannicus folded and unfolded his hands as if weighing what to say. "I don't think he wanted to share them with God. I suspect Jacob doesn't quite trust they are in a better place. His life experiences haven't taught him to trust a father's love. He feels betrayed, and he includes God in that."

"That is sad. There is much comfort in believing in an afterlife," Pius said, wiping beads of sweat from his brow.

"Perhaps, but if you're unprepared, there can be much anger and fear."

Pius nodded. He had sat with many parishioners as they approached the last moments of their lives. Joannicus reached over and picked the Salsify seedpod. He wiggled it. Seeds flew away like a giant dandelion blown on by a child.

"Will he return? I don't mean to sound judgmental, but I often wondered when he would leave us," Pius said.

The sound of squeaking sandals alerted Pius that Brother

Ambrose was approaching. Ambrose confronted Pius the afternoon after Jacob quit.

"If I had known it was you, I would never have allowed you to punish Paul. You tricked me, and that was wrong. It won't happen again. I will be watching." Then, having said his piece in true Ambrose style, it was over. That was a definite quality to desire, the ability to move on.

"From your expression, Joannicus, I would say that you are talking about Jacob." Ambrose stood, casting a shadow over them as the downy seeds collected on his habit.

"We were speculating if he will return to us," Joannicus said.

"He will. The sheep recognize where they belong, and so does Jacob," Ambrose said. "He needs us."

"We were parish priests. We are aware of the world. We weren't kept away from it," Pius said, always resenting the secular accusation that religious were hiding from something.

"True, but haven't you heard what the college kids call us? The oblivious are blinded by God's light. But they couldn't identify a Merino from a Dorper, but Jacob does," Ambrose said, nodding.

What is a Merino?

"Seriously, Jacob is not a sheep," Joannicus said.

"No, he's a shepherd. He'll see we need him as much as he needs us. He won't be staying long at the farmhouse."

Joannicus gasped. Apparently, he wasn't aware that Jacob had gone home. A Dorper was bred for slaughter.

"How do you know this?" Joannicus asked.

"I asked Rebecca where he was, and Vincent confirmed it," Ambrose said, tucking his hands into his waist belt, causing his habit to rise above his ankle, revealing hairy legs.

Father Pius learned from talking with Father Vincent that home life in the Mackenzie house had not always been pleasant. Sometimes, what called a man to monastic life puzzled Pius. Ambrose was an unlikely monk, unkempt and uncouth, and yet he had a faith that connected earth to heaven. Then there was Joannicus, raised by a

Baptist minister. He supposed ministering in any sector of Christianity is like the priesthood. The Mackenzie household produced three Benedictine religious, two priests, and a nun. Perhaps a troubled childhood allowed for a compassionate and open heart.

"I worry about Father Vincent. Jacob is unaware of how much influence he has over him," Pius said.

"Vincent has to decide for himself who is calling him—Jacob or God," Ambrose said. He bent over and pulled a weed from the garden. Clumps of dirt and dust floated in a cloud in the dry air.

"Let's hope he can," Pius said, realizing Jacob's vocation inspired Vincent. Father Pius was sure that many had someone who they admired. Perhaps, in Joe's case, his father opened his eyes to the possibility of a vocation. More likely, Joe's desire and joy in serving God led him to become a Catholic and a monk. Still, he wondered what that calling sounded like to Jacob.

A heathen until he was eight, Jacob must have found his new religion confusing. Pius was born a Catholic cloaked in faith. The foundation was firm. Even the shame of his actions did not shake his conviction that he was one of God's chosen. Pius frowned. Each man had his reason for answering the call. Vincent had a vocation. He wanted to serve God's people, and he wanted a balance. Benedictine priesthood gave him both. Maybe that is what Jacob sought: balance. Father Pius recalled the words of Father Hilary when Jacob was a novice. "Jacob is here to rest and to gather strength." Is that why he left? Was he rested, or did he find his strength, and for what battle?

"And what about Jacob?" Joannicus said.

The sound of students celebrating the end of finals resounded from the college below. The loud music floated up the hill, disturbing the calm.

"Jacob needs to get his ass off the grave and join the land of the living," Ambrose said, wiping his dirty hands on the front of his scapular.

Joe's eyes opened wide. "That's rather callous. He lost his family. You told me some wounds never heal."

"Well, just because your tail's bobbed doesn't mean you can't wag it. He's been in the grave, spent his time in hell, and now it's time to rise," Ambrose said, shaking his head.

The Jesus analogy amused Father Pius.

"Who will roll away the stone?" Pius asked.

"Good question," Ambrose said, looking at Joannicus and crossing his arms.

CHAPTER 30
BAD BOY

Psalm 56: 5
My soul lies down among lions,
who would devour the sons of men.
Their teeth are spears and arrows,
their tongue a sharpened sword.

J acob stiffened as he sat at the dining room table of his childhood home. It was a beautiful table, hand-hewed and carved—twice carved if you counted his name on the underside of the table. Jacob smiled at the thought.

Dinner with the family made Jacob wish for silent monastic meals. His mother was a mediocre cook with a philosophy of quantity, not quality. His youngest sister, Vicki, baked well, and there was always an array of baked goods, a balance between good and bad food. Tonight's menu included overcooked vegetables and bland meat. At least the plates were pretty. French and old, hand-painted scenes of the pastoral countryside, shepherds, and maidens. He missed Brother Barnabas's savory meals. Even the leftovers were delicious at Saint Alberic's.

"Nice of you to bring preserves, Rebecca, and share dinner with us. That boy ate the last of my reserves," Judith said, patting Rebecca's arm. The gesture was odd. He let his eyes avoid the scene and instead focused on the faces of the family portrayed on the wall. All the children were there, frozen in timeless innocence.

"Not a problem, *Ihkaa*. The girls and I made a lot. I had a twofold mission. I wanted to check up on Jacob and bring an invite to give the invocation at the tribal gathering," Rebecca said, eyeing Jacob.

Vicki's eyes narrowed. The look on her face reminded Jacob of one he had seen on Judith's face—sour and envious—whenever someone showed him attention. Was Vicki jealous? Paul reacted that way when Jacob and Joannicus did things that excluded him.

He wondered if his kids were ever jealous of each other.

Judith's hand jerked as if static electricity had shocked her. "Well, that's very nice of you. I'm sure Todd and the kids are worried about you. It's getting late and all."

Jacob's leg bounced up and down. He hid his smile behind his napkin.

Vicki scooted her chair closer to Judith. Vicki was being a silly girl. Judith loved her daughters. Marie was her favorite, but she had entered a convent. Rebecca was like loving a cat with claws that would strike. Vicki's place in her mother's heart was secure.

"Are all the kids going to participate?" Terence asked.

"Well, Dawn and Sabrina are. As for Holbrook, he's at that difficult teen stage. So, we'll have to see." Exhaustion settled around her face.

"Yes, I remember that stage. Boys seem to wallow in it. Some never really move beyond," Judith said, pulling her slight frame to its full height.

She is picking a fight, the Elder within whispered. *Bend like the prairie grass.*

"Good thing I am no longer a boy," Jacob said, running his fingers under the table, searching for his name.

Rebecca sighed softly. No bending today.

"I would beg to differ," Judith said as she gathered her silverware onto her plate.

"Mind your tongue, *Ihkaa*. There are witnesses," Jacob said, knowing he was jumping off the cliff of good sense.

"Jacob," Terence said, his voice harsh and commanding.

"Well, I never," Judith said. Her plate banged on the table, silverware rattling.

"Indeed." Jacob started as a sharp kick met his shin. Like a light bulb that flickers before it dies, Jacob knew he had set the spark.

"I feel a sick headache coming on," Judith said, gripping the back of her chair with such strength that her knuckles turned white.

"Not feeling well, myself," Jacob said as he rose. "Hope it was not something I ate."

Terence's chair scraped the wood floor, and Jacob took that as his cue to head upstairs to his room before another arrow-tipped word entered the room. The insolence would have gotten him a beating as a boy, but not today.

Jacob sat in the room of his childhood. The heat of the attic space made little beads of sweat drip down his cheeks like tears. The Jesus crucifix glowed on the wall.

His room was a place of solace and a source of information. The heating vents carried voices from below. As a youngster, this activity gave him knowledge and, with that, leverage. Today, the voices just made him sad. He opened one vent to eavesdrop on the conversations from the foyer.

"How long, Terence?" Judith said, her voice strained and shrill.

"Until he's ready. He's our son," Terence said. There was a long pause. "Not long."

"I don't like it. A visit is one thing, but you have given him a job. He will not leave. You're making his stay pleasing."

"As soon as he has money, he'll go. No grown child wants to live with his parents."

Judith's voice sounded like a tap dancer, ticking off Jacob's offenses. "I don't like him lurking around and not eating meals with us. He drinks too much coffee. He locks his door at night. What is he doing in there?"

That was who rattled the doorknob. She was the reason for his inside lock. Her threats when he was a child caused him to put a lock on his door. In retaliation, she had installed one on the outside of his door. It came off because Terence pointed out that it was a fire issue.

Now he understood why Paul didn't believe him about Pius. He was glad he installed that lock on Paul's door. He should tell Joannicus about the hidden key. Paul had no reason to lock his door, not after he had exposed Pius. The power over Paul was gone. The monks would keep Paul safe.

Even if he couldn't be there, they would protect Paul.

"Why did they kick him out? What did he do?"

"He left, dear, no wrongdoing," Terence said, his voice smooth and calm, almost cajoling.

What had he done to be banished from her heart?

"That can't be true. Nobody quits the priesthood."

Paul had said that to him: "You left me. You can't quit; you took vows." Then after the angry words came the begging: "Come back home, I miss you, I need you." Every call from Paul left Jacob parched. He had sent Paul postcards with no return address to keep peace within himself.

Jacob wished he could go to the monastery and pretend nothing had happened.

Why can't you? the Elder asked.

Because things have happened, and they haven't punished Pius. They forgave him. Where is the justice in that?

Jacob moved to the south wall and switched the vent to the kitchen. Rebecca and Vicki talked in hushed tones while Judith's enraged voice echoed in the background.

"He's making Mom crazy," Vicki said. She sounded sincere in her concern.

"How so?" Rebecca asked.

"He is repairing things, like the porch rail, weeding the gardens. She doesn't like having him around."

At the sound of running water, Jacob contemplated a trip downstairs to help with the cleanup.

"How're things with Dad?" Rebecca asked.

"He gave him a job." Vicki's voice took on a sneer, betraying her jealousy. "Mom is worried he'll stay forever."

Not likely. He was leaving within a month or two.

The clinking of dishes being stacked mingled with Rebecca's words. "Mom's just fussing. She likes to fuss. Jacob won't be here for long."

Jacob closed the vents and listened for his sister's footsteps. The floorboards squeaked and groaned down the hall.

"Hey," Rebecca called up the steps, "I know you were listening, so you may as well come down."

"Yes, ma'am," Jacob said as he planted himself four steps up, resting his feet on the bottom riser.

"I'm supposed to stay out of this," Rebecca said, not looking at him. Jacob wondered who had given her that advice. Probably her husband Todd. The advice was sound. They were too close as siblings go. That was not healthy. Too close did not bode well in either white or Apsáalooke culture. The connection forged in childhood could not be severed. They had been through so much. She sheltered him as an infant, dragging him around in a red wagon until he was old enough to walk. She protected him. When she could not keep him safe from physical harm, she schooled him on how to avoid it. Sometimes he listened and, sadly, sometimes not. Her advice to him had always come from the heart. Even when he had impregnated her roommate, Faith, she still stood by him. Rebecca was his warrior.

"But," Jacob prompted.

"You need to leave here. Be aware, you bring demons."

"Are you saying I am a demon?" Jacob said, picking at the curling wallpaper seam next to him.

Rebecca ran the toe of her boot along the worn floorboards. "Just listen. It is not good to be here. Not for you, not for her. Have you not seen the signs?"

He shook his head.

"The bushes out front are dying. There is a skunk under the porch. You know that is a sign, a warning of danger."

"There is a spider web in my window every morning. He is telling me I need balance. I am trying to do that. Find the balance."

"Then go home."

Home? Did she mean the monastery?

The aroma of freshly baked apple pie crept up from the kitchen.

"Maybe Mother needs to come to grips with her past. I am not her demon."

"Just look at her, Jacob. She has lived a life of torment. Please, just let her be." His entire life, Judith had tormented him.

A childhood of "wait until your father gets home," a set of words that were almost a call of endearment, for those were the times she acknowledged his presence. Why had Terence believed his wife?

Was he such a rotten kid? What made him so despicable to his mother? He didn't wish them harm, even when angry with his children or Paul.

The realization that Judith could not love him made him sad.

"Becca, I am not running from her hate. She only makes a fool of herself when she points a finger at me. Terence cannot physically hurt me anymore. I am bigger than him."

The odor of freshly brewed coffee wound its way into the hall.

"Don't be the raven mewing at the cat. Don't play that game. She's a weak opponent, and she always has been. We just didn't see it as kids. She left you in the hospital to die, and in her mind, you died. You don't remember because you were a baby. She didn't even acknowledge you existed. I fed you and changed your diapers.

Me." Her voice cracked, and she swallowed hard, turning away from him.

He might not have remembered, but he realized she was the one who loved him.

"Thank you," Jacob said.

"I don't want thanks, you moron," Rebecca said as she turned back to him, thrusting her chin into the air. "Stop haunting her. You'll not be happy with the results. Just remain dead."

"But I am not dead," Jacob said. He wanted to understand why. He hadn't asked to be born early.

"Then go home. Leave the past where it belongs."

Now she sounded like Terence and Abbot Gordon. Leave the past and go home. She meant the monastery. That place wasn't home. As for the past, it lingered like the stench of a ferret.

"I cannot," Jacob said, knowing that he was lying to her again.

Her face hardened. "Why the hell not?"

"Hot apple pie," Vicki called from the main floor.

The smell of cinnamon and nutmeg tiptoed up the stairwell.

"There is nothing there for me."

"Paul is there."

Jacob closed his eyes. A searing pain ripped at his heart. He raised his hand to his chest but grabbed his braid instead, holding it like a lifeline. "Paul has Rose and Joannicus. He will be fine."

He couldn't risk losing another person he loved.

"The boy needs a warrior," Rebecca said, her voice waning. She looked tired, as if she had spent days in battle without sleep.

She was still worried about him. He wasn't a little boy. Their parents held no power over him.

About time, mocked the Warrior inside of him. Would it take as long for Paul to realize that Pius held no power? The warrior had strength, not fear, superiority, not weakness. The frightened blue-eyed boy he had once been peeked out from behind his soul, watching and waiting.

CHAPTER 31
WAITING

Psalm 21: 1

My God, my God, why have you forsaken me?

J acob drove the familiar path to Saint Alberic's Abbey. He turned off the main highway, following the road past the prominent hill where the monastery, with its large cross and glistening picture windows, silhouetted high on a flat land-scape. He paused and, like a weary traveler, looked yearningly in its direction. Jacob lived within a chrysalis of a life for more than a year, waiting.

Since leaving the monastery, the only thing that changed was the seasons. Every morning, he rose and prayed, even without the bells to summon him. He prayed what he knew, the Divine Office, and thanked the Great Spirit. The words of the psalms had seeped into his bones and rained out of his pores as nature manifested itself before him each day.

He parked his motorbike and unbraided his hair as he walked into the graveyard, heading for the secular section for a visit with his loved ones.

Familiar headstones lined up in rows, marking tribute to a life well lived. He walked by the only crooked headstone belonging to Brother Mellitus. One year, it leaned forward; the next year, to the left—every attempt to level the stone and make it uniform failed. The ground was wrought with issues. Vole holes pocked the dusty ground, barren of grass, while other graves sported green. Wildflowers grew in dense patches as if the cantankerous monk were laughing at their attempts to change his ultimate resting place.

"I'm saving you a spot right next to me," the man used to say to him. Jacob thought the idea of spending eternity next to the mean monk was not resting, but today, he missed the old coot. The old monk found his heart in the end. It just took Paul to bring it out.

Jacob paused, glancing at the hilltop. *What am I waiting for?* Thanks to his stepfather, Terence, money wasn't an issue, and as of last week, he looked at a studio apartment. He could invite some of them over. Paul could spend the night.

His head shook at the awkward thought. *Would Paul want to be with me? Would the monks want me as a friend rather than a confrère?* He walked away and sent Paul back to the monastery. He turned from the graves, mindful of their eyes upon him. They were good at that, watching and waiting. They practiced patience with such fortitude that Jacob was sure that God himself often forgot what the waiting was for.

He needed to find out why they were holding on to his dispensation papers. What were they waiting for? There was a process, paperwork, and an interview. He signed a contract with the abbey, one that was not just spiritual but also legal. Yet, for a break from the priesthood, he needed Rome's stamp of approval, and then he could be a disenfranchised priest.

The words *You are a priest forever* rang in his heart.

The fog of depression and grief hung around him like the first time he considered being a monastic. At least then, after his family's deaths, he was aware of what he was doing, waiting for God to answer. God answered.

One day, his anger and grief melted like a candle, and peace settled within him. A faint glow in his soul stirred. Being with the monks felt right. The Warrior remained silent, and the Elder whispered, *Go forward.* He approached Abbot Sebastian and asked to enter. Could he approach Abbot Gordon and ask to come back? He would start again from the beginning as a novice. Could he do it all over again? Would he be able to complete it in the usual four years, excluding the year as a postulant?

Jacob stepped into the small secular graveyard to the right of the monastic cemetery. The ground held the remains of monastic loved ones: mothers, fathers, siblings, and for Jacob and only Jacob, his wife and children. His two worlds, monastic and secular, sat side by side yet worlds apart, not to mention his Native faith. The realization was obvious to him now.

He couldn't believe they let him enter and live as one of them. Were his heart and soul here? He bent over and plucked the yellow bells growing wild near the sandstone wall.

"They always have had a thread tied to you," Faith said in his mind. Jacob smirked.

He placed the flowers on the graves of his family, reflecting that marriage and fatherhood had completed him. He read the name on the headstone: Faith Mackenzie-Knows the Song. Dates and a feather, then written in Lakota, *wife, mother.* He rubbed his fingers over the curved stone's top, smooth like his lover's skin.

Half a man has little to offer. Half of him was buried in this secular cemetery, and the other half would have been buried beyond the wall with his second family of confrères. Would they let him be buried with Faith?

In front of her stone, he let the weight of the moment ground him. Today marked over 15 years since his family had been ripped from his life. The tree they had planted stood strong and straight.

"Look at me. I am an accountant. Perhaps if I had just accepted this job when Terence offered it to me instead of the Theology scholarship, I would not be standing here with flowers. Maybe I would be placing a blanket on your shoulders."

Faith's face appeared before him, pouting. "You linger, fret about things you cannot control. Let it go."

She always told him to let life flow, to follow the current. He could feel her disapproval.

The rusty gate screeched open. An urge to run, mixed with the hope of a warm greeting, caused him to hold his breath. This wasn't Paul. The boy liked to climb over the wall.

He glanced over his shoulder; he saw Father Joannicus with his arms full of leftover church flowers.

"Hey," Jacob said, surprised that Joannicus remembered this anniversary, for it was not a Church solemnity. That was what they did—they covered you with kindness and compassion. From the scholarship he didn't deserve, meals that fed his family, to a cell in the safety of the monastery and a parish of primarily Apsáalooke parishioners.

The heavy scent of lilies punctuated the air.

"Brought these for your family," Father Joannicus said. Jacob's single yellow bells dimmed against the altar arrangements.

It was a quick visit in and out. Just as a drop from an icicle slides away, Jacob's resolve weakened. Had they heard his motorcycle? Were they waiting? Where was Paul?

"Thanks," Jacob said, pushing his hair back from his face. He blinked to keep his eyes from tearing up—*damn empathy.*

Jacob placed lilies around the headstones of his children. He paused, and noted that Joe's face looked ashen. His once-cherubic cheeks looked boney.

"Are you well?" Jacob asked, realizing that Paul's worry was not exaggerated.

"Lent, fasting, and all. I was overzealous," Joannicus said, not looking at Jacob. "You've been gone a long time. Things change."

Jacob recognized the lie. Paul had told him that Joannicus was often ill. He wanted to ask, but chose to include Joe's health in his prayers.

"Like what?" Jacob asked, steeling himself for a fall into the abyss of caring. His self-imposed exile left him parched for human contact —genuine connections—like the fellowship of the monks. He tried to appear on Sundays for Mass but found it hard to restrain himself from action.

Why couldn't he listen to their suffering and just nod?

His mother's lecture on the matter of his Sunday obligation tainted his efforts to connect.

"You should be at Mass. We are Catholic in this family. I won't abide with heathen ways," she said.

She was Apsáalooke. Jacob bit his tongue, refraining from asking, "What heathen ways?" His curiosity soared with his longing to understand her. She had really meant that she didn't like him.

Joannicus coughed weakly and continued. "We've finished our education. Ms. Carr found someone who came and taught sixteen modules on subjects from anger management to communication. I think it has been helpful and unifying, but I don't believe I am any more qualified to raise a child. There is too much to remember. Someone should write a manual." Joannicus brushed his hands and pulled wool gloves from his pocket as if it were December instead of April.

Jacob imagined the community listening to lectures on emotions and self-control. He swore he could hear Ambrose snoring. Anger rose like water from an artesian well. This forgiveness crap was too much. They should have listened to him, and opened their eyes when they opened their hearts. Things went too far.

The thought that everyone deserved a second chance didn't vanquish others' sins for Jacob. He exhaled forcefully and hung his head. *Really, are you any better?* He acknowledged he was disappointed. They all needed to heal.

"Too bad I missed it," Jacob said, grateful that he wasn't a part of the lessons. Pius appeared to be forgiven. *Would they forgive me?*

"How did Father Pius take it all?" Jacob asked, hoping that he was pointedly uncomfortable at the very least.

Joannicus turned and walked toward the main graveyard. "For all of us, change is hard. He's back at Saint George's parish now."

"What happened to Vincent?" Jacob asked, holding his breath. Paul never mentioned Father Vincent in his weekly updates of the monastic community.

"Things didn't work out for him."

"What do you mean?" Jacob's voice rose as he called after Joannicus. What wasn't he saying? "He did not hurt anyone, did he?"

Joannicus stopped and straightened a toppled urn. "He's not cut out for parish work. A parish priest needs a strong sense of balance. Vincent is suited for brief moments with a variety of people. He would make a great hospital chaplain." Joannicus stood straight and shook his head. "He's your brother. See his goodness."

Jacob stumbled forward, inhaling deeply. "Is there goodness in people? Show it to me."

"I will continue to show you. Seriously, I know you believe in it."

"Then why did Paul get hurt?"

"Bad things happen—to the Jews and to the Apsáalooke. I don't have the answers. Is that the reason you are hiding? You need to be here." Joannicus crossed his arms under his scapular. "Jacob, it is not your fault—none of it. You can't change the past by going back to it."

Jacob held his braid. "I have messed everything up. Where Paul is concerned, I was not helpful."

Joannicus moved down the row of dead confrères, stopped, turned, and rubbed his arms. "Paul isn't your issue. Why are you at Terence and Judith's home? They can't give you anything healthy."

Why was he there? What was he seeking? Reconciliation? Punishment? Even Faith questioned his attendance at family gatherings. The events always turned ugly. He told her they were family, and he needed to honor his parents. The children deserved a connection to their ancestors. But he realized that wasn't his reason for going home. He hoped that by returning, he could find love and be loved. He could show his mother he was worthy and his stepfather that he forgave him.

"Healing," Jacob croaked. He watched a patch of unfrozen earth move as a nearly eyeless vole wiggled out of the freshly turned soil.

Joannicus shook his head. "Looks like flagellation to me. It's not possible to heal your folks. You're not a professional. You gave them forgiveness, something I struggle to give them. Seriously, come home."

"Come home for what?" Jacob asked.

"If not for Paul, then for Brother Moses. He needs someone to play checkers with while he convalesces from his fall."

Jacob frowned.

"Why didn't anyone tell me?" Brother Moses had come and sat with him, keeping a silent vigil during Jacob's grief.

"If you came around, you would know," Joannicus said, his voice clipped with anger.

If he hung out, every visit would shorten that rope they lassoed around his soul until he surrendered himself completely. Every cell in his body wanted to stay, but his stubborn heart pulled back.

"I am not ready. How is Paul?" Jacob asked, moving past Joannicus to the cemetery gates.

Joannicus ran his hand over the rusty metal. "Why ask me? You communicate with him regularly."

Jacob stared at the headstones.

Joannicus picked off a flake of iron. "Paul is fine. He and Abbot Gordon meet weekly. Paul seems content."

Jacob paused. *Paul and Abbot Gordon*—hairs prickled on his arm.

"Is that wise?" Jacob asked.

"It isn't any worse than you two sneaking around the monastery at night or playing raiders of the lost dessert in the kitchen," Joannicus said with a slight smile.

Paul is a little snitch.

"Seriously, I notice he writes you, and you write him. Do you think after all that has happened, I'm oblivious to what he's doing?" Joannicus asked, gradually moving toward the trail that led to the hilltop.

Jacob lifted his head to the sun and let its warmth kiss his cheeks. They were protecting him.

"Paul misses you. We all do."

"I miss Paul, too," Jacob said, his throat constricting.

"Then come home."

Jacob nodded and turned, knowing he should leave this place now before he found himself inside the monastery, dressed in his former habit.

CHAPTER 32
ACCEPTANCE

Psalm 89: 12
Make us know the shortness of our life
That we may gain wisdom of heart.

J une 28th started out the same as any monastic day, with the bells ringing an invitation to pray. Father Pius stood, smoothing the wrinkles of his black habit. He walked silently with a few other monks down the hall to the church. He took his seat to the right of the Abbot. It felt odd. Abbot Gordon asked him to be sub-prior. He was third in rank from the top. In reality, it was like being the errand boy at the castle. The job left him with a human view of the community.

I don't belong in this position. This is not an honor. Father Joannicus was sub-prior, but he asked to be relieved. Abbot Gordon then requested that Pius step in.

Father Pius glanced over at Joe's empty choir seat. Lately, he was worried that Joannicus did not make it to morning prayers. With all the requests, responsibility, and accountability, he found himself anchored to the community. His mind wandered. The concluding "amen" signaled the end of prayers as he apologized to God for being a little preoccupied.

Pius headed to the monastery on the first floor. He approached Joe's cell door, where he heard violent coughing. He waited, and then softly knocked.

"Come in," came the raspy response.

Pius entered. The smell of camphor and menthol assaulted his nose. Joannicus sat hunched over his desk, wrapped in a wool sweater and several blankets.

"Father, I missed you at prayers, and came to see if you needed anything."

"Thanks, Pius. As you can see, Brother Barnabas thinks I'm suffering from malnutrition. He's kept me supplied with soup."

A stack of bowls and an urn for hot beverages stood in the corner. Pius moved toward them. If nothing else, he could return them to the kitchen.

"It's just a cold. I didn't want to disturb everyone's prayers with my coughing," Joannicus said with a weak smile. "Seriously, don't look so worried. God hasn't sent me a pink slip."

Pius chuckled, feeling a great love rising for this man.

"What can I do to help?"

"Continue to pray for me," Joannicus said.

Pius nodded and gathered the discarded kitchenware before leaving. He collided with Paul as he exited. The bowls wobbled and clattered. The boy glared and grunted, carrying a tray of food into the cell.

"Say 'excuse me,'" Joannicus scolded.

"He ran into me," Paul protested.

Pius didn't stick around for the apology. He knew that saying something and meaning it came from two separate places. The boy was fast approaching his teen years with a pudgy awkwardness before a growth spurt that would leave him unfamiliar in his own body. He saw the signs of hormones and confusion dripping from the boy. There would be no mending the rift between them anytime soon.

The thought of Paul being a teenager caused Pius to wince with pain. He let his mind fill with worry for Joannicus as he spread jam on his toast. Surely others had seen Joe's pallor and absences. He had lost weight and seemed to have a continual cold.

His mind jumped to the upcoming day as he mentally prepared for the meetings. The prior and sub-prior ate meals with the Abbot at a table separated from the rest of the community. He watched his confrères eating in silence, punctuated by the clanking of cups and scraping of chairs. As he ate, he remembered that many disapproved of his reassignment. Yet, Abbot Gordon wanted him. Obedience stopped him from objecting to the request.

Jacob's departure had caused pain—the kind that tore men apart. Shame, humiliation, anger, and distrust captured and carried them away. They had almost lost Father Vincent, for he could not understand Jacob's departure. Father Pius tried to explain that not all vocations were pure.

Vincent saw Jacob's faith as being evaluated and forged, as if losing one's family gave him a leg up on the holy scale. Pius did not see it that way. It was like comparing Jonah's call to the apostle John. One man crossed his arms, stomped his foot, and needed to be stripped of everything before he heeded God's voice. John heard the call, and with a burning desire, he accepted it. In the end, he recommended Vincent pray. Every monk experienced a test of vocation during his lifetime. Abbot Gordon sent Vincent to Rome to study. Abbot Gordon was wise to surround Vincent with Catholicism and fan the embers of his soul. Vincent remained a monk.

Pius shook the crumbs from his scapular as he stood and blessed himself after his meal, grateful that Abbot Gordon knew his monks better than they perceived themselves. Gordon had brought about a change in Pius.

"A penny for your thoughts, Father," Abbot Gordon said as they walked back to the monastery after breakfast.

"I'm concerned about Joannicus," Pius said.

"Yes, that's a concern, but he'll tell us what he needs," Abbot Gordon said.

Pius was skeptical. Would Joannicus burden them with his health issues or offer his suffering to God in silence?

"I worry that this illness is serious. I don't think we are ready for him to leave us," Pius said.

"As Abbot, one learns you can't hold all hands at once. Men need to decide. Joannicus may put the needs of all before his own, but he understands he lives within a community. We need to wait and be ready, just as Simon of Cyrene stepped up when Christ fell."

Exhausted, Pius sat in his chair in the darkened church. The bells rang, calling all to evening prayer. Pius rubbed his eyes. He cracked his knuckles in the silence. The lights clicked on one by one, and monks shuffled in from evening strolls and fellowship.

Abbot Gordon sat down next to Pius and smiled at him before dropping his chin to his chest and leaning his head on his hand.

"O God, come to my assistance," called out a monk as prayers began.

"O Lord, make haste to help me," answered the community in unison. Pius glanced at Abbot Gordon, who had not risen at the invitation to prayer.

Throughout prayers, Pius stole glances at Abbot Gordon. *Is he asleep?* The rigors of the monastic schedule must have worn him out. The words of Abbot Gordon echoed inside his mind. *Give them what they need. God would not be offended if one slept through prayers.*

A half hour passed from the beginning to the end of prayers. The concluding "amen" resounded, and still, the Abbot did not rise. Pius held his breath. Abbot Gordon looked even paler. He reached out and gently touched his shoulder. Gordon fell, hitting the chair in front of him and landing on the floor with a thud.

The church filled with gasps and exclamations of distress, like smothered explosions. Pius stepped back from the fallen man and cracked his knuckles. Brother Jude, with his nursing experience, rushed forward and turned the Abbot onto his back. Someone shouted to call an ambulance. No blood dripped from the gash on Gordon's head—he was gone.

He probably made haste at the beginning of prayers, thought Pius.

"I can't find a pulse. Should we start CPR?" Jude asked as Brother Ambrose lifted an unresponsive arm to check again for a sign of life. Pius turned to his confrères, who stood in confused silence or ran from the phone to the door. Several wept; others moaned. Paul shouted angry words to nobody in particular.

He should have checked for life instead of waiting until the end of prayers.

Give them what they need.

Pius opened his prayer book.

"Come to his assistance, you saints of God," Pius said, his voice shaking.

The pandemonium shifted. A hush rippled through the room.

"Come to his assistance, you saints of God," Pius repeated.

"Come forth to meet him, you angels of the Lord. Receive and offer his soul in the sight of the Most High," Joannicus answered as he tugged Paul's arm, moving him away from the Abbot's lifeless body.

Choir two continued, "May Christ who has called you, receive you now, and may the angels lead you to Abraham's bosom."

Sirens wailed in the distance, getting louder as they approached, but the subvenite restored order to the shocked community of Saint Alberic's Abbey.

The paramedics rushed in. They hovered over the fallen Abbot as equipment cases clicked open and voices asked questions. Notes of discovery and chaos collided with the solemnity of the moment.

Pius concluded the prayer over the noise: "To you, O Lord, we commend the soul of your servant, our brother, Abbot Gordon Mace, that, being dead to this world, he may live unto you, and that whatever sins he may have committed through the facility of human nature, you may wash away by the pardon of your most tender love."

The prayer for the dead ended. With heavy hearts, the monks silently filed out of the church. A lone bell tolled 63 times, one for every year of Abbot Gordon's life.

A clunking sound woke Father Pius. The phone he held slipped from his hand and landed on the desk. Startled, he listened. The prerecorded message repeated, "If you need to make a phone call, please hang up and dial again."

He couldn't remember if he had been talking. He glanced at the clock and wiped the drool from the side of his mouth. Morning prayers would start soon. A knock on the Abbot's office door caused him to jump. Brother Ambrose entered, his rubber boots squeaking as he approached. He set down a steaming mug of coffee on the desk.

"I noticed you were up and thought you might need this. The novices will be in the cemetery later this morning preparing the ground. Shall I dig to the right or the left of Abbot Sebastian?" Ambrose asked.

Abbot Sebastian was the third of four—now five—abbots to lead the monks of Saint Alberic's Abbey.

"The left side."

"Try to get some rest," Ambrose said, running a hand through his uncombed hair. He looked as if sleep had escaped him, too.

Father Pius nodded, fighting a yawn. He stared at the phone, aware that it would ring continually with questions, explanations, decisions, comfort, and sympathy. The call to Mrs. Van Horne, Abbot Gordon's mother, was hard. No mother should outlive her child. He told her that Gordon passed in peace during prayers. Pius sighed.

Lost souls would fill his day. He took a sip of the coffee and let it burn his tongue.

He wrote out a list of people, family, friends, and benefactors to call. Should he call Jacob? Would this event bring Jacob home? Jacob didn't handle death well and would probably avoid this event.

A rush of sadness ran through Pius. For all his flaws as Abbot, he had been a good friend and a blessing.

The stack of today's work sat on the corner of the desk, calling his attention away from his sadness. Pius noticed the documents for Jacob's dispensation were on the pile. The testimony hinted that Jacob should not have been ordained. The words were harsh.

He believed, and he wondered if Jacob did.

Pius heard they would consider Jacob's absence as a sabbatical—a time for a monk to pursue other interests. Some who left did not return. When it comes to serving God, sometimes God wins, and the man comes back. Pius flipped through the stack. He glanced at the note from Jacob stating that he had requested these forms several times. It looked as if Abbot Gordon was ignoring Jacob's pleas. As he dug through the papers, he found the signed document.

Gordon said that God's will was complicated, requiring one to listen and allow God to work His wonders. Abbot Gordon suffered with each of his monks. Jacob's departure had disturbed Abbot Gordon. When Pius came struggling over his place in the community, Abbot Gordon listened without judgment.

Should he stay or go? Was he the better man? The realization of his actions echoed inside Father Pius.

"We all change, Father. You are a better man," Abbot Gordon said.

Pius smiled. *Perhaps Father Abbot was right.*

The bells rang. Pius placed the signed request in the envelope and placed it with the outgoing mail.

CHAPTER 33
DESPAIR

Psalm 87: 4-5
For my soul is filled with evils.
My life is on the brink of the grave.
I am reckoned as one in the tomb:
I have reached the end of my strength.

J acob heard the phone ring down the hall. He listened as his sister Vicki called out, "Are you here today?"

He rose and left his father's office. They hadn't called in six months, and now six times.

Perhaps it's important, the Elder suggested.

Vicki stood next to the phone. With her hand on her hip, she looked like an arrogant teenager instead of a 31-year-old woman.

"You hung up?" Jacob said, shaking his head.

"I thought you would say, 'Take a message; I'm busy.' Besides, it's plain stupid not to answer the phone."

"And it is plain rude to announce that I am not taking the phone call," Jacob said, stepping past her. "You could say I am not here."

Vicki shook her head as her short black hair whipped around her face. "That's a lie."

Irritation filled him. He found this sister lacking in qualities that his other sisters owned. Jacob shook his head again. *She is the twin of Vincent, and they are total opposites.*

"And your point is?" Jacob said, trying hard not to goad her.

"Priests don't lie. You lie. So, you really aren't a priest."

Jacob frowned, wondering if Rome would accept the testimony of a spoiled sibling on his dispensation papers.

He had given her a chance, but she was immature. She flitted from job to job, hanging on the rodeo circuit. A fear darkened his mood.

"Who called?"

"Which time?" Vicki asked, adding, "So now I'm your secretary? It wasn't that kid, but some guy. John? Jonas?"

"Father Joannicus?" Jacob asked as his breath caught in his throat.

"Yeah, that's the one. What kind of name is that?"

"We do not pick them, the Abbot does. They are to be inspirational," Jacob explained as the shadow dissolved and a weight lifted.

Jacob walked to the kitchen to refill his coffee mug. Joannicus wasn't dead. A rush of relief rattled him. The brown contents sloshed as his hand shook. He wiped up the spill while his mother tsked and measured ingredients into a large mixing bowl. Jacob dismissed her as best he could. He could handle a tsk.

His encounter with Joannicus had pushed him to move into a studio apartment, taking nothing but his clothes and an old set of bath towels.

Where did he belong? What was his purpose? These thoughts rolled around his soul like marbles on a tilting wooden floor.

"They gave you the name 'Jacob.' How does that fit? You don't have twelve sons," Vicki continued like a yappy dog.

Jacob closed his eyes and squared his shoulders against Vicki's sharp and venomous tongue.

"I had a son and three daughters," Jacob said in a whisper.

"Forgive her. She was just a kid when they died," Faith murmured in his heart. He countered it with emotion: He didn't like her. "Perhaps she doesn't like you," Faith echoed.

The contents of the bowl thumped onto the counter as Judith kneaded the white lump specked with herbs. She punched as she spoke. "Jacob of the Bible tried to control life by manipulating others."

"Oh yeah, he cheated his brother out of his birthright."

Jacob glanced at his sister in her expensive jeans, which would have been more suitable on a teenager.

"He was the child of his messed-up parents, Rebecca and Isaac. That is not how the story ends. He wrestled with God and received a new name, Israel, and a new life. Jacob returned to the promised land," Jacob said, thinking once he gave into God's will.

His mother was right. He had lived up to his namesake, the man who wanted to control God.

"It is just a name," Jacob said, sipping his coffee.

The white man's name, not your Indian name, said the Elder.

What would they name him now? He was past due for an adult Indian name. They would probably call him *Lost* instead of *Dreamer*. The tribe had given him that name. He remembered being insulted that they'd thought him asleep.

"This isn't the Promised Land," Vicki said, interrupting his thoughts. "And weren't he and Laban always scheming?"

"That sounds familiar," Jacob said, looking at his sister and then his mother. They were so alike. Now, instead of barbs between mother and son, the battleground was between brother and sister.

"Stop picking on your sister," came Judith's voice as she punched the bread dough with her small fists.

The tone of her voice hit Jacob in the gut, and he recognized he had just stepped into an ambush.

"Yes, ma'am," Jacob said through a wired jaw as he gripped the counter. Everything told him to leave and to do it now.

"I don't like that tone," Judith said, turning from the task in front of her. Her slight frame advanced toward him. He stepped backward, not wanting her out of his sight. With his back against a wall, she had cornered him. He spied his coffee cup standing triumphantly, alone, and out of harm's way. She stood in front of him, babbling menacingly, waving the doughy wooden spoon in front of his face. A prickle akin to being cut off at a traffic light washed over him. He looked down at her, devoid of love.

"Who do you think you are? You wait until your father gets home."

The spoon barely grazed his cheek. Jacob grabbed her wrist. It was slight and boney.

"I am not eight. He cannot beat me anymore."

A look of repulsion clouded her face. She struggled against him as he took the spoon out of her hand.

So easy to do.

"Let go of me," she hissed in her native tongue of Apsáalooke. "He never beat you. It was your father who did the beating."

"I am not him, *Ihkaa*. I am not Endow." The words came out like pus from a rancid boil.

"Oh, but you are," her voice snarled. The truth at last in her eyes —he was his father's son.

Endow was her first husband—the father of her first four children. He was a man she'd loved. He learned that because Jimmy, his older brother, had told him. He was also a man she'd hated because he was a violent drunk. Judith never left Endow. That fact had haunted Jacob all his life, especially after he recognized the cycles of abuse. She was not a weak woman. She was headstrong, yet she allowed herself to submit to the fists. She had not stayed for the sake of the children. Had she succumbed to the same morbid need, an ounce of love after a beating—that Band-Aid for a gaping wound?

Then he saw it: she could not stand to be alone. That was why Vicki still lived there.

"I wish you had died," Judith said as drops of spittle sprayed and burned him like acid.

"Which time? When you left me as an infant?" Jacob's vision grew minuscule, and the spoon clunked to the floor. His muscles tightened as Jacob shook the woman.

"You should have died. They told me you would, yet somehow you cheated death." Her voice faded, and her eyes glazed over with a memory.

Jacob knew why he was alive. He had been saved when Rebecca had fashioned a talisman and slipped it into his incubator. Judith was unaware of that.

"You look like him, you smell like him—an almighty Crow warrior. You are nothing. I don't care if you have the blue eyes. You're not blessed. Those eyes are a curse." Her words sounded forced, like a lie invented on the spot.

Vicki made a whimpering sound. Judith was denouncing the ancestors. The white man Cold Feet had given his eyes to the blood-line in the Apsáalooke tipi of Sings in the Night. The story was passed down from the 1700s, and it reappeared every time a blue-eyed Apsáalooke child was born. Jacob learned that by the 1800s, whites and Natives had frequently interbred. His father's side had always bragged about being "pure." But it took two blue-eyed genes to make a blue eye appear, so there was white blood in both of his family lines.

His maternal side saw it as a blessing; his paternal side saw it as an unfortunate event. When a blue-eyed baby was born within his family, the tribe saw it as a sign, like the birth of the white buffalo. The blue-eyed one had a duty and a destiny. But, he was a man now, and he recognized that dreams die and fates change. Jacob didn't believe his blue eyes made him significant or blessed. Rage filled his mind and steeled his heart.

"If I am cursed, then it is because I have you as a mother."

Judith spat in his face.

Jacob tossed her against the wall, and the impact caused a framed photo to slide to the floor. The glass spiderwebbed across his family's smiling faces before falling into shards on the floor. He looked up to see Vicki transfigured in the glow of the kitchen lights, her mouth hanging open. The same confused look had wrinkled her brow when she was three.

Jacob stepped back. His mother lay crumpled on the floor, diamond shards of glass glittering around her. Jacob was filled with regret. He knew he shouldn't have done that.

"Get away from me, you monster," she screamed. Vicki came out of her trance and joined the trill.

Jacob headed to the front door with a numb calmness. He opened and softly closed it behind him. The realization that he had just given her validation smacked him in his face.

Thanks, the truth has finally spoken. Great move. He had become his father's son. He glanced at the heavens. He hoped the sun would blind him.

The door behind him opened, and he bolted forward like a hungry wolf. With no pattern, intent, or path, he ran. Branches and brush whipped and cut him, giving him the punishment he so desperately needed. His throat burned, his lungs ached, his side throbbed, and his stomach knotted. He stopped and vomited. He recognized this place. The world spun around him.

"Why the hell am I still here?" he screamed.

A startled squirrel scampered up a hemlock tree and scolded him.

He made his way to an overhang and squatted, hugging his knees to his chin. Memories and emotions swirled and dipped like the river below. The spring rains had made the waters rough and raging. He heard arguments from childhood, and questions still unanswered. The key to letting go is understanding.

Nobody could ever name the event—the unspoken horror. He couldn't talk about it, but he understood the emotion. At an early age, he had perceived that she hated him. Today, the confirmation of her rejection wasn't imagined. He was her sacrifice to the gods.

His biological father, Endow, had beaten her, and he was born early. The weekend binges falling into the brown bottle had been regular events in his early childhood, coinciding with a paycheck, food, and more violence. That had been Jacob's normal world until Endow died. His death brought a disjointed peace within the small band of siblings. That peace had been shattered when they joined Judith in her new marriage, one in which the husband didn't beat his wife.

Only her son.

Jacob's voice dripped, thick with anger. "I hope you are happy, both of you." His mind would not be quiet. *Wait till your father gets home.* He could almost hear the words chanted in the rustling leaves.

"Wait till your father gets home."

It was a war chant—a siren's call. The words rattled in his mind, as did the fear and the triumph. He controlled the beatings—that was his childhood fantasy.

His heartbeat drummed.

A carefully coordinated dance between white man and Indian and stepfather and son played out for crimes he had committed and for the imagined ones, too. Each event was filled with tension and a crescendo when punishment was meted out.

Terence.

Emotions like two dogs fighting over a scrap of meat tore at Jacob's heart. *He loves me, he loves me not. Lame excuse, control for obedience.* He would have listened without the beating.

Jacob wiped the moisture off his face.

He was a good kid. He didn't do half the things he was punished for. Why couldn't Terence see that? Not once had he acknowledged his cruelty. *Why?*

Judith's face filled his mind, and he beat his fists against his skull. *Who hears silent screams?* Tears dripped, making dark spots on his jeans. Jacob wiped his nose with the back of his hand and then wiped his hand on his thigh.

He listened. The water in the river below sparkled with kisses from the sun. It was a beautiful distraction from the fight within. He wondered how fast the current was.

He wasn't Pius, or Terence, or Endow.

The sun dappled the perch where Jacob sat. Oppressed by remorse, Jacob struggled to stand. Enslaved by the past, his soul was drowning from broken dreams, broken hearts, and a tainted life from the beginning.

Sing your song, Mother. He wouldn't listen.

Like the sun on a gray day cracking through the clouds to shine, the light whirled inside of him.

He would find strength through this pain.

He fought as memories seeped into his veins. He untied his shoes, and tossed them aside. He needed to connect with the Earth. His thoughts turned to Faith, who had been his reason for living, now his entrance ticket to heaven.

Jacob danced without drums or bells. His bare feet thudded on the ground.

He needed a connection, a reason to continue. He struggled to find truth in his life's many lies. He shouted to the blue sky above.

"Great Spirit, it is time. Set me free."

In a circle, Jacob pounded the ground and chanted, "Oh Lord, where do you want me to be?"

Lightheaded, he thought he heard Ambrose say, "It isn't where we come. It's where we're going."

"Our bodies will cease one day, but our souls, our love for one another, will go on," Joannicus whispered.

"That's your answer?" Jacob said with a laugh. Exhaustion claimed Jacob's balance, and he teetered as he spun around. The edge of the cliff, softened by the rain and kneading, gave way, and Jacob found himself weightless and tumbling.

His prayer to be united with Faith was being answered.

CHAPTER 34
SINS OF THE MOTHER

Psalm 51:5
O see, in guilt I was born,
A sinner was I conceived.

The old Ford truck stood defiantly in the front of the farmhouse.

Wait till your father gets home echoed in his mind.

Jacob limped up the steps, shivering. Wet clothes stuck to him like papier-mâché. His body hurt from the inside out. At least this assured him he was alive. Jacob wiped his hand across his face and looked at the smear of blood. The top of his head throbbed where he had grazed it as he fought the river for his life.

He entered the house, and his mother screeched like an eagle. Jacob ignored her and headed down the hall to his stepfather's office for punishment, as he had done so many times as a child.

"Oh my God," Vicki said, opening the office door and stepping into the hallway. "What happened to you?"

His mother's torrent of rage reached a crescendo.

"Dear, please," Terence said, approaching his wife. He stepped between her and Jacob.

"I demand he leave," Judith said in Apsáalooke. She called him the spawn of Satan. Vicki gasped, and Jacob wondered what that made her since she'd given birth to the abomination.

Jacob entered the office, leaving Vicki and Judith in the hall.

Terence gently pushed the frothing madwoman out the door, closing and locking it behind her.

"Open this door now. Don't lock yourself in there with him. He's crazy." Her voice sounded like the cry of a child, complaining and piercing.

"Son, about this afternoon," began Terence, talking over the banging on the door.

Jacob stood, dripping.

"Are you all right?"

"Yeah. Fell and hit my head. Got some sense knocked into me."

"Maybe you should see a doctor."

Jacob smiled, now confident in the future and secure about the past. There was nothing here for him. He had lain to rest this past, just as he had lain to rest his wife and children. The time to begin again was now. "I'll get my stuff and leave."

"My goodness, you are jumping to conclusions. I just need to know what happened."

Jacob's lips curled, his head pounding. *What happened this afternoon is in the past.*

"What, her version is not good enough?"

Terence sighed heavily. His shoulders sagged. "Your mother is hurt."

Jacob trembled. The pounding on the door continued like a military air strike. *Should I explain?* There was no changing the past. Faith had been right; he had wasted his time.

"Son, I have seen the bruises on your mother's arm. It might even be broken."

"Oh, now you see bruises," Jacob said, regretting the words that flew out of his mouth. He didn't want to fight.

"Let's not make this about me. Parents make mistakes. You recognize that. That is why you brought Paul here."

"I didn't hurt Paul. Another man did. I only meant to keep him from harm, but I realized he needs more than me."

"It's good that you can recognize when you need help. I'm not apologizing for the past. I cannot change the past, son."

Jacob faced Terence. This man was no longer powerful. Jacob searched for the frightened boy inside of himself. He was silent. The hammering on the door stopped.

"I don't need an apology. Why was it only me?" Jacob asked, his voice tight. Ah, there was the little boy. A glint of anger twitched in Terence's eyes, his face devoid of sorrow. His face spoke the answer. There was no reason.

"Open this door now, or I'm calling the police," Vicki called as she jiggled the knob.

Jacob stepped toward the door. Nothing was going to happen today. The little boy was safe. The cycle of abuse had ended today with him.

"No, wait," Terence said, trying to stop Jacob from unlocking the door. Jacob pushed his stepfather away. The surprised expression on Terence's face told Jacob that his stepfather had not expected resistance. Their eyes locked as Terence stumbled to gain his balance, narrowly missing the wooden desk. In slow motion, Terence fell with a thud and did not rise. Jacob moved to help him to his feet. From Terence's grimace, Jacob realized that something wasn't right.

"Mom, I got it open," Vicki shouted as the door swung and banged against the wall.

Judith pushed her daughter aside and stepped into the room. Jacob looked up from where he had placed his stepfather. The small woman was holding a long gun. She swung the barrel around like a firefighter with an open nozzle, aiming as best she could with an injured wrist. Jacob took a step toward her. The gun looked familiar. *Is it a musket or shotgun? It is a deer rifle.* Jacob took two steps back. A rifle would surely end his life, and distance was his only hope. As he turned, the barrel of a shotgun searched for a target. The gun roared, and glass shattered.

Jacob felt sharp stings worse than stepping on a hornet's nest rip through him, and the smell of gunpowder filled his nostrils. But he was still standing. Vicki had a lemur stare on her face, and her eyes were bigger than he had ever seen. She gripped the doorjamb. His ears whistled from the blast in the small room. Something wet seeped down his left arm.

She had shot him.

Terence and Judith danced an awkward dance as they wrestled for control of the gun. Jacob stepped in, grabbed the gun barrel, and yanked. He bellowed, "Let go!" To his surprise, the gun was now his.

Judith wailed, "Don't kill us."

Jacob's left shoulder throbbed as he struggled with the gun, unloading unspent shells onto the floor. He set the gun on the desk. His mother sprang at him. She pummeled him with her fists and clawed at him with her nails. Jacob endured her wrath in the way that one accepts hugs and kisses. Terence finally pulled her off.

The disinfectant in the emergency room nauseated Jacob. It smelled like death. Too many visits and terrible memories threatened to crowd this moment—his wife and children dying once again in his arms. The voice of Faith chided him: "When will you let us go?"

The world sounded muted. He felt oddly numb as if nothing more could harm him.

"Okay, let's hear a story." The young doctor looked from one Mackenzie to the other. Who was the real victim? Jacob shook his head, trying to clear the dull drumming that continued in his ears.

He reconsidered his earlier wish. He was good with living.

Judith sobbed. Terence comforted her. Neither had sustained a major injury other than a sprain and concussion. Jacob recognized the moment for the code of silence about the violence. Even as a child, Jacob realized that lies, plain and fanciful, were used to explain injuries requiring an MD.

"An accident; a misunderstanding," Jacob said loudly as his hearing faded in and out.

"Anyone pressing charges?" asked the doctor, as if he had inside knowledge—another wild night on the Rez. The fact that Terence was white was probably the only thing keeping them from being given a Band-Aid and sent home.

Rebecca appeared, dressed in scrubs. She was working this evening, and Jacob felt the space change with her presence. She leveled a gaze at the young intern, who darted for the door. Vicki appeared. Color had returned to her face. She had gone and found Rebecca.

On the ride from the farmhouse to the hospital, Vicki turned ashen. Tears dripped down her cheeks. Jacob had walked her into the ER like a baby in a stroller. He wasn't sure how they arrived at the hospital safely, but he was sure someone had parked on the sidewalk.

Funny what details stuck in one's head.

Rebecca's eyes narrowed as she looked from her stepfather to her brother. Fingernail scratches decorated Jacob's cheeks like war paint.

Terence spoke. "We are all fine. Nobody is seriously hurt."

"Mother, how could you?" Rebecca said. Judith's mouth opened with astonishment. Clearly, she felt her actions to be justified and could not understand her daughter's disdain. The brief family reunion was interrupted.

"Okay," the officer said. "Let's have the basics."

Jacob shrugged. In the Apsáalooke versus the white world, the truth didn't matter. "I got a little too forceful with my folks. But, in my defense, she did try to shoot me."

Judith let out a sob. Rebecca's eyes narrowed as her lips flattened.

"So, none of you are ready for a family portrait. What's the actual story?" the officer asked. His pen clicked as if he had important calls to deal with.

Jacob thought for a moment. *My mother hates me, so she tried to kill me. After years of physical abuse from my stepfather, I shoved him.*

Jacob licked his swollen lips. "I didn't tell my folks I was coming home for a visit, and they thought someone was breaking in and they attempted to defend themselves. As you can see, the kickback from the rifle sent her flying. My father, who was next to her, fell back, hitting something. It all happened so quickly."

Jacob's steel-blue eyes bore into the officer. *Would the man believe that?*

"Barroom brawl. I hooked up with the wrong woman," Jacob added, pointing to his face and dried blood.

Rebecca didn't give the officer time to think as she ordered Vicki to escort Judith to the truck.

Judith continued to whimper like a scolded puppy. The truth of this evening's events would remain a family secret. Judith was too proud to be seen in a bad light. Jacob wondered how wounded he would be if she had used a bow and arrow. He realized as he watched her being led out by his half sister that she was a woman undeserving of his love.

"Good, no charges," the officer said.

Jacob and Terence nodded, agreeing for the first time.

The odor of iodine lingered around Jacob as he limped to Rebecca's old Ford Falcon. The bump on his head throbbed in time with the stitches in his arm. Rebecca headed north at a speed that clocked above the limit. Jacob thought she was taking him to the Reservation to smack him over the head and dispose of his remains in a shallow grave. He glanced at her.

"Shut up," she said, barely taking her eyes off the highway.

He figured out where they were going before she turned onto the

267

winding road. The monastery stood proudly in the setting sunlight. She parked the car, stepped out, and opened his door. The aroma of hops and freshly baked bread wrapped around his senses as his stomach growled.

"This isn't where I belong," Jacob said.

"Don't be a fucking idiot," Rebecca said. "You can't stay with them. She tried to kill you."

"A small woman with a big gun, but it was a relatively low-powered weapon," Jacob said, feeling his insides trembling. If she had been a better aim, there'd be a hole in his head instead of his arm.

"At point-blank range, she could do it with a ballpoint pen. Stop trying to make her into a mother she will never be. I don't understand why you keep trying to make them love you. You have others who love you."

"The ones I love seem to go away," Jacob said, amazed that he understood what she was saying. He could only hear every other word.

Rebecca marched toward the refectory. "Oh really? I think not. Yes, you had Faith and the kids, and they walked on. You've got a life here; a damn good one, I might add. And you have Paul, who you walked away from."

Jacob stood and watched her. "He could be taken away. God doesn't play fair. Besides, I left because they don't live up to their own standards. I can't live with hypocrisy."

"Your entire childhood has been that, and you lived it," Rebecca said as she turned and stood with her arms crossed. "Where is my brave brother? Stop judging the world by your standards. We don't measure up. It is not right for you to hold on to the past, her death, and our parents' mistakes. Put it to rest. The farmhouse is out. You have touched the enemy and lived. You are meant to be the leader."

"I know," Jacob said, amused.

"I'm not arguing with you. The community needs you."

Jacob cocked his head and shook it slightly. They didn't need him as much as he needed them.

Who was he serving? God? Himself? Or man? If he stayed, would they make him a novice again? To return meant giving up his place, rank, and status.

He liked being a novice—one monk in a sea of monks—not a leader. Decisions were made for you. Life was set and orderly. One spent a lot of time breathing in and waiting with expectations.

Yes, that was what he wanted.

"Are you listening to me? Abbot Gordon died. Didn't you get that message?"

Had he heard her correctly? *Crap. That was the reason for the calls.* There would be an election and a funeral. *Joannicus.* Jacob's spirit soared.

"He went quickly. We should all be so blessed. You should take calls—then you wouldn't get surprises," Rebecca said, shaking her head.

Abbot Gordon had gone, leaving another hole in his heart for the wind to whistle through. Their unfinished business would linger like the heat of a summer day. He had been foolish to stay away. As he stood, he realized he had spent too much of his life planning, rescuing, running after, and running away. He had thought of himself as a warrior. Only *brave* wasn't a word; it was an action. He kissed Rebecca on the cheek before opening the refectory doors.

CHAPTER 35
ELECTION

Psalm 118:105-108
Your word is a lamp for my steps,
and light for my path.
I have sworn and have made up my mind
to obey your decrees.
Accept, Lord, the homage of my lips,
and teach me your decrees.

Abbot David, the president of the Benedictine Confederation, led the community in the process of discernment. The time dragged. Jacob's hearing had returned except for the occasional ringing. But he had kept that information to himself, enjoying the bits of knowledge he received when people assumed he still couldn't hear them. *I've become Brother Mellitus, that old trickster.* In his last years, Mellitus feigned sleep and confusion, ending up in places he shouldn't have been. Jacob smiled at the thought of the white-haired curmudgeon.

The triangle football, punted by Paul's fingers, flew past Jacob's finger goalpost and landed in a coffee cup. Father Pius frowned and shook his head.

The names appeared on the whiteboard: Father Joannicus Brookes, Father Pius Carrington, Father Vincent Mackenzie, Father Hilary Saint Clair, and Father Jacob Mackenzie-Knows the Song. Five men were being considered for the position of Abbot.

Jacob shrugged and mumbled an apology as the meeting broke up, and the monks headed to lunch. Father Jacob stopped at the whiteboard and erased his name with his thumb. He didn't want that job. Why was his name on that list?

That was precisely what Father Pius had been thinking as he watched Jacob erase his name. Pius wondered why his name was on the list, but he could not take it off. This was no man's doing. It was God's. If the vote went in his favor, who was he to second-guess the Divine?

It had taken almost two years, but he was grateful that the community had forgiven him and now considered him worthy. *Abbot.* The word weighed heavy and, like a worm, burrowed into Father Pius's brain. Abbot David had led them in conferences focused on the qualities of an Abbot and the future needs of Saint Alberic's monastic community. He glanced again at the now ghost letters of Jacob's name.

How had Jacob's name gotten on that board? Should he tell them they had sent the paperwork to release Jacob from his vows? *He's such a distraction.* Irritation rose inside Pius.

Between Jacob and Paul, it had been hard to concentrate on what Abbot David was saying. He noticed, too, that Moses and Ambrose were watching the silent game of paper football instead of listening to the words of talk. This election was important. Each candidate would bring something different to the community. The new Abbot would change life at Saint Alberic's. Change was hard, even for monks who sought the Divine will within all events.

Pius walked outside to the refectory as the sun warmed him, consoling himself with the notion that Jacob's presence was like a visit from family, short-lived. The official documents would arrive as they prepared to install the new Abbot. He smiled. *That's my gift to the community: the removal of Jacob and his drama.* Pius cracked his knuckles. The only other disruption to their lives was Paul. If they chose him, he would see that when the boy turned 18, the monastic gates would slam shut behind him. That sounded cruel, but the boy had no vocation. Just because Paul lived with them did not mean he had a vocation.

Father Pius entered the hallway.

"What are you still doing here? You weren't here for the funeral. Abbot Gordon loved you. It's your fault he's gone. You broke his soul," Paul said with heated words.

Squeaky sandals alerted Pius that Brother Ambrose had arrived. He turned to see the large man marching toward the arguing pair.

"Oh, for crying out loud, little one," Ambrose said. "Abbot Gordon died of an aneurism, not a broken soul. Besides, Father Jacob is deaf to your complaints, so you might as well be talking to the wall."

"Then justice is served, for God is punishing him by taking away his hearing. He should have listened to Abbot Gordon and come home when he was told. That's what a real monk does," Paul said.

"It's temporary, and more a blessing than a punishment," Ambrose said. He grabbed Paul's arm, giving him a piercing glare showing that he had overstepped. Pius had to agree with Ambrose. Blessing, punishment... sometimes it came down to interpretation.

It was a temporary hearing loss. Rumors were whispered among the monks about how Jacob had received his injuries. Pius questioned the story of a hunting accident, yet it seemed plausible that a hunter had mistaken him for a deer. Jacob liked to walk at twilight in Native garb. This lack of hearing was a blessing for the community. It kept Jacob's controversial comments at bay.

Father Pius watched Jacob perform magic with words whispered in the boy's ear. Paul hung his head, his eyes hooded and cheeks reddening. Teenage boys' emotions were so erratic—one minute up and then next down, like a yo-yo. Father Pius wondered who the lucky string holder would be. He said a prayer of thanks: it would never be him.

The monks ate lunch in silence. The community needed time to discern the voice of God. A joyful hope filled Pius as he ate.

Abbot Pius.

He folded his napkin, prayed, and exited the refectory. Brother Ambrose was pacing the walk. The man stopped and looked at Pius. Father Pius felt like Ambrose hoped to see a message on his forehead: *This one is the Abbot.*

"This may take a while," Pius said, joining Ambrose. "That list is long."

"I know who to vote for, don't you?"

Pius looked at his large confrère and noticed that the man's habit was inside out. The deep pockets hung at his waist like wing buds. Why hadn't anyone informed him? Pius was not sure whom Ambrose wanted as Abbot. He knew Ambrose had always had a soft spot for Jacob. Pius played it safe and said, "Yes, but Father Joannicus will not accept. He has said so."

Brother Ambrose looped his thumbs inside his belt. Bits of tobacco that clung to the pocket wings fell to the ground. "He doesn't have to do it alone."

No, he'd follow him to hell and back if he asked. He wanted to vote for Joannicus. Everything in his heart insisted he was the one. Hadn't Ambrose noticed?

Something was wrong with Joannicus. What were they afraid of?

They watched Jacob and Joannicus talking at the far end of the garden between the church and the refectory.

"Seriously, you know you can't just erase your name," Joannicus said as he sat on the bench near the statue of the Blessed Virgin Mary.

"You know, I am not that obedient."

Joannicus chuckled and then coughed. "Also, I know you aren't deaf."

"Do not tell Paul."

"Sorry about your family. I'm grateful you survived the war, and it's a sign. What did Mellitus say? Four requirements. You just snatched a weapon from an enemy. You have met all four."

Jacob frowned. This was not his goal—to be a Warrior Chief or Abbot.

"I am glad I survived. How do you know what happened?" Jacob said, confident that Rebecca had confessed to Brother Ambrose and he to Joannicus.

Joannicus looked up at Jacob and shook his head. "Rebecca, she is convinced you are here for a reason. Why not to Chief of the Benedictines?"

Jacob shook his head and laughed. "I cannot wait to be a novice again, especially after we elect you," he said.

Joannicus rubbed his sandal on the gravelly ground, scooting the rocks and exposing the firm surface below.

"Seriously, you will not be a novice. Senior Council still assumes you were on sabbatical."

"Senior Council will change with the new Abbot," Jacob said, liking the vision folding out before him. He wouldn't have to work on his vow of obedience if Joannicus were Abbot.

Joannicus shifted on the bench, and a groan escaped his lips. Jacob recognized the sound of pain.

"You and I must acknowledge that I can't accept, even if elected. I have health issues." Father Joannicus folded his hands in his lap. "You'd make a good Abbot."

"Let us not go there. Vote for Hilary," Jacob said, fearing that if Joannicus spoke that idea to others, votes would shift in Jacob's favor. "So, what exactly are those health issues?"

"The new Abbot will disclose what everyone needs to know," Joannicus said with a wry smile.

"You and God do not play fair," Jacob said, sitting on the bench, folding his scapular into his lap, squelching the desire to be chosen to know what Joe's health issues were.

"I'm glad you figured that out and that you're staying. You seem content."

"How come you and God never give a direct answer?" Jacob asked.

"I don't know what you mean. Seriously, God always answers. It isn't what I expect most of the time, though."

Jacob pursed his lips and listened to his friend wheeze.

"I beg to differ. Take the birth of Samson. His folks asked directly, 'What shall we do with the boy?' 'In time,' the angel said. What kind of answer is that?"

"Nothing is set in stone. Time would reveal," Joannicus said, his voice taking on some of his former enthusiasm for healthier days.

"Fine, I will accept that, but they were asking for hope, and neither God nor his angel gave that to them. So much for a loving God."

"You're right. They got the gift of faith instead," Joannicus said, as he wobbled a little to his feet. Jacob held out his arm as they returned to the room, where conviction and hope waited.

Pius stood nervously outside of the community room. Having been present for the election of Abbot Gordon, he understood what was happening—the process of scrutiny. The community discussed the merits of the man being considered. Several juniors and novices stood a few paces away. Since they were not permanently vowed, they did not have a vote. The air was heavy, and sweat trickled down his neck, making his clerical collar itch. He watched Paul enter the community room, look around, and exit. What was that boy up to? They had allowed Paul too many liberties. Pius feared that the boy's unbridled ways would prove to be their downfall in the next few years. *If I become Abbot, the boy will be a permanent novice. That should squelch his teen angst.*

"This is excruciating," one novice said as he twisted his scapular into a knot, wrinkling the long black cloth that hung over his shoulders.

"It is," Pius said.

They were talking about him. He wondered what they were saying. His faults are many. Would they see his merits? Since Jacob's absence, Paul and he had a truce, and he had turned his life around.

Pius felt the loss of Gordon and hoped that his premature death was for the greater good.

"Seems kind of silly. When you hire a boss, you don't send him out of the room. You ask him questions."

"They'll do that, but this isn't an interview. The discussion focuses on who can do the best job. This isn't a short-term job; more like a lifetime appointment. The Abbot manages the entire community and every one of our souls," Pius said, feeling the thrill and the weight of his words.

"Do you want the job?" the young novice asked.

Father Pius pondered the possibility. *Abbot Pius.* He could see the heavy pectoral cross hanging shiny on his black habit. *Yes, I want this job. I'm the best man for it. I have run a thriving, profitable parish.*

"Who wouldn't want the job? Everyone must answer to you. On top is better than on bottom," the junior said.

Pius placed his hand in his side pocket and let the cool beads of his rosary slip through his fingers.

"It's not in my hands," Pius said. "But yes, I would accept if my community felt I deserved such an honor."

Fathers Vincent and Jacob walked outside to the patio through the community room. The words of Chapter 64 of the Rule rattled Jacob's brain.

"The Abbot must profit others rather than precede them. He must be learned in the divine law (the Scriptures), chaste, temperate, and merciful, and always put mercy before judgment. He should hate vices but love the brothers. He must correct prudently and without excess, adapting himself to the individual monk. He should try to be loved more than feared. He should not be restless and troubled, nor should he be extreme and headstrong. An Abbot should be farsighted and thoughtful, giving prudent and moderate orders. He should always be discreet and create a life where the strong are challenged, but the weak are not discouraged..."

Could anyone live up to those lines? It was like his argument about a modern-day Apsáalooke chief: lead a successful war party, steal a horse from the enemy camp, snatch a weapon in combat from the enemy, and be the first to touch a fallen enemy. There wasn't an opportunity to fulfill those requirements.

"You were smart to take your name off the list," Father Vincent said.

Jacob smiled at his youngest half brother as he reached into his habit pocket, pulled out a bottle of pain pills, and took two.

"Talk said you were leaving us," said the older novice.

"Talk is dangerous. Do not listen to rumors," Jacob said.

"You filled out papers," Vincent said.

"I did, over a year ago, and nothing happened. I cannot imagine that Abbot Gordon would have sent the papers at this late date."

"They got mailed, Jacob," Vincent said, his brow creased with concern. "Someone finished the office work after Abbot Gordon's death."

Thanks, Pius, but which papers? The papers that would release him from his priestly duties or the papers to release him from his vows as a monk? The pain in Jacob's arm made his thoughts swirl and then calm. A brother wasn't so bad if that was what God wanted. A deep sadness pulled at him. He repeated the words of his wife aloud: "It is what it is. I guess the final decision rests with the new Abbot."

The door to the patio opened.

"What are you doing out here?" Paul asked, seeing Jacob. "You took your name off the list."

"How do you know so much?" Jacob asked, wincing as he turned.

Paul gave him a look that meant, *Are you stupid?*

"They are scrutinizing me," Father Vincent said. "Father Jacob is my half brother, so he has to sit out."

"They are not talking about you anymore; they are talking about Father Jacob," Paul said. "I have to stop this. I don't want them electing the wrong person."

Jacob shook his head. "I wonder who that would be. It will not be me. They are just discussing. We vote this evening."

Paul stopped and gave Jacob a critical look.

"You will have time to influence the vote," Jacob added, graciously nodding to Paul. He was aware that influence came from others' comments. Heartfelt words often changed the minds of men who, moments before, thought themselves firm in their decision.

Vincent's jaw dropped. "This does not concern Paul."

Father Jacob smiled. *Little brother, you are so young.* "I disagree. This vote affects his life as much as anyone who lives here."

An epiphany registered on the faces of the juniors and novices.

Indignation rose in Vincent's voice. "You aren't suggesting he has a vote?"

"No, but nothing prevents him from expressing his opinion to others."

The voting had begun. The community elected Father Joannicus as Abbot.

Joannicus smiled and stood facing the community.

"What a wonderful honor! Nothing would please me more than to serve my remaining years as your Abbot. In all honesty, I can't perform the duties."

Sadness wrapped around Jacob. He could feel the regret in Joe's voice. This was the man for the job.

The voting began again. To elect a new abbot, they needed a two-thirds majority, which meant someone had to get at least 26 votes rather than the 40 Joannicus had just received.

"Sixteen votes for Father Joannicus, eight for Father Pius, six for Father Vincent, four for Father Hilary, and six votes for Father Jacob," Abbot David said.

He should just announce that he was not in the running.

Ever since his discussion on the back patio with Vincent, Jacob had been reflecting on a job on the Rez. He could do a lot for the Apsáalooke people with the wealth of archival information that Mother Rocky Cliff had shown him a month ago. Her wrinkled face smoothed with a grin when she explained the museum plans. Jacob had inspected a dozen dusty boxes and marveled at the ancient arti-facts she had collected and stored.

"Ten votes for Father Joannicus, fourteen for Father Pius, four for Father Hilary, eight for Father Vincent, and four votes for Father Jacob," announced Abbot David. His voice showed signs of exas-peration.

The words of the afternoon bounced around inside Jacob's head. *The Abbot must see the possibility of conversion and change. The Abbot must be able to encourage each brother. The Abbot must lead a successful war party.*

Jacob looked at Father Pius.

No.

Jacob looked at his half brother, Father Vincent. He was young—too young to be Abbot. Could he give direction to and correct Brothers?

Another vote. Four votes for Father Joannicus, nineteen for Father Pius, four for Father Hilary, eight for Father Vincent, and five votes for Father Jacob. A two-thirds majority still eluded the community.

Father Joannicus leaned over and poked Jacob's sore arm.

"Stop voting for me," he whispered.

"Only if you stop voting for me." Jacob wondered who the others were who had given him five votes. He was sure that Moses had voted for Joannicus.

The monks broke to stretch. Jacob looked out the window. Pain pills clouded Jacob's mind. The afternoon was still. He watched the smoke from Ambrose's pipe rise and drift to the heavens as if it knew where it would end. The slow lines of wispy gray stretched like fingers as the sun filtered into the room. The vapors hung in long tendrils, gliding nowhere and everywhere.

Let my prayer rise like incense. Oh, that is what that means, reflected Jacob.

A commotion drew his sleepy attention to the front of the room. Paul. The boy stood waving something and protesting before they forced him to leave the room, and the voting resumed.

"If there is no objection," chuckled Abbot David, "it seems we have a member from the grave who would like to cast his vote." Brother Mellitus had prepared a vote and wanted to be counted in selecting a future abbot. If nothing else, the name on the paper would prove interesting.

Although there was mumbling, most remembered Brother Mellitus's antics, but no one objected. Abbot David ripped open the envelope holding Brother Mellitus's vote. Jacob wondered if the name written on the paper made one win. Would they take it as a message from God?

"Father Jacob," Abbot David said. "I, Brother Mellitus, vote every time for Father Chief Jacob Mackenzie Knows the Song, for that is the only way his soul will be redeemed."

Chuckles drifted through the community. Jacob smiled. That old devil. He would never quit with his jabs.

Jacob put three ballots in front of him. The voting had narrowed: Pius or Vincent. On the first ballot, Jacob wrote Father Vincent. On the second ballot, he wrote Father Pius. He looked out the window and toyed with the idea of writing Brother Mellitus but knew a Brother rarely became Abbot, let alone one who was dead.

Jacob printed the name *Father Joannicus* on the piece of paper.

The swallows dipped and swooped up the wall in gleeful abandonment, circling the cloistered patio in a mad game of chase. Jacob marveled at the speed and grace as they dodged branches and buildings, landing gingerly on a sculpture of St. Placid as if to bless it with their holiness. He moved the papers around on the table and selected one, placing it in the ballot basket as it came around. Leave it up to God.

One more vote. Jacob closed his eyes, feeling the sun sink into his black habit, warming his injured arm. He propped an elbow on the table and leaned his head into his hand.

"Well," Abbot David said in an astonished tone. "We have two votes for Father Joannicus, two votes for Father Vincent, seven for Father Pius, and the rest go to Father Jacob. At last, the community of St. Alberic has elected a new Abbot. Congratulations, Father Jacob Mackenzie-Knows the Song."

Jacob's eyes fluttered open.

Oh, dear God, what have we done?

ACKNOWLEDGMENTS

A big thanks to the Benedictines in my life who answered all my questions about monks: Father Jude Anderson, Father Alfred Hulscher, Father Benedict Auer, and Father Gerard Garrigan. Oblates Margaret Mazeski and Jane Woolson also shared how to live a Benedictine life in the world.

Thanks to Eddie and Lori Big Medicine for teaching me so much about Apsáalooke culture, correcting my misunderstandings, and helping me shore up the Native American voices in this tale. Thanks also to Connie Ambrose and her sister for helping me with a last-minute change to ensure more authentic dialogue from a Native American character.

Thanks to the Puget Sound Writers' Guild, who endured the evolution of these stories, chapter by chapter, and gave me their helpful thoughts.

Acknowledgement to Wayzgoose editor extraordinaire, Maggie, who has made this story wonderful.

THE SERIES: THE BENEDICTION OF PAUL

Thank you for reading Book 2 of *The Benediction of Paul*. Here is the full series.

Book 1: *Winds of Life*

Book 2: *Less Thunder, More Lightning*

Book 3: *All for One Child*

Book 4: *Counting Coup: The Making of an Abbot* (prequel to the series)

For ordering information, please see the Wayzgoose Press website:

https://www.wayzgoosepress.com/authors/patricia-mcclure/

www.ingramcontent.com/pod-product-compliance
Lightning Source LLC
Chambersburg PA
CBHW020415260626
47156CB00007B/2394